Also by Tim Green

Fiction
Ruffians
Titans
Outlaws
The Red Zone
Double Reverse
The Letter of the Law
The Fourth Perimeter
The Fifth Angel

Nonfiction
The Dark Side of the Game
A Man and His Mother: An Adopted Son's Search

THE FIRST 48

TIM
GREEN

WARNER BOOKS

A Time Warner Company

Warner Books, Inc., 1271 Avenue of the Americas, New York, NY 10020

Visit our Web site at www.twbookmark.com

A Time Warner Company

Printed in the United States of America

First Printing: February 2004
10 9 8 7 6 5 4 3 2 1

Library of Congress Cataloging-in-Publication Data
Green, Tim.
    The first 48 / Tim Green.
        p. cm.
    ISBN 0-446-53144-8
1. Investigative reporting—Fiction. 2. Fathers and daughters—Fiction. 3. Kidnapping victims—Fiction. 4. Washington (D.C.)—Fiction. 5. Women journalists—Fiction. 6. Missing persons—Fiction. 7. Legislators—Fiction. I. Title: First forty-eight. II. Title.
PS3557.R37562F56 2004
813' .54—dc22   2003015146

For my Illyssa,
because the day I met you
was the best thing that ever
happened to me.

ACKNOWLEDGMENTS

Some of the best things in this book, and the book itself, couldn't have been without the help of others: my agent, Esther Newberg; my editors, Rick Wolff and Sara Ann Freed; and my parents, Richard and Judy Green, for their careful reading and constructive criticism; my friends in the Syracuse Police Department, Inspector Michael Kerwin and Detective Pete Patnode, for their endless patience in answering my questions; Exec Air manager Mark Germia and chief pilot John Leary; Pat Scova of the Valhalla (N.Y.) Town Clerk's Office, for helping a stranger; and all the people from my Warner Books family, including Larry Kirshbaum, Maureen Egen, Jamie Raab, Chris Barba, Dan Ambrosio, Mari Okuda, Flamur Tonuzi, and Tina Andreadis.

I thank you all.

In addition, once again, a very special thanks to my brother in words and my particular friend Ace Atkins.

A Special Tribute to the Memory of Sara Ann Freed

In June 2003, Sara Ann Freed, my coeditor and friend, left this world much sooner than she should have. For those of us at Warner Books who knew her, a light went out, but we will always remember her easy smile and the warmth she brought with her to share wherever she went.

Sara Ann, you will be sorely missed—but never forgotten.

"I sometimes think that all you tell me of knighthood, kingdoms, empires and islands is all windy blather and lies."

Sancho Panza
Don Quixote, Book 1, Part 15

PROLOGUE

His name was Nobody. Nobody Jones. Nobody Smith. His passport and cruise ship ticket said Mott, a name he'd found on a bottle of apple juice. You could do such things without much effort when you knew the right people and you had the money. Official documents and tickets were only what you told people you were. He liked being Mr. Nobody. Especially Nobody on a vacation.

On the third day, they'd cruised out of Jamaica and headed over to Grand Cayman. He spent most of his time on deck by the pool, watching the women slather themselves with suntan oil and drink funny little drinks with umbrellas. There was nothing like this in Ukraine. This was like Mars.

But now he had a feel for it all. He knew the ship. He knew the people, their habits, and the way they talked to one another. There was a group of twenty-something men who sat around a glass table under the eaves of the bar playing a drinking game they called quarters. He had practiced in his cabin, bouncing his own quarter off of the small bathroom vanity and into his drinking glass.

There was an empty chair. He bought two pitchers of beer at

the bar, and standing there in his flowered shirt and khaki shorts, he asked if he could play.

They looked at him, grinning, red-faced from too much sun and too much drink. Two laughed out loud. One grin turned into a frown.

"Sure," someone said.

He plopped down the pitchers in the middle of the others. Beer sloshed up over the lip of one and spilled into the swill that already lathered the tabletop. He sat down and adjusted his straw hat. He stroked his thick mustache, and the game began again. Quarters bounced off the glass. Some went awry, finding the deck. Many plunked into the drinking glass full of beer and they shone brightly from the bottom amid the swirl of bubbles and golden liquid.

You had to point with your elbow, or you were the one who had to drink. He learned fast though, and soon his own dark hairy elbow was flashing around the table, making the others drink. There were groans and a few cheerful curses. He flagged a waitress for four more pitchers and then lost his turn on purpose so as not to hog the game.

The laughter grew hot, like the sunbaked wood beneath his feet. They began to call him the Russian Bear. He had to roll back a sneer. He was a Soviet from Ukraine. He'd told them that. Hadn't he shown them the CCCP lapel pin stuck to the collar of his shirt? Leave it to a handful of American jackasses not to know the difference.

It was his turn again. He reached into his pocket and fingered the little wax bead until it broke. Then he bounced the quarter into glass after glass, sending beer all around the table.

It was half an hour before a tall thin man with bad skin and a shock of short blond hair popped up out of his seat, turned, and vomited in the general direction of the pool, spattering three rows of deck chairs. Screams erupted, and two of the people in deck chairs got sick as well.

The Soviet stroked his wiry mustache and left the table in the midst of the uproarious howls of his new friends. He climbed the stairs to the deck that overlooked the bar and pool. There was a chair by the railing with no one in it. He removed the soggy towel from its back and sat down to watch. Within a half hour, two more young men lurched to their feet, also sick. The game broke up, and he went to the casino.

The next day the ship stopped at Cozumel. The Soviet was in the casino again when the fat lady next to him at the blackjack table turned green, clutched her stomach, and hustled for the bathroom. Later, a farmer from Ohio lost his ham sandwich at the roulette wheel and the casino shut down amid the twittering laughter.

That night less than half the vacationers showed up for dinner. People stared accusingly at one another and if someone coughed, heads turned and hands gripped the table's edge. Waiters in cheap tuxedos shot nervous glances at one another and spoke in subdued tones about the three-layer chocolate cake. The Soviet drank a good deal of the tart cork-tainted Chardonnay and grinned around at the others, who sat at the half-empty table picking at their food.

On deck at 2 A.M., a helicopter sputtered secretly down out of the dark sky. Medivac. Two gurneys were hurried out across the deck. In the flashing lights of the helicopter, he could see the wincing faces. Tubes in their noses. IV bottles swinging above them. Nobody knew that they probably wouldn't make it. Word spread fast. By 6 A.M. there was an angry crowd outside the bridge demanding that the ship return immediately to port.

Later that day, as they were pulling into Miami, a line snaked in front of the ship's hospital, all the way out onto the deck. People covered their faces with T-shirts and makeshift masks. A dozen people were trampled by the crowd pushing to get down the stairs and off the ship. The Soviet waited patiently, then tugged the wrinkles out of his flowered shirt and marched ashore with his leather briefcase, trying not to smile at other people's misfortune. But who could have blamed him for smiling? After all, it had been a very fine vacation.

CHAPTER 1

Tom Redmon didn't need to hear more, but he knew the couple needed to talk. Beneath the desk, he clenched and unclenched his hand, squeezing the tennis ball, trying to be patient. Finally they finished. The mother was sniffing and dabbing her eyes with a napkin from McDonald's. He looked past them and out through the old glass to a bright locust tree, wavy and distorted.

In his office, the paneling of one wall sagged under the weight of diplomas. A 1996 calendar of a German castle high on a mountaintop hung by a pushpin. In a wood frame was a cheap print of van Gogh's *View of Montmartre with Windmills*. Tom loosened his tie and unbuttoned his collar. Size nineteen. If he could have, he'd have taken off his coat.

The couple was young. Their little girl sat between them, her eyes hollow, her head bald and white. When she smiled, her teeth shone gray, with great gaps between them. The father worked at the power plant, stoking coal. The mother stayed at home. There were four other kids too. None of them were sick. Yet.

Tom slapped his hand on the desk and said, "We'll sue them."

"Who?" the father asked.

"Everyone," Tom said, standing. "GE. The State of New York. The City of Ithaca. The Power Authority. The EPA and the DEC."

"Everyone?"

"I mean it," Tom said. "I've done it before. I just sued the New York State Dormitory Authority and won.

"These big corporations. These colossal government entities. They need to be taken down, and that's what I do, Mr. Helmer. Don't you worry, Mrs. Helmer. They'll pay."

"I just want her to be okay," she said through the napkin.

"We all do," Tom said.

He patted the little girl on the shoulder. She smiled up at him.

"I'll have the papers ready for you to sign by the beginning of next week," Tom said. "Say Tuesday. How's ten?"

He opened the door and Sarah, his secretary, looked up from her romance novel. She was sixty. Yellow hair. Cat glasses and chewing gum.

"Tuesday at ten for the Helmers, Sarah," he said. "We'll start on the papers first thing tomorrow morning."

He showed them out and turned to Sarah. She sat staring blankly at him.

"The property management company called again," she said.

"That's the problem," he said, smiling. "When one man owned this building, a favor here and there wasn't forgotten. Now it's a nameless, faceless LLP that you can't appease and you can't kill."

"We *are* two months late."

"Let them evict me," he said. He winked and grinned and

took off his blazer and lost the tie. "Take the rest of the day, Sarah. Get some sun."

"You've got Mr. Potter scheduled for three-thirty."

"Cancel it."

"Tom, they *will* evict you."

"Cancel it. This Helmer case could be the big one."

"We've had a lot of big ones, Tom," she said. "They never pay. The small stuff is what pays."

"We got the janitor."

"That's one. They settled because their witness died, remember? Mr. Potter will pay a retainer up front. I told him that on the phone and he agreed."

"Sarah," he said. "I know you care, and I appreciate that. But I'm sick and tired of DUIs and shoplifters and aggravated assaults. I'm tired of drug dealers, pickpockets, drunks, crackheads, motorcycle gangs, and dregs. These are the people I used to put in jail."

"You're a defense lawyer, Tom. You need money to file that suit. You need an index number. You need an investigator," she said. She was standing now, with her hands on her thick hips. "You already owe Mike Tubbs six thousand dollars."

"He sent a bill?"

"Of course not," she said, pressing her lips tight.

Tom flattened the tennis ball and rubbed his chin.

"Then reschedule Potter for Thursday and go get some sun," he said. "It's beautiful out there. And do me a favor, will you? Dial up Mike Tubbs and tell him I'll meet him at Friendly's at three-thirty, sharp."

"Of course," Sarah said.

CHAPTER 2

At Friendly's Ice Cream, Tom edged past a sunburned crowd of summer tourists wearing visors, shorts, and golf shirts to where an empty booth waited for him in the back. The waitress set down two sweaty glasses of water just as Mike Tubbs stumbled in, jostling the tourists. Thirty years old. Flirting with the three-hundred-pound mark. A head of thinning hair with small matching ginger mustache and goatee. Extremely capable.

The broad forehead beneath his fine hair was beaded with sweat. A streamer of toilet paper rode in on the bottom of his sneaker.

"Sorry I'm late," Mike said as he wedged his way into the vinyl booth.

Tom took the younger man's meaty hand and shook it.

"A good investigator," Tom said, "respects time."

Mike smiled, but his cheeks went pink.

"Sorry, I—"

"Two chocolate Fribbles," Tom said to the waitress.

"Could you make mine light on the chocolate?" Mike said, raising an inquiring finger toward the waitress.

She scrunched up her face.

"You just make it with vanilla ice cream," Mike said.

The waitress looked confused.

"Forget it," Mike said. "It's okay."

"Okay," she said.

"And miss," Tom said.

"Yes, sir?" she said, barely forcing a smile.

"You better take this now," he said, handing her his American Express card.

"This one's on me," he said to Mike with a wink.

"Hey, you don't have to do that," Mike said.

Tom raised his hand, signaling an end to any debate.

"Now," Tom said, "you and I have some things to discuss . . ."

Mike looked down at his hands and pattered his fingers against the tabletop.

Tom smiled and leaned back into the booth, feeling a cold blast of air-conditioning on his face.

Over Mike's shoulder, he noticed a man who had just entered the restaurant wearing a three-quarter-length army coat. His eyes were small and shifty. His face was dirty with stubble, his dark hair long. Tom squinted and started to slide out of the booth.

"Tom?" Mike said, turning to look over his shoulder.

"Shh," Tom said. His hand was on the tabletop, his butt on the edge of the booth, his feet tucked up under his knees.

"Who would wear an army coat in the middle of summer?" Tom said in a low hiss.

"I don't . . . know," Mike said.

The man looked around and then marched up to the cash register. His hands were jammed in his coat pockets. He spoke to the cashier. A young girl with a paper hat whose face went suddenly pale. Her mouth, pink with lipstick, formed a perfect O.

"The price of greatness is responsibility," Tom said under his breath, his eyes on the man.

"Churchill?"

"Yes," Tom said. He was on the move.

"Tom?" Mike said, from somewhere behind him.

Tom was halfway there. When he hit the cluster of tourists, he shoved them aside.

"Hey," someone said. Irate.

The girl was nodding to the man now. Frightened. Teary-eyed. She reached into the cash register, saw Tom and hesitated. The man looked over his shoulder and spun around, his hand clenching something inside the jacket pocket. Tom was in his stance. He uttered a cry.

The man's hands darted from his pockets. In one was a dark heavy object.

A woman screamed.

Tom shot in. He chopped one hand, then the other. The object fell to the floor. The man lunged. Tom had his arm. He pivoted and tossed the man over his hip to the floor.

When the man hit, his breath left him in a great gust. Tom was on him instantly. One hand expertly clamped to his throat. The other pinning the wrist that had held the weapon.

"I've got him!" Tom yelled. "Everyone back! I've got him!"

Someone was crying.

The robber's eyes rolled into his head. Tom looked up. The cashier. Her pink face was crinkled. Mascara streamed down her cheeks.

"It's all right, young lady," Tom said. "It's all right. Someone call the police."

The girl cried harder.

Mike was there, bending over. He had the weapon.

"Tom," he said, putting a hand on Tom's shoulder. He held something in front of Tom's face.

"Come on, Tom," Mike said in an urgent whisper. "Let him up. It's a wallet."

A uniformed policeman burst in through the front door with his gun drawn. More people screamed. The herd of tourists broke past the hostess's stand for the rear of the restaurant.

"Freeze!" the cop yelled.

"I've got your man," Tom said. "He was trying to rob her."

The girl behind the cash register, still bawling, said, "He wasn't. He wasn't. That's my dad."

The store manager popped up from behind the counter. He put his arm around the girl and patted her back. He glared at Tom.

"What?" Tom said.

"Mr. Redmon," the cop said. "What the hell did you do this time?"

"I . . ."

"It's my fault," Mike said. "I'm sorry. I told him it was a robbery. Tom is a martial arts expert."

"Jujitsu," Tom said, getting up and dusting his hands. "I'm terribly sorry. It's a martial art with roots in feudal Japan, a period lasting from the eleventh to the sixteenth centuries of near-constant civil war."

"Jesus," the cop said, holstering his gun and kneeling down beside the fallen man. He began to chafe the man's wrists.

"I'm very sorry," Mike said. He pulled a fat wad of money from the front pocket of his pants and stripped off a hundred-dollar bill. He slapped it down on the counter. "This is all my fault. Come on, Tom. I'm sorry."

Mike led him out by the arm.

"Holy shit," Mike said.

"Hey, my credit card," Tom said, turning to go back.

"Tom," Mike said. "Later. Please."

"Who the hell wears an army coat in the middle of summer?" Tom asked, shaking his head.

"Please," Mike said, tugging at his arm, looking frantically around, his cheeks burning with color, "let's just get out of here."

"Now you're not going to cover my back?" Tom said, shaking free. "When I was a cop, a partner covered your back."

"How can you say that?"

"How can I not?"

"You . . . I . . ." Mike's face bunched up. "Who helped you dig up that federal judge's wife to see if she died of natural causes? Who was that?"

"I'm not talking about that kind of stuff," Tom said, getting into his old Ford truck. "That was a mistake. I just have discipline. I've trained myself to react."

"I've got discipline too," Mike said, raising his chin. His nostrils widened.

"In what, Mike?"

"Fiscal discipline," Mike said. His lips were smashed together tight.

Tom's face went slack. He opened his mouth, then stopped to catch his breath.

"Is that what this is about? Money?" Tom said. He looked hard at Mike. "And I'm buying you a Fribble?"

Mike threw his hands up in the air.

"I knew about your doubts. Ellen said something to me . . ."

"Ellen?" Mike said, his face losing tension. "What?"

"She . . ." Tom clamped his mouth shut. He had slipped. How could he tell anyone that sometimes she was still there? There and gone. Sometimes whispering. Sometimes it was just her laughter. He wondered himself.

"I've got to go," he said, closing the door.

"Tom . . ."

Tom backed out of his spot and got onto the road.

Halfway to the marina, he pulled into the convenience store and bought a six-pack of Labatt Blue beer. Next door he picked up a small brown bottle of Knob Creek. His heart pounded in his chest just watching the deep brown liquor swish in the thick glass.

The summer in upstate New York brought with it a rich canopy of trees. But even the sweep of broad green maple leaves and the whispering blades of the huge locust trees couldn't entirely conceal the crumbling gray concrete, the sagging metal roofs, and the corrugated walls washed in rust.

Like so many small upstate New York cities, Ithaca was pockmarked with structures that had long outlived their usefulness. The worst of these buildings butted right up against a lush green park that capped the south end of Cayuga Lake. Tom drove through the worst of them—grafittied brick, plywood for windows—kicking up gray dust in the heat.

The marina lay nestled in the midst of this eyesore. Tom's boat was a once-proud twenty-one-foot Regal with an open bow. *Rockin' Auntie*. Previously owned by the spinster from L.A. who spent her summers on a lake home up in Aurora.

The hull had been battered up one side and down the other

by nearly twenty years of minor accidents. The windshield wiper had no blade. The prop was gouged and bent. Its red racing stripe had faded to a drab dirty pink. It rested between two sailboats, sleek and white with long sweeping lines. Tom didn't know how to sail; that was for people who grew up with money.

He was the son of a cop who was the son of a cop. Their combined experience on the lake could be traced to a couple of fishing poles and a bag of ketchup and bologna sandwiches on board a battered aluminum skiff. In his mind, he could still hear the wheezy seven-horse Johnson outboard motor and smell the oil that bled from every seam. It had been the sole constituent of the Redmon family fleet.

Tom popped open the first of the Labatt Blues. He dropped down in a cushioned seat and leaned back, cutting off the wax around the whiskey bottle's neck. When he tilted his head a certain way, that first bit of whiskey heating the inside of him, he almost felt like she *was* there.

Had it really been ten years?

"You know the secret everyone wants to forget," she said. *"It's why you are who you are."*

He looked at her foggy shape, his cheeks feeling wet.

"You know there's evil in this world," she said. *"True evil. And it's only a matter of time before it enters your life again."*

He nodded.

And he drank.

CHAPTER 3

The newsroom was a jumble of metal desks painted in primary colors. Bland white columns thick enough for a person to hide behind stood guard along the outside wall, and the few glass-fronted offices were against the windows. For the rest of them, light spilled down from a pattern of square fluorescent panels throughout the ceiling's grid.

"Look at this crap," someone said.

Jane looked up from her computer, tapped a few more keys, then got up and slipped into the small crowd clustered around the little TV on Gina's desk.

"TV," someone else said in disgust.

A man on the television screen doubled over and emitted a stream of vomit.

"Can you believe that?"

Jane felt slightly ill.

"I believe it. Who in hell would go on a cruise anyway?"

"I went on one once," Gina said, turning from the TV to face the small group. She was sitting at her desk, and she looked up at them all. "It was like a frigging floating Motel Six. If a guy didn't have a tattoo, his nipples were pierced."

Gina turned back to the TV.

"I went on one once too. Motel Six has better food."

"At least it didn't kill you, right?"

"I mean can you believe they put that on TV?"

"Why not?" Gina asked. "They show people practically screwing on network television at nine o'clock at night."

The small screen was now filled with a big white ship. In the foreground a reporter with a solemn face talked about the outbreak and the dead.

Jane turned away. She had a deadline. As if on cue, Don Herman stood up at his own desk across the big room. Face like a mastiff. Overweight. Fifty. Bald with tufts of frizzy brown hair decorating his freckled skull above the ears. He looked at her and pointed at the clock. He held up two fingers, then three. She had twenty-three minutes.

Jane twisted her lips and looked away from him. She sat and put her fingers to the keyboard. There was Gina. By her side.

"Deadline?"

"Yup," she said, her fingers pounding out a flurry of words.

"Big one?"

"Big load of horse crap," Jane said, still pounding. "Unless you think anyone runs out in their bathrobe and tears through the morning paper to find out what happened in the Senate Finance Committee's meeting on funding for the Department of Weights and Measures."

"You gotta start somewhere," Gina said. "I told you that from the start. Just because you got a Pulitzer nomination doesn't mean you don't have to pay your dues. This is the *Washington Post*, sister."

Jane's maniacal patter stopped. She looked up at Gina, past the short frosted hair and the thick eyeliner.

"I don't have to like it, do I?"

"I'm going out for a cigarette," Gina said. "Meet me when you're done and we'll get a drink."

"You're on."

"That's what I like," Gina said. "We'll pull that hair of yours into a ponytail and they might mistake us both for college girls."

Gina was almost forty. Divorced. No kids. Nice figure, but a face Jane had overheard two copy editors describing as five miles of bad road. She drank too much and always regretted the men she slept with.

"Leave my hair alone," Jane said.

"Just trying to help."

Jane swept a long dark lock out of her face and back behind her ear, then continued to type. Gina repeated her instructions and left. Jane looked up at the big white clock on the wall. The thin red second hand swept around quicker than she would have liked. She flexed her fingers, cracking their knuckles, and got back to it.

She finished and sent the document to Don Herman. It wasn't what she would call good, but it wasn't bad, either. She got up, looked in her satchel, shut it, and slipped it over her shoulder. That's when the phone rang.

"Houston's at eight," the thin voice grated at her. "Manhattans and big Greek salads."

"It's seven-thirty, Frank," she said. "Why didn't you wait a little longer?"

"God, the market was crazy today," he said. He was a financial consultant for Dean Witter. "But we made a freakin' ton."

"I've got plans with Gina," she said. "Sorry."

In truth, she was sick of having the bill arrive and the two of them sitting there, looking at it, waiting for some magic trick that would make it disappear. She believed in chivalry. He regularly forgot his wallet.

"And do me a favor," she said, "don't come knocking on the door at midnight. I've got an early morning tomorrow."

"Sometimes I just need you," he said.

"I know what you need."

She hung up and was already on the other side of her desk when it rang again. She tried to walk away, but for the same reason she couldn't shit-can him altogether she picked up the phone.

"What, Frank?"

"I've got something for you," the voice said.

It wasn't Frank.

All the noise around her, all the typing, all the talk was reduced to a low hum.

"What?" she asked.

"Have you checked out everything else?"

"Yes," she said. She picked up a pen. She squeezed it. She twisted it. "It's good, but I still need more if I'm going to get it in. I have editors and they have editors. Something like this will have to go all the way up the line. You can't just attack a United States senator with some loose allegations. We don't print rumor."

"This will get it in. Meet me at L'Enfante Plaza at nine. 3-F."

"Can't we—"

She was going to say "meet someplace normal," someplace where she could see his face, know who he was. But he'd already hung up the phone. The thought of section 3-F in the damp bowels of the Plaza's parking garage made her skin crawl. But this could be it. He'd teased her with enough information that she knew he had it. It was just a question of when he was going to give it up.

This could be more than just a Pulitzer nomination. This could be the prize.

CHAPTER 4

One always had to be certain about leads. Jane was a young reporter, and still she got at least two dozen voice mails a week from people she didn't know. Crackpots with goofy ideas. Incredible stories. Wild stories.

Mrs. Kibble—she called once a week—had it straight from Jesus that the senator from Kansas was being guided by Satan to vote against the tax bill. A secretary in the office of a congressman from Rhode Island who wanted Jane to do a story on what a bad guy he was for not sending flowers on Secretary's Day, not even a card. This Mark Allen guy was extreme, though. He had left three messages a day for almost a week until he finally caught her answering the phone. Tidbits and leads that only an insider would know.

She told him to send an E-mail or fax but to stop calling. She'd check it out. But in the end, it took only one sentence to really grab her.

"Don't you want to know about the senator's connection to your father? He's Tom Redmon, right?" he asked.

Then the information began to pour out. Still he wouldn't answer questions about her father.

The air was still quite warm, even in the deep shadows of the buildings, when she exited the *Post*—the sun unseen, but glowing yellow in the west. Gina leaned against a concrete planter full of geraniums. Legs crossed. Pall Mall between her index and middle fingers and held up beside her ear. Lipstick stain on the white filter.

"I can't do drinks," Jane said.

"What?"

"I'm not even going to tell you. I was only *nominated* for a Pulitzer. Remember?"

Gina twisted her face sideways. She covered crime for the Metro Section. Two heads in a Dumpster wasn't a big deal to her.

"It's about Senator Gleason," Jane said.

Now Gina actually rolled her eyes.

"Not again."

It was a short walk to Jane's apartment. Out of her skirt and blouse and into jeans and sneakers with a sleeveless top. She didn't like to dress this way on the job. Casual made her look too young. She checked her face in the mirror. Some of the many freckles there were showing through so she dusted on some fresh makeup, then added a touch of lipstick.

Not bad. That was how the copy editors described her when they didn't know she was listening.

She caught a cab to the L'Enfante Plaza Hotel, got out, and circled around to the back of the building until she found a brown metal door. The opening led out onto a concrete pad just to the other side of a loading dock. She scanned the area to see if anyone had seen her. She went back around front, into the hotel lobby, and took the elevator down to the garage. The thick concrete columns bore the black scuff marks of a hundred bumpers. Above that were thick-painted bands, orange, green, and red, with numbers and letters stencil-painted in black.

Section 3-F was at the bottom, in the far corner, away from the light of the elevator bank. Right near the red door of an emergency exit stairwell. Jane cleared her throat and looked around. The lonely sound of her footsteps echoed off the concrete with just the hint of a twang. She glanced from the dark interior of one car to the next, then made herself stop. The hair on the back of her neck was beginning to rise.

"Mark," she said, peering into the dark corner.

She jumped. A rat scrabbled across the floor and between two small cars and disappeared beneath a box with a series of quick scratching sounds. Jane sniffed the dank air, then swallowed.

"Mark," she said, softly now.

"I'm here," he said. The dark shape of a man materialized in the shadows behind one of the thick columns.

Jane hurried over.

"That's close enough," he said.

She reached out and felt the smooth curve along the trunk of the Audi coupe resting beside her.

"I'm going to have to know who you are, you know," she said. "If you want me to keep spending time on this."

"I told you my name," he said.

"There are about a million Mark Allens," she said. "And you still haven't told me anything about my father. You said you would."

"I said when the time was right."

"I think the time is right, right now," she said.

"I know everything there is to know about him," he said. "I've spent two months. Watching. Listening. Everything. I've read everything there was to read about him. I tracked down every rumor. Some were. Some weren't.

"The whole time, your name kept popping up. Twenty-seven hundred dollars in unpaid parking fines. Another on campaign finance problems. One on . . . one on—"

"A seven-hundred-and-eighty-six-dollar credit card payment to a mob-operated strip club in Atlanta—which I forgot to mention, by the way, has since been shut down by the feds," she said. "We've been through this."

"Yes."

"So I don't like dirty rich egomaniacal politicians. They kind of suck."

"Neither do I."

"I don't have time for this. Give me what you have or leave me alone."

He bent down and slid a manila envelope down the length of the Audi.

She reached down and felt for it, keeping her eyes on him. Straining for a glimpse. The voice was young. Strong. His frame looked that way too. Just over six feet. Wiry. The shadows were too dark for anything else.

She straightened up and opened the envelope.

"It's all you'll need," he said. "Credit card records. From his foundation. Look at them. More strip clubs. Charter planes. Cases of French champagne. Escort services in Las Vegas. Those are hookers."

"No shit," she said, angling the first sheet into the dull light coming from the other side of the garage. "Hookers. Man, this guy is a professional politician. Almost quaint."

"This will get it in, right?" he asked.

"I'll check it out," she said, still reading. "It's a start. What about my father?"

She read on.

When she looked up, he was gone.

Jane heard the creak of the fire door. Instead of following the sound, as she'd done two other times, she turned and began to run. She sprinted up the ramp, full speed. Up and around. Up and around. Up and around. Her head swimming now. Her lungs burning.

She streaked past the cashier's booth. A thin dark man in a powder blue uniform. Thick glasses. He looked up and she raised her hand briefly on her way past. Like she knew him.

Outside. Clean air. She tore around the corner and froze. A man was walking swiftly away from the metal door. It was already closed, but it had to be Mark Allen. She watched him walk to the guardrail. Dark pleated slacks and a black knit shirt with a collar. Thick dark hair. Thick eyebrows. A tan chiseled face. A lean build. He looked around. She ducked behind a utility box, then popped her head out the other side. He disappeared over the edge.

Jane ran for the guardrail and peered over. A steep concrete embankment. A sidewalk along the bending road. He was walking down it, moving fast. Looking back. She waited until he rounded the corner of another building. He was headed for the Mall. Jane scrambled down the embankment. She slipped and landed on her bottom, scraping the palm of her left hand. She sprang up, tasted blood and dirt, and sprinted off after him, into the night.

CHAPTER 5

Jane watched him go back down Independence. He crossed at the Smithsonian, disappearing into its shadows. It rose like a gingerbread fortress from the street. Red stone. Turrets that reached into the night sky. Tall ornate windows, arched and gothic. She followed, pushing through a group of tourists shuffling along the brick pathway. Shorts and sneakers. Bags full of souvenirs. He looked back and she ducked behind a massive urn. She could smell the fresh-cut grass and just a hint of the flower beds glowing red and orange under the lighting along the sidewalk.

She stalked up to the path that encircled the park. Cinders crunched beneath her feet. To her right was the Capitol, a glowing white marble mountain. Mark went the other way. The Washington Monument lanced the sky. She passed it, then the Reflecting Pool. He cut across the front of the Lincoln Memorial, outlined black in its blue glow. Jane passed a group of teenagers sitting on blankets with a guitar and smoking pot. She began to jog, afraid she was losing him.

Suddenly, he glanced back and broke into a run. Jane followed. He darted down the path that led to the Vietnam Memorial. When Jane got there, she stopped and looked down into the space in front of the jet black wall. Flowers lay in clusters. Flags. Photos. Half a dozen small groups of people stood quietly. No one moved. Jane studied them, one by one, from her vantage point. He was gone.

She turned and ran toward Constitution Avenue. When she got there, she sat down on a bench and scanned the sidewalk up and down the street. Her breathing came in short shallow gasps. A bum stumbled out of the darkness and asked her for some change.

She heard the honk of a horn. Two blocks up a cab screeched its brakes.

A single figure dashed out from in front of the cab for the other side of the street. She sat and waited. When he got across, he leaned up against a tree and waited. After a few minutes, he came out of his shadow and turned up 21st Street. Jane paused for just a few seconds, then sprinted across the street herself.

She followed him up 21st. He went left on G Street. Halfway down the block, he went into an elaborate building. Italian Renaissance. White stone and a green bronze cornice. Jane crossed the street. When she saw the sign, she gasped.

DUFFY & MCKEEN, LLP

One of the most powerful law firms in the capital. She had seen McKeen at some of the bigger Senate fund-raisers. A little red-faced rooster of a man. She'd even shaken his hand once. He said hello, never taking his eyes off the senator from Michigan who was on the other side of the room.

Jane mounted the thick marble steps and peered through the

glass door. Mark Allen—it had to be him—stood there having a small laugh with the aging guard behind the front desk. Allen looked early thirties. His dark hair was neat, but longish and wavy. His high cheeks were tan and his skin contrasted sharply with the brilliant green of his almond eyes. A strong wide chin and white teeth.

She thought about going in, but instead waited across the street in the shadow between a van and a locust tree. It was only a minute or so before Mark Allen emerged. Jane felt her heart double its pace. When he was halfway up the block, she followed. In Monroe Park he stopped and bent over between a trash can and a park bench. Jane ducked behind a tree.

She squinted her eyes and craned her neck. He was lifting something up from the shadows. It looked like a big rug, but then she realized it was a person. A bent and wrinkled woman. Her long gray hair was kinky and matted. Mark Allen guided her by the arm across the street to a small coffee shop. Jane crossed also and watched from behind a car. She could see them inside the diner. He sat her in a small booth by the window and put something into her hand—money—before appearing back on the sidewalk and continuing on his way.

Five blocks later he entered a three-story brownstone. A small wooden sign hung above the door: THE TABARD INN. As groups of people came and went, she realized it was a restaurant as well as a small European hotel. She paced the sidewalk for nearly ten minutes before she decided just to go in. To the left of the small entryway was a sitting room lined with books and small table lamps. People sat in clusters, dressed in slacks and summer skirts. Jane looked down at her Levi's and gave them a cursory dusting.

There was no sign of Mark Allen so she moved on into the

dining area, past a narrow lively bar. Each of the small linen-covered tables was full. The air was scented with saffron and rang with banter. She scanned the room twice. Nothing.

Jane walked through a narrow doorway and out into the aging redbrick courtyard. It was quieter there, the sound muffled by two trees and the vines that blanketed the brick wall. Mark Allen sat at a wrought-iron table by himself, looking at the menu.

Jane slid into the seat across from him.

"So you want to tell me why Duffy & McKeen is so bent on ruining Senator Gleason?"

The menu dropped to the table and Mark Allen peered up at her. His eyes went past Jane, flickering as if he expected others to be there as well. Then he took a deep breath.

"What are you doing here?"

"I'm a reporter," she said. "I report."

"On me?"

"If it's a story I do," she said. She was sitting on her hands, but leaning forward. It was hard not to look at his eyes. "You ever heard, 'Consider the source'?"

"Maybe," he said. "You considering me?"

"Perhaps."

The waitress set a menu in front of Jane and asked if she wanted a drink. Jane said she didn't.

"Have something," Mark said. He smiled.

"No, thank you. What's this all about?"

He shrugged. "It's about a corrupt senator."

"Blah, blah, blah," she said. "What's new? What do you know about my father?"

"Did anyone ever tell you you have a beautiful neckline?"

"My father, please."

"I really can't say," he said. "Hey, if you don't want it, just give me back the credit card statements. I thought you'd be interested. I thought you'd be following Gleason, not me. No offense, but you're not the only reporter in this town."

She stood up.

"My father," she said.

"Good. Ask *him* about Gleason. Ask your father why he went from a respectable young prosecutor to representing old ladies slipping on grapes."

"My father fights for people," she said. "He has more balls than anyone who works at McKeen."

"He used to put people in jail," Mark said, his face grim. "Remember? He could have ended up a judge the way he was going. Then there was one little regular person he didn't help, and after that . . . Well, people do talk. They say he's a little off."

"You say that about my father again and I'll call a friend in the IRS. She'll give you and your friggin' law firm an enema. You hear me?"

Mark Allen let out a snort.

"Look. I didn't mean it like that. We're on the same side here. Talk to your father and call me."

"Whatever, Mr. Allen," she said. "I'm tired of playing games.

"I look forward to more of your consideration."

CHAPTER 6

The next day, Jane skipped the committee meeting she was supposed to write a ten-inch daily about and left a message for Don—she was working on a story project he'd love. Instead, she drove herself out to the edge of town near the old RFK Stadium. It was a strange place to headquarter a charitable foundation, and she was a strange sight. A white girl in a skirt. A small red convertible. A rough part of town.

If it was true, then Gleason was writing off millions of dollars each year by funneling money through something he called the Good Samaritan Foundation. He was then using the funds to finance his own weird adventures. The foundation had a Web site complete with pictures of smiling children and their mothers, claiming it built homes for impoverished single-parent families in the capital area.

She couldn't seem to reach her father.

Even his secretary said he hadn't been in. Some kind of problem with the local police again. At a Friendly's. What could you mess up at a Friendly's Ice Cream?

She found the building. Three stories. A board on one window. Spray paint on the door. She looked at the address again.

It was correct. She got out of her car and looked around. Smoke and laughter floated up from a group of young men on the sidewalk. They wore sports jerseys, baggy pants, and crooked hats, and they stood underneath a half-dead cherry tree that strained against its metal collar. There was a stain on the sidewalk and the wall of the building. Jane smelled stale urine. She turned her head to the side and took a breath.

She focused on the painted door. It was unlocked. She glanced at the group of young men. They stared. She went in anyway. The first office on the right was open. An olive-skinned man with a thin beard sat talking on the phone. He had a cigarette in his free hand, and a cloud of smoke eased out into the hall. He glared up at her. She went on. The address said suite 102. Two doors down on the left. It was locked. Jane knocked softly. No one came.

She walked down the hall. Other than the man on the phone, there was no sign of anyone. She looked one way, then the other as she removed the driver's license from her satchel. She slipped it between the frame of the door and the lock and jimmied it open. She looked around once more. Her heart pounded. She went in.

No one. A bound stack of magazines in the corner of the cracked linoleum floor. Broken glass. Cardboard taped on the missing part of the dirty window. It smelled like an empty can of tuna.

She stopped at the smoky doorway on her way out. She waited there while the man talked in Spanish and glared at her through the gray cloud.

Finally, she held up her hand and said, "Can I ask you a question, please?"

The man put his hand over the receiver and said, "What?"

31

"The Good Samaritan Foundation," she said. "Are their offices here?"

The man gibbered something quickly into the phone and hung it up. He rose and started to come out from behind the desk.

"And who the hell are you?"

"I'm with the *Washington Post*," she said. "My name is Jane Redmon."

The man was almost toe to toe with her now. She smelled cigarettes and mouthwash.

"You got no business coming here," the man said. "This is private property."

Jane stifled a laugh.

"I'm looking for the Good Samaritan Foundation offices," she said. "Their Web site gave this address."

"So what do you got to do with them? You don't work for them."

"I want to ask some questions about the foundation," she said. "Do you know the people involved? Are they tenants here?"

"I think maybe you should just mind your own business," he said, frowning. "That's what I think."

"Unfortunately," she said, "that's my job."

He moved even closer to her. His voice became throaty.

"Well, maybe you ought to think about changing jobs."

Jane felt his hand brush her hip. She slapped it down and stepped back.

"What's your name?"

The man began to laugh.

"Get your hands off me, you cockroach," she said. "I know

about twenty ways to knock your nuts into the back of your throat."

He stepped back and unconsciously blocked his crotch with a fist.

Jane turned and left, hurrying to her car. Tires squealed as she pulled away from the curb and blew through a yellow light.

The summer air warmed her face and hair. The broken glass and graffiti began to dry up and she raised her face to the sun, inhaling the green bloom of the trees. She rolled past the Capitol Building and felt a twinge of guilt for the story she'd missed. She kept going. There was a spot for her car down the alley behind her apartment. She went up the rusty iron stairs in the back. The slider was unlocked.

She had to have all the angles covered before she took this to Don Herman. On-line, she got corporate records for the foundation and Gleason's tax returns. She called a handful of people she knew back in New York, constituents; she got their comments. Finally, she picked up the credit card statement off her desk and began to call the businesses where Gleason had spent the foundation's money. Strip clubs. Escort services. Limousines. Private jets. Luxury hotels. Jewelry. Cigars. Fine wine. A Madison Avenue furrier. Custom-made suits. It was all right there. Some weren't helpful, but enough of them were.

She had what she needed, so why were her hands sweating? More. She needed another day. Everything in a tight package for that tight-ass Herman.

The phone rang.

She let it ring. But for some reason, her voice mail wouldn't kick in, and she picked up the receiver. "Talk to me."

"Didn't I teach you better manners?"

"Dad?"

"Sarah said you'd called."

"You going to be around tonight?"

"Sure—there's this piece on A&E about the Trojan War. Did you know that Helen of Troy was the daughter of Zeus himself? That's a lot of weight."

"Dad, please. Yes or no?"

"Yes."

"I'll take you to Madeline's."

"I'll cook. I have two fillets in the freezer that were made by the gods, and I'll make my special steak sauce. You know Redmon's Best. Makes A-1 seem like motor oil."

"Sounds great," she said. "But before we eat, we talk."

"About?"

"The past."

CHAPTER 7

By the time Jane drove through Ithaca, the sun was ready to disappear behind the clouds. They had congregated in a thick cluster above the western ridge of Cayuga Lake. Jane drove up and out of town, climbing the massive ridge to the east until the rooftops and the water lay below.

The top to Jane's red Mazda was still down. A silk band held her hair in a single soft whip and it dashed away at her long neck. The air was beginning to cool now. She struggled into her dark blue denim jacket without bothering to slow down.

Home was an old white farmhouse on a hill. Fields stretched in every direction. Russet. Green. Yellow. Colorful even in the diminishing light. Hundreds of acres before the lush woods staked their claim. The house's gables were somehow majestic in the auburn light. The windows were tall and rounded at their tops. Narrow, with gingerbread shutters. Columns, carved in the Corinthian style, supported the broad front porch. As Jane drove through the thin stand of large oak sentries, she narrowed her eyes, looking past the house at the magnificent view, purposely ignoring the peeling paint and the rotten gray joints that she knew were still there.

The old house had been her mother's bane. Tricky plumbing. Fickle heat. Mice. And five massive fireplaces that attracted a slew of swifts year after year. Her father was always going to fix it. All of it. Just as soon as he had a windfall of cash. He promised. Jane and her mother both knew in their hearts that he really meant it. But the money never came, and then the promise died alongside her mother.

Jane walked up the front steps, avoiding the third from the top, where rusty nail heads stood proud amid the horde of soft jagged planks. The screen in the door was torn. A dark furry fly bumped against it twice before finding its way in. Even before she crossed the threshold Jane detected the scent of steak and charcoal. The door opened with a creak.

To her right, the parlor of the original owner, a gentrified farmer, opened like an Egyptian tomb. Beneath the gilt crown molding of the spacious room, she saw a huge castle built of empty beer cans.

"Xanadu," said her father in his Tabasco apron. He stood there in the hall, in his hand another Labatt brick for the fortress.

"You named it?" she said.

"Why not?" he said with a shrug and a smile. "I'll have grandkids one day. Maybe. Can you imagine them running through that thing?"

"That's a long way off, Dad," she said.

"A man without dreams is a man without hope," he said. "How about a hug?"

Jane hugged him, turning her nose away from the smell of alcohol. Out on the deck she saw a platoon of empty beer cans mustered on the glass-covered cocktail table. The deck was the one improvement he had made. Pressure-treated wood with thick lag bolts. Nearly two centuries removed from the rest of the house. Smoke boiled from beneath the cover of the grill. The day was fading fast. The sky pink. The clouds scarlet trimmed with charcoal wisps.

"Want a beer?" he asked.

"Okay."

Her father's dark eyes glimmered in the soft light. He bent down and dug into a green cooler that he'd set up next to his chair.

"God, the view," she said, opening the beer.

He turned and looked out at the long dark lake. To the north, it stretched clear to the horizon.

"Sometimes I sit here and I feel like it belongs to me," he said. "All of it. Then your mother reminds me that only five acres came with the house."

"Dad?"

"What?"

"What do you mean she reminds you?"

Her father turned to the grill, picked up his fork, and lifted the lid. A great cloud of smoke hurried away.

"In my mind," he said. The steaks hissed and spat until the grill clanked shut.

He sat down in an old folding chair and brought the beer can to his lips, looking out over his kingdom.

Jane pulled up a chair and sat down beside him. He sighed and reached over to pat her leg, his eyes fixed in the distance. Jane filled her mouth with beer, letting it fizz out before she swallowed it.

"Now you gonna tell me?" he asked.

"When I was a little girl," she said, "everything you said, I soaked it up. Little things and big things. You read books. I read

TIM GREEN

books. You didn't like golf, so I thought it was stupid to chase a little white ball around on a nice day. You always tip twenty percent. So do I. I even tried to learn that self-defense stuff."

"Jujitsu."

"Yeah, that. And you always fought against corruption, Dad, and I wanted to fight too."

"And you're doing good," he said.

"Thanks. And there was always one thing you railed against nonstop, and I guess I have too. You always zeroed in on one particular politician. Every news article about a backroom deal. Every press conference. Every fund-raiser. Every election. I picked up on that. How could I not? But I want to know why, Dad. What happened with Senator Gleason?"

"Is that what this is about?"

"Kind of."

"You heard about Friendly's."

"I don't care about Friendly's."

Her father finished his beer and fished out another one.

"Gleason is just a bad man who owned this town," he said. "And now he owns a lot more than that. The whole state."

"And us?"

"What?"

"Does he own us?" she asked. Her hands were shaking, and she took a gulp of beer from her can.

"No one owns me," he said, glaring at her.

Jane looked away and said, "What happened, Dad? I know something happened. It has something to do with a story I'm working on and I don't want to have to find out on my own. I want you to tell me."

He slowly dropped his face into his meaty hands and massaged his temples for a minute. His fingertips moved to his eyes,

38

then he sat up and tipped back the new can of beer until it too was gone. The empty can made a quiet tinny noise when he set it down on the cocktail table next to the others.

He got up and shut off the grill.

"Who told you?" he asked before he started.

"A man I met but don't trust."

"Is he with Gleason?"

"No," she said. "I know that much."

Her father wiped his hands on his apron and pulled it away from him. He cracked open a beer and looked out into the lake as if it held all the answers.

"I don't know where to begin," he said, rolling into the story.

Her father told her about a college girl named Sook Min who was beaten and raped. Of a young assistant district attorney named Tom Redmon. A former cop who worked his way through law school. A year in property crimes. Another trying assaults. Then sex crimes. The precursor to homicide, a young lawyer's dream.

The girl, a math student from China with broken English, was a baby-sitter. She said her assailant was the father of the children she watched on a regular basis. A young state senator. Michael Gleason of the Gleason Truck Lines empire.

"Then I got a call from Walt Tipcraft," he said. "He was the DA and a good man. I have no idea why he did it. He's in a nursing home down in Binghamton. Anyway, he told me the case was to be dropped. The girl wasn't credible. She was credible to me, though, and I said I wasn't going to just drop it . . .

"They took the case from me. I tried to raise the roof, but it came down on me instead.

"They trumped up some sexual harassment charges against me with one of the secretaries in the office," he said, staring at the lake. "God, that hurt your mother. It was all lies. I think she finally believed me, but you know, I never really knew. I tried to go to the papers, but he bought them, too. Anyway, I was finished and I knew it. They not only canned me—they blackballed me at every firm in town. But they couldn't take my license. They tried, but that I kept.

"I know he did it," her father said. "So did a lot of people. I tried to fight, but some things . . . I just watched him keep going, keep doing things. There were other people along the way. A girl who worked on his campaign who disappeared. Some people said he was involved with her. They kept it quiet. There was an opponent who suddenly dropped out of a race when his kid got arrested with some cocaine. The kid swore it was a setup, but the damage was done. That's how Gleason operates. No rules but his."

"I remember the girl," Jane said, "but no one ever accused Gleason . . ."

"People who get in his way are either crushed or ruined," her father said. "It ate at my gut to know that no one could stop him. So I . . . railed."

He reached into the cooler, fishing around noisily in the ice until he came up with another can. He flipped the top. It hissed and he sat back. Neither of them spoke. Crickets played their nighttime serenade. Fireflies blinked across the back lawn. Jane sighed.

"I'm going to stop him," she said.

Her father's face sagged from the alcohol.

"You can't," he said.

"Why? Because you didn't?"

She was sorry before the words even left her mouth, but she couldn't stop them.

40

"Because. I. Couldn't. No one can."

"I can," she said, raising her chin.

His massive frame was slumped down in his chair, his face sagging again. At the sight of him, she felt herself come uncorked. She stood up and looked down at him. Her knees shook. She could barely breathe.

"You ran after all these crazy dreams," she said. "And we stood by you, Dad. We stood there and watched you throw yourself away on—on injunctions against the government and lawsuits against billionaires, fighting noisy battles against giants who swatted you down like a gnat."

"I want you protected from all that," he said. "That's the ugly world." He smiled at her and winked. "You're too pretty for that."

"I don't need your protection," she said. "I'm not afraid of him."

"Well you goddamn well better be," he said.

He walked back inside the house and she heard him add another can to his castle with a clink.

CHAPTER 8

Jane woke in a sweat in the sheets of her own bed. She looked at her watch and sat up. It was nearly ten. She'd driven the whole way back last night.

She got out of the twisted sheets and into a cool shower. Refreshed, she made strong Starbucks coffee, filled her mug, and went for some cream. On the fridge was a picture of her on spring break from five years ago. One hundred twenty-eight pounds and looking not bad. That's what she should be. She shut the door and drank it black.

She looked at her watch. Don Herman would be rolling out of his morning editorial meeting any minute. She stuffed her leather satchel and went out the front door.

By the time she arrived, she was breathing hard. Her upper lip was damp, and she tugged at her linen pants, adjusting her underwear as she hurried up the steps. Don Herman was at his desk, on the phone. His coat was slung over the back of his chair, and he displayed the coffee stain next to his tie without apparent concern.

Jane stood waiting for him to finish the call. When he hung up she said, "Can I talk to you?"

"Talk."

"Can we talk in a conference room?" she asked.

"This is a newspaper," he said, getting up from his desk anyway and leading her toward the small glass conference room, "not a GD monastery." Don Herman never swore. He just used the initials for whatever curse he wanted to express. His wife was a devout Catholic.

Don sat down at the table while Jane closed the door. When she turned to him, he was looking into her.

"I have a story," she said.

"Let me guess," he said. "You've got something that's gonna change the balance of power on the Senate Appropriations Committee with shocking implications for our nation's morality."

"I . . . ," Jane said, her mind tumbling, "you . . . How did you know?"

A smile crept onto Don Herman's face. His eyes twinkled briefly and the furrows thinned out, but just for a moment.

"You're slightly obsessed," he said. "You think you're GD Carl Bernstein and Senator Gleason is Nixon."

"You believe that?" she said. She pursed her lips and felt her eyes straining at him. "Gleason couldn't wipe Nixon's ass."

"Please watch your language," he said, still smiling. "This would make the fourth article you've written on Gleason blasting the guy since joining the paper."

Jane slid the file across the table to him and watched while the furrows of his brow grew deeper and deeper. When he was finished, a low whistle slipped out of his puckered lips.

"Where'd you get these credit card statements?" he asked, holding one up in the air.

"I have a source who wants to remain anonymous," she said.

"How credible?"

"Very," she said. "My boyfriend—uh, a guy I know—went to Princeton with the CFO of the Bank of Bermuda and I verified the account."

The credit card bills were the linchpin of her story. Everything else could be explained away, but not the charges to Gleason's foundation credit card. She had a strip club owner in Tampa who was drooling over the chance to pin a U.S. senator. Gleason had been disruptive and rude in his club. And there was a woman who ran an escort service in Las Vegas who shared the strip club owner's sentiments. Those were the things that gave life to the story, the things that would destroy the senator.

"I mean, this doesn't make sense," Don said, shaking his head. "Some people are talking about him running in '08. His family's got money."

"Yeah, and how do you think they got that way?"

After a pause, Don said, "You know Simon's sure as F not going to want to let you do this."

Simon Wahl was the managing editor of the paper.

"Are you kidding?" she said with an incredulous laugh. "This is front page. This man chairs the Senate committee that oversees the expenditures for health and human services and he's committing tax fraud. He'll go to jail."

Don waved his hand in the air.

"I don't mean it's not going to be written," he said. "I mean he's not going to want you to be the one to do it."

"It's mine," she said, gathering up the papers.

Don stared at her for a moment, then said, "Jane, you work for this F-ing paper. Nothing is yours . . ."

Jane felt the floor shifting beneath her.

"I've already got most of this thing written," she said. "I don't give—excuse me—a fuck. I'm writing this. You lose my byline and I'll quit."

"Written?" he said.

"I've verified everything. I went to the offices. They don't exist. I've got his tax returns, the corporate records, the credit card bills. I've got comments from his constituents. All I need are comments from Gleason and some other members of the Senate, and I can get those today . . ."

"Listen," he said. "I'm not promising anything. I'll try. I just know Simon. He's going to want Bob Woodward or someone like that to do this thing. This is GD big. Maybe you can work together. We'll see."

"Don," she said. "Please."

"I'll talk to him," he said, rising from the table. "Don't get your hopes up, but I'll go talk to him right now."

"That means yes."

He shrugged.

"I'll be at my desk. Writing."

He clenched his jaw. "Shit."

CHAPTER 9

Jane watched the show from the corner of her eye. Don Herman and the invisible Simon Wahl. Herman's arms moving wildly around behind the glass in the corner office. His frizzy brown hair protruding from the sides of his head, changing shape. Then he pursed his lips, nodded, and reached for the door.

Jane turned quickly to her computer. She began to type. She could feel Don Herman standing there behind her. Finally, he cleared his throat. Jane turned and looked up.

"Don?" she said.

Then his eyes were back on hers, locked and probing.

"All I can say to you is, you better not fuck it up."

Don Herman turned and marched right back to his desk without another word. Jane looked around her at the other writers staring. Gina grinned. Jane sucked in her lower lip and bit down, not wanting to smile, not wanting to appear smug. It was an effort, but she did her best and spun back around to her computer, where she tilted her head down and began to type.

When Jane settled down enough that she could think, she

picked up the phone and dialed Gleason's office. Her hands trembled.

"Senator Gleason's office."

"Hello, my name is Jane Redmon," she said. "I'm with the *Washington Post* and I'd like to talk with Senator Gleason."

"Oh, you again. I can give you to his press secretary, Mr. Canter."

"No," she said, "I don't want to speak to anyone but the senator."

"I'm sorry, he's in a meeting right now anyway, but Mr. Canter would be the person you're going to want to talk with. He handles all the senator's media relations."

"Tell him I'm writing a story that involves funneling money from Good Samaritan Foundation into the G-strings of hookers and prostitutes. Tell him I'll make sure I spell his name right and I'll use the standard family photo he likes with the family and dog."

"The senator can't speak to you right now."

"Fine," Jane said. "Tell him he can read about it then. It's your job."

Jane made nearly two dozen more calls to different senators, hoping to get at least two return calls so she could get quotes from Gleason's colleagues. Chuck Schumer, the other senator from New York, actually called her back and gave her a noncommittal quote before she realized the newsroom had gone quiet around her for a second time. When she turned in her seat, there was Don Herman.

"We just got a call from Senator Gleason," he said, a rare smile tugging at the corners of his lips. "He's very unhappy. I told him we'd certainly include whatever he had to say to you as part of our story. He didn't say he'd talk to you, but he didn't say he wouldn't, so . . . go get him."

She was on her feet. She loaded her satchel, glanced at the clock, and wondered which would be faster, a cab or her feet.

She took a cab. At Columbus Circle, they got hung up in traffic. She hopped out and ran down First Street. The dome of the U.S. Capitol loomed over the tree-lined street, the bronze Statue of Freedom at its crest, nearly three hundred feet from the ground. Her right hand rested upon the hilt of a sheathed sword. In her left was a laurel wreath of victory. Beneath her gaze was the Senate Office Building. Jane's destination.

She cleared security and went up to Gleason's office. The secretary directed her to have a seat, a spindly wooden chair with no cushion. After that, the woman sniffed sharply and paid her no attention whatsoever. Jane took some papers from her satchel and pretended to be busy. After nearly an hour of eaves-dropping, she gathered that Gleason wasn't even there, but getting a workout in the fitness center downstairs. Jane politely inquired where the rest room was, left the office, and hurried down the fire stairs to the basement.

Down the hall and through a door of frosted glass was a reception desk. Behind it sat a woman Jane's age with a blond ponytail. She wore a white nylon sweat suit.

"Senator Gleason's office sent me down here," Jane said, making eye contact, but continuing right on past.

Rich blue carpet covered the floors, and the machines were widely spaced. The air was crisp and cool and smelled not of sweat, but of new carpet, with just a hint of fresh paint and grease. She saw a handful of people working out, talking among themselves to the accompaniment of classical music, the slick whisper of well-oiled chains, and the light tap of weight stacks.

Gleason stood in the corner facing a mirror, a dumbbell in each hand. A dark blue towel draped around his neck. He was a short man in his early fifties, but the muscles in his arms were clearly defined beneath the tight short-sleeved shirt. His waist trim and even beneath the dark blue sweatpants.

Seeing him this way, out of his custom-made dark suits and silk ties, was somehow embarrassing, as if he were naked. Jane stole a quick glance around. The woman at the desk had her eyes glued to Jane. She was on her feet. Jane swallowed and waited for Gleason to lower his arms. With a huff and a thump, he returned the weights to their rack. His tan face was flush, and Jane could clearly see the plugs of dark yellow hair that sprouted from above his brow.

As if he sensed the target of her attention, Gleason flipped his part down and over and raised his small nose, its nostrils flaring.

"Can I help you?" he said. His eyes were dark and round like a beetle's. Even so, the cleft of his jutting chin and his full cherubic lips made most people describe him as handsome.

"I'm Jane Redmon from the *Washington Post,*" she said. She set her satchel down on a padded bench and removed a notebook and pen. "I'd like a comment from you about your personal spending with credit cards from the Good Samaritan Foundation."

A porcelain smile slowly revealed itself. Crow's-feet appeared at the corners of Gleason's eyes, and Jane noticed the liver spots normally camouflaged by the orange tan.

"I have no idea what you're talking about," he said. "But I do know that this is a private club. You have no business being here."

He signaled past her to the girl at the desk.

"You don't remember charging twenty-five hundred dollars

with the Paradise Escort Service in Las Vegas on December thirty-first? Or one thousand seven hundred and seventy-five dollars at Mons Venus Men's Club in Tampa in mid-March?"

Gleason's dark eyebrows pinched together above his nose and rose precipitously up and out toward his sharp ears. His small mouth was pulled into a tight flat line and his lips puffed out. The color of his face began to change. Orange. Pink. Red. Scarlet. His hands gripped the towel on either side of his neck, the beds of his sharp manicured nails fire engine red, the knuckles white.

"You are making a mistake," he said. "We're talking about libel and slander."

"I know my facts," Jane said. "I have the credit card statements and the witnesses who can corroborate it. So what do you have to say? Anything about the love of your family and country? Or maybe just of brass poles?"

Someone was beside Jane now. An angry scowl. A quivering bleached-blond ponytail.

"Senator? I'm sorry," the attendant said, "this woman said she was sent down by your office."

"Remove her, please," Gleason said. A shiny line of perspiration was now evident along the furrowed ridges of his brow.

"You'll have to leave," the attendant said, taking Jane by the arm.

Jane snapped free. "I take it that's a 'No comment.'"

"You're making a mistake," he said, laughing. "I hope you like being unemployed."

"I have a story to write."

CHAPTER 10

Bob Thorne set down his book and got up out of the chair where he did his reading. He wore a white tank top undershirt, a pair of light blue boxers, and dark socks. This was how he spent most of his time, reading in his underwear. He dressed only when he went out.

His books lined the walls of his living quarters, floor to ceiling, covering almost every inch of the painted cinder-block walls. They were the finest works of literature the human race had ever produced and they spoke to him in four different languages, led by Voltaire, Tolstoy, Faulkner, and Márquez. He had read them all and was halfway through reading them again. According to the actuary tables, he would have the opportunity to read them no more than three times. At that point, he would be ninety-eight.

The kitchen was spotless. That made sense. He never used it. He lived entirely below the earth's surface. He came out once a day before dawn to walk the perimeter of his grounds for an hour, then shoot at the range in the detached garage for thirty minutes. As the sun came up, he retired to his quarters.

Every meal he ate came from a can. The distilled water he drank came in one-gallon plastic jugs. His pantry was quite orderly. He went to any single store no more than once a year. No one knew who he was. The last person who could identify him had died three years ago of a sudden and unexpected coronary.

He wasn't being self-important in considering himself the perfect killing machine. He had proven his worth through the years. There were very few of his kind anymore. Young people were too brash. Too self-centered. They wanted people to know who they were. What they did. Bob Thorne was a ghost.

The phone rang.

He crossed the room and picked up the phone on his desk.

"Hello?"

"Mr. Thorne?"

"Yes."

"I was told to call this number and mention the King of Clubs."

"Yes, of course," Thorne said, flicking a switch by his phone to secure the line.

"Now?"

"Of course. You are free to talk. Our line is clear."

"There's a reporter from the *Washington Post* who has some very damaging things to say about the King of Clubs. He is very concerned. I was thinking you could clean up the entire matter. Everything. I think everything needs to just . . . go away. Right away."

"As in . . . today?"

"Yes," the voice said. "Tomorrow would be too late. It could get messy and it could be a disaster."

"Everything is possible," Thorne said.

"The King of Clubs can pay you. Money isn't an issue."

"Everything has already been taken care of," Thorne said. "My job is to do a favor. Tell me about the problem."

The voice did.

Thorne's clients were few, but their needs were usually great. That was his job.

He sat at his desk when he hung up and pondered the King of Clubs. Wasn't there a key vote in the Intelligence Committee back in '92? Something about Colombia? No matter.

He found the girl's address by dialing directory assistance. He wasn't fond of computers, didn't trust them. He wrote small neat letters in a pocket notebook and found a map of D.C. in the cabinet beside his desk. He traced his pen along the route from where he was in rural Maryland to where she was, jotting down directions for himself in his notebook as he went.

When he was finished, he took the master list out of his desk drawer. Using a ruler, he put a line through the King of Clubs. Fifty-two cards in the deck when he began. Only the Seven of Diamonds and the Three of Clubs remained. After that, he would get a phone call. He would go to Grand Cayman and cash out an account for $2 million. He would change his identity for the last time and buy a small time-share on St. Martin. The only things he would take with him were the books.

He went to his closet. Three suits hung neatly. A pair of khaki pants. Two shirts. A raincoat. On the floor were two pairs of polished shoes. One black. One brown. Rubbers. Also a pair of work boots. Matching belts hung from a hook on the door. He chose gray and black. The blue shirt. No tie; domestic work didn't require a tie. He would, however, need the coat and rubbers—the forecast called for rain.

A can of Lysol stood next to the shoes; its blue plastic top was free of dust. He gave each black shoe a gentle blast before slipping his feet inside with an ivory shoehorn he'd purchased many years ago in Cambodia. Next he went to his gun drawer and removed the .22 revolver. Small. No jamming. He filled the cylinder with hand-loaded cartridges. Quiet. Under his other arm he strapped the Walther PPK. Efficient, with adequate firepower in the event of an emergency. He'd never had to use it outside his shooting range.

His thin gray hair was already combed neatly through with pomade. A gray felt hat with a black band went on top of that. Suit coat on, he went upstairs, stopping at the metal door to peer through the fish-eye lens into the kitchen. It was impossible that someone could be there without having tripped the series of warning systems encircling his hundred-acre compound. But Bob had been able to reach the age of sixty-seven because he had always considered even the impossibilities.

He walked outside into the sunshine, blinking as he felt for the clip-on sunglasses in his breast pocket. He fastened them onto the black plastic rims of his bifocal glasses and crossed the driveway under the eaves of a massive red maple. The tree whispered to him as he crouched down and opened the garage door. A nondescript Buick Regal.

He set the coat and rubbers on the passenger seat and set off down his long straight driveway. Once he was through the electric gates and out on the open road, he indulged himself with a little whistling. His own rendition of Beethoven's Fifth. The approach of death. He had never failed on an assignment. He had never even come close.

CHAPTER 11

Conrad Duffy of Duffy & McKeen had once been presented to the Queen of England at Buckingham Palace. He was part of a small delegation invited to tea. The library where it was served was carved from black cherry, a rare material that gave life to the carved men and creatures in the burgundy plains of its panels. To preserve the memory of that day, Duffy tried to replicate the feel of that place in his firm's main conference room. From the center of that room, amid the swirl of wood, hung a Lalique crystal chandelier. Mark Allen found himself not listening, but staring at the seam of a particular bauble, fascinated that from the empty space of glass could come an explosion of colors.

Today, Mark Allen wore a dark blue Armani suit and a two-hundred-dollar burnt orange tie. When he realized the room had gone quiet, he leaned back in his leather chair and unbuttoned his jacket. They were waiting for him to speak. He glared back at the half-dozen attorneys assembled around the massive table. When you didn't know what to do in a meeting, you glared. He'd learned that from his mentor.

"We're talking about eleven figures," Mark Allen said, leaning forward with his hands flat on the wood. "Billions. That says it all. It has its own set of ethics. If you have to step on someone's throat . . . you do it, or it will be done to you . . .

"I want you to remember this: If we get this contract, it's more than a deal. It will change the balance of power in corporate America, and this firm is going to be a part of it."

The meeting ended on that note, and he returned to his office. Mark Allen hadn't ended up in the offices of Duffy & McKeen by chance. You didn't just get to a midpoint in your career and happen to find yourself there. You had to reach for it. If influence was the currency of politics, Duffy & McKeen was a mint. Its partners included six former senators, ten former congressmen, and thirty-two high-ranking members of past administrations.

Mark was there for different reasons, but his development was equally impressive. West Point. Four years as an officer in Military Intelligence. Then back to school. Men in their early thirties didn't usually move other men and companies like chess pieces, but Mark Allen did.

He made phone calls until the light coming through the window began to fade. Rain pattered on the sill, and as he packed his laptop into his briefcase, he called for a car. Dinner was at eight at the Capital Grill. After a thick red steak and two bottles of Franciscan Magnificat with the senator from California, he threw his coat over his head and dashed through the rain into the waiting Town Car.

He sprinted from the car up the steps and into his brownstone. It was a spartan apartment, with a few pieces of rented furniture. Mark looked down at the floor and thought about finding a cleaning service. Without bothering to remove his wet shoes, he grabbed a can of Sprite from the refrigerator, loosened his tie, and sat down on the couch to watch the news. He carefully watched an ad for a Porsche. That was one thing he planned on getting. Then one day, a yacht. For parties with important people. A helicopter, too. He wanted to have meetings and land on the tops of buildings. He wanted someone with an umbrella waiting for him in the rain. The real rain had dried from his face by the time he went upstairs.

His mind was on a shower, but the small red eye on his monitoring device glowered at him. He flipped off his shoes without untying them and sat down at the table. He put on the headphones, went back to the beginning of the recorded disk, and took a thin notebook and a pen out of his briefcase.

Over the months of listening to what went on inside Gleason's office, he had become adept at being able to advance through the mundane conversations. It was just midnight when he got to the part of the disk where Gleason stormed into his office irate and made his mysterious phone call to Bob Thorne.

When Mark heard the words "go away," his heart grew tight and his breathing short. He jotted them down. They were going to kill her. When he heard "Tomorrow would be too late," he ripped off the headset, stuffed the notebook back into his briefcase, threw on his running shoes, and dashed out the door.

CHAPTER 12

Jane got up and changed the music. It wasn't happening with Holst's *Planets*. It hadn't happened with Mozart's Piano Concerto in D Minor. John Coltrane was next. The words were stuck. Maybe it was the ideas.

She had no distractions. The phone was unplugged, her cell phone turned off. She never wrote at home. She always wrote on the clock and in the chaos of the newsroom. But she wanted this filed tomorrow morning. She didn't want Herman to pull the damned thing at the last second because she hadn't dotted some i or crossed a t. She just took the whole thing home with her. She'd work all night if she had to to get it all straight in her head.

They were clearing the lead column on page one for her. She had to make this the best piece she'd ever written.

There was one distraction. The image of Mark Allen kept popping up, unwanted graffiti on the inside of her mind. What was his deal in all this? What was his agenda? Everyone had an agenda.

She huffed out loud and changed into a pair of shorts and

sneakers, muttering as she tied them. She pulled a nylon shell over the top of her favorite Syracuse basketball T-shirt and flipped up the hood. The cell phone went into her pocket.

This was what she needed. It didn't matter that the rain was spattering the glass in an unending staccato. It might cleanse her mind.

In the front hall of the brownstone, the warm smell of incense and spices filled the air. She considered the door to the young Indian doctor's apartment, and thought she heard the muffled sound of laughter. Out on the front step, there was a single silent flash of lightning. Not chain lightning, but a glow from horizon to horizon. Heat lightning. The rain poured down, mincing the puddles and flooding the street. The glow of the streetlights was muted by the torrent, and the yellow rectangles of light coming from the front windows of the apartment building across the street were blurred.

A single car crawled down the street, pushing cones of light that swarmed with rain. It slowed in front of her steps, and she thought she saw the glint of someone's eyeglasses from within. The vague, gray form of a face. Someone looking. Then the car drove on, its taillights bleeding into the night.

Jane went the other way, for Potomac Park along the river. If it had been nice, she would have run the streets. But the nasty weather would keep the darkness's usual dangers under cover, even this late at night. She preferred the long slow winding path along the edge of the park, where she wouldn't have to stop for traffic lights.

She looked back over her shoulder for the car. It was gone. Strange. Something told her to go back. She slowed her pace, then stopped. She turned to search the street. Rain pattered off her hood. Her socks were already wet and heavy. She felt a wave of disgust. Childish fears of the dark.

Growing up, she was afraid of swimming in the lake after dark. Irrational. She'd beaten that by forcing herself to endure small doses. Then she'd increased them, like poison, until she was immune.

She turned for the park, running hard now. Pushing herself. Splashing through the puddles. By the time she got there, she was winded. The smell of rain and warm pavement was drowned out by the tangy scent of worms. She slowed her pace and started up the path that ran alongside the road. She caught herself looking back over her shoulder again. Something darted into the trees.

Jane turned and jogged backward, looking. Was it a trick? Adrenaline coursed through her veins. More foolishness.

When the path split off, she forced herself to veer left, into the heart of the trees. There were lights along the path, but the space between them was like ink. Her heart rate went up and down according to the level of illumination. She was going to force herself to be brave. When she hit the bottom of the loop, she started to run fast. She had done it. Now she wanted to get out. The dark shadows between the trees seemed to sway. The rain hissed.

She was almost back to the road when something moved in front of her. She stopped. This time she was certain. A shape. Someone had scurried off the path in front of her. She stopped and stared. Then, in a panic, she shot into the shadows herself, ducking behind a tree, her hands pressed against its thick rough trunk. The ripe smell of wet bark filled her nostrils. Her heart was a jackhammer against her ribs.

She had to move. She went farther into the trees, using the

light of the path. It filtered weakly through their limbs, guiding her toward the street. She wanted to cry out, but there was no one there to help and she knew if she did, he would only find her. She knew it was a man by the cunning and deliberate way he had moved. Crouched like a Neanderthal.

When she saw movement again, it was no more than twenty feet from her. For an instant she froze. She reached inside her jacket pocket. Her cell phone. She yanked it free and felt for the buttons as she bolted for the light of the path. She flew across the grass.

She was too horrified to scream. Her mouth was open, but she couldn't get enough air to come out. She couldn't get enough air to come in, either. She was choking. She felt him behind her, reaching. The phone slipped from her hand. Her legs ached. She felt him grab her shell. She tripped and went headfirst into the darkness. She hit something immovable. Stars exploded. Then everything went black.

CHAPTER 13

The green water stretched out in front of the boat's bow like a flat creamy sheet, unspoiled by the usual traffic. But then, the sudden break in the thick gray clouds had been unexpected. Tom knew the forecast called for rain, and rain it had for the better part of the day.

For him, the summer was never long enough, and he knew he would be stuck inside a courtroom for most of the next week. He relished the smooth feel of the cool water against his skin and the breathtaking sight of the green hills, rising loftily on either side of the emerald lake. With binoculars, he could see his house.

He closed his eyes and felt the gentle rock of his new boat, a cold beer in his hand. November would be here in a blink. The landscape would fade to drab browns and pewter after the briefest flash of fiery reds and oranges.

With the new client he met today and his retainer, Tom would now owe Mike only a thousand dollars, and what was that between friends? Mike hadn't answered the phone, but this development was still cause to celebrate. Even alone. He stretched his legs on the cushioned seat and looked across the bow. Ellen.

"I'm sure she's fine."

Tom felt a dizzying ache.

Ellen disappeared. The empty bow swayed gently. Time sometimes shifted for Tom. It was confusing, and it didn't only happen when he drank. This was his first beer, and he'd barely nicked the Knob Creek.

There was a phone call last night. Late. Tom had been pulled from his slumber by the sharp ring of his cell phone. He'd rolled over, knocked it to the floor along with two beer cans, and put on the light. By the time he found the phone, he had missed the call. The Caller ID showed a private number. Jane had a private number. Tom dialed Jane's cell phone. He got her voice mail. He called her apartment and got the machine there, too. When he hung up, there was a message on his voice mail. He retrieved it. Nothing. A low hissing that could have been static, or rain, but no voice.

He hadn't spoken to Jane since she'd left and she hadn't returned his three phone calls from earlier. Sometimes he went a whole week without hearing from her, and given their harsh words he hadn't expected a call anytime soon.

Tom docked his boat and drove up to the house. Windows down. The summer breeze rustling through his hair. A buzzing in his head. He called the *Post*.

When Jane didn't answer at her office, Tom asked for Don Herman.

He was being crazy. Maybe he should call Mike. When he had these instincts that were always wrong, he should call Mike. Yeah, Mike could bring him down. He wasn't psychic. He wasn't a superhero. He was paranoid and fat and tired. Maybe he and Mike could get some coffee. He didn't need to drink more. But he wanted the Knob Creek, he wanted Ellen there.

From the cove in the kitchen, he closed the drapes over his old rust-stained farm sink.

He was about to hang up when Don Herman came on the line.

"Mr. Redmon, we've been trying to reach you at your office."

"I'm not in my office. It's a beautiful day. Where I live, only a criminal would waste a day like this."

"A police captain should be contacting you shortly," Herman said. "Where can he find you?"

"Jesus God," Tom said. He felt the hair prickle on his neck.

He turned around and walked backward with the cordless phone into the parlor.

Ellen stood in the corner, spinning in fading daylight and dust motes, nodding at him. He looked away. He could not see her eyes.

"Jane didn't show up for work this morning," Herman said. "A newspaper isn't like Wal-Mart. People don't just not show up. And to be more specific, people like Jane don't just not come to work. We sent another reporter to check on her. She found her apartment ripped apart. Papers torn up. Her mattress ripped open. I want to assure you, Mr. Redmon, that the police are doing everything they can."

"Stop."

"Sir."

As Tom walked backward, he heard the clatter of thin metal sounds all around him. His beer can castle toppled inward, and he stumbled and fell to a knee.

"Mr. Redmon?"

He caught his breath and looked at the door. Ellen was gone.

He kicked the cans out of the way and stood.

"I had a call last night," Tom said. "She called me last night. I was asleep. Why was I sleeping? I knew."

"Sir?"

"I'm coming to Washington."

"I can have someone meet you."

"I'll call when I get there."

Tom looked at his watch. Five-seventeen. The phantom phone call came in around midnight. Seventeen hours. Gone.

"We have thirty hours."

"Mr. Redmon, I'm sorry?"

"Tell the police it's Gleason. Everyone knows it's Gleason. I'm coming for him."

"The police are working as hard as they can. Please."

"Thirty hours," Tom said, again.

"I don't understand."

"Look, every cop knows that if someone isn't found in the first forty-eight hours they aren't coming back," Tom said, swallowing hard. "No one will tell you this, but after the first forty-eight, we quit trying. People vanish."

CHAPTER 14

Mike Tubbs was awakened by the sudden blast of his own snore. He lifted his massive bulk upright in the bed and stared around him. Where it showed amid the tangle of sheets, his pale skin glistened with a film of sweat. A large slab of his belly heaved. He blinked his eyes two times distinctly at the brassy late afternoon sunlight glaring at him through the window, then scratched his head.

The computer on his desk emitted a quiet chirrup. Mike looked at himself in the mirror, silly with his short tousled thatch of thin red hair, a neck as big as his head. His dark eyes stared back, set like raisins in a vast sheet of dough. He narrowed them in a predatory scowl and stroked his goatee, imagining his opponent, a grand master in Hong Kong.

He stared up at his Jackie Chan poster and struck the same pose with his fists.

Tacked to the wall above the computer hung a haphazard series of colorful certificates. Mementos of his past victories. Other masters on other continents. Mike swung his massive legs over the edge of the bed. His feet were wide and flat, his calves like two powder kegs. He rose with a wheeze. The wooden floor complained under his weight, creaking as he crossed the small room, duck-footed, to bring his computer screen to life. No, he hadn't imagined the small noise. The black knight was now poised to strike either his king's rook or his queen's bishop. His Asian opponent had been unable to resist the bait.

Mike smiled. Nine more moves and checkmate. Mike looked up at his certificates. He could remember the game behind each one of them. Every move.

Mike pulled on a pair of olive green cargo pants along with a black T-shirt from the White Stripes concert. He took a large pack of Big Red gum from a drawer in the kitchen and stuffed it into his side pocket along with his fat money roll.

Quietly, he closed the door to his apartment and stepped softly down the stairs and outside into the light. Even the waning heat was too much for Mike and he crossed the street quickly, stopping only to pull a newspaper out of the box before ducking into the Lost Dog.

The hostess led him to his usual table in the corner of the colorful dining room, by the window.

Mike sat down and hid behind the paper. A small girl pointed her finger his way, looked at her mother, and puffed out her cheeks. The girl's mother gave her hand a gentle slap and Mike retreated a bit more.

"Hi, Mike," said the waitress, Jeannie, an elfish little girl with twenty body piercings and a T-shirt that read A LESBIAN TRAPPED IN A MAN'S BODY. "You working nights?"

"Yeah," he said, lowering the paper just enough to avoid being rude. "How about a double order of the French toast?"

The house specialty. Doused in bananas. Walnuts. Real maple

syrup. Available on the menu all day long. Eggs were a different story.

"And you think I can get Max to whip up a skillet of eggs with cheese, onions, and potatoes?" he asked. "I've got to get breakfast, lunch, and dinner in all at once."

"No, you can't," she said with a mischievous smile, holding forth a tiny clenched fist, "but I can."

After a few mouthfuls, he looked at his watch. He had time, but he couldn't dawdle. This was a big job. Working nights to keep tabs on the little redheaded wife of a stockbroker. She'd told her husband that after she dropped him at the airport for his trip to Chicago tonight, she was going to drive up to Skaneateles with a girlfriend to spend a couple days at Mirabeau, a fancy spa.

When Tom Redmon appeared in a pair of khaki work pants, Mike jumped to his feet, knocking over his chair.

"Tom," he said, waving his arms, "over here."

Tom crossed the room, swinging his thick bowed legs with their purposeful arc. His stubby graying hair, like his shape, seemed cut at right angles. His chest was thick, like a small refrigerator. The short sleeves of his navy blue 2X polo shirt escaped up the slabs of his upper arm.

"Mike," Tom said. "Man, I'm glad I found you."

Mike pulled back a chair. Tom's face looked drawn, as if he'd had a stroke. Mike was reminded of Ellen's funeral. Tom's hands shook.

He was sober.

"Sit down, please," Mike said. "I'm sorry about the other day . . ."

Tom waved his hand as if it didn't matter.

"I can't," he said. "Here . . ."

"What's this?"

"A check for five large. I still owe you a grand, but I want you to have this."

"Tom," Mike said, his face growing warm, "I can't take this. I don't want your money."

"I owe you."

"I owe you for everything I have," Mike said. He tore up the check and dropped the pieces into his syrup.

"Mike," Tom said, his words choked, "something happened to Jane."

Mike swallowed hard.

"She's working on a story about that Senator Gleason and she didn't show up for work," he said. "Someone trashed her apartment. And I got a call last night and I think it was her. I didn't know it then, no one said anything, but . . . I'm going to Washington."

Mike slurped down his coffee and flicked a twenty onto the table.

"What are you doing?" Tom said.

"Going with you."

"Mike, I can't ask—"

"You didn't ask," Mike said, grabbing his friend's shaking hand. "But we ride together."

CHAPTER 15

Tom's big white F-350 diesel sat rumbling in front of the fire hydrant. The big commercial camper top covering the bed was white, too, but had faded to a different hue. The banged-up rear quarter panel bled rust.

"Give me two minutes," Mike said, touching Tom on the arm.

"Hurry," Tom said.

As Mike crossed the street, Tom looked at his watch and said, "I need to set this thing to go off forty-eight hours from when she called me last night."

"When did she call?" Mike asked, turning his head, but still jogging for his apartment door.

"Twelve twenty-three A.M."

"What time is it now?" Mike shouted, pulling open the door.

"Six oh-six."

"That's thirty hours and seventeen minutes," Mike said as he disappeared inside.

Tom nodded and punched 30:17:00 into his Ironman watch. Mike was better than a calculator when it came to numbers.

He climbed into the truck. The light went on in Mike's apartment. Tom tapped his foot, then revved the engine.

Mike came out and almost got hit crossing the street. He tossed a big duffel bag in the back with a clank and threw himself into the front seat, clutching a soft leather briefcase to his chest.

"Go," he said.

Tom slapped his foot on the accelerator. The big truck lurched away from the curb and grumbled down the street. The engine whined and groaned at the same time.

"What's in that?" Tom said, angling his head toward the backseat.

"Some guns and stuff," Mike said. He patted the briefcase. "Got my computer in here."

Tom nodded. He reached down and patted the snub-nosed .38 strapped to his ankle. Standard issue back in his day. They both leaned into the turn as he whipped around the on-ramp to the highway. Mike braced himself on the dash. Tom looked at his watch. 30:10:22. It was a seven-hour drive to D.C. Tom planned on doing it in six.

"We missed the last commercial flight," he said to Mike, "otherwise we could have flown. I even called Randy Kapp for his plane. He's in Vegas."

He looked over at Mike to see him nod.

Everyone around Downstate New York knew who Randy Kapp was. You could see the Kapp trademark sky blue equipment at construction sites from Buffalo to New York City. Two years ago Kapp was accused of beating his wife's boyfriend with a bedroom lamp. Mike helped Tom on the case. They won. Tom used the money from that one to pay his back taxes and he still had enough left over to buy *Rockin' Auntie*. But he'd won more than just the case. If Kapp's jet had been available, it would have been at Tom's disposal.

Tom zipped past an eighteen-wheeler. He looked at the speedometer. Eighty-three and feeling good.

"What was the math problem all about?" Mike asked.

"The first forty-eight," Tom said.

"Forty-eight hours to find a missing person," Mike said, pursing his lips. After that, the odds said you'd never find them, but neither of them needed to say it out loud.

"I'm going to make a call, okay?" Mike said, taking out his cell phone.

"Help yourself."

Tom watched the hood vacuum up the white stripes on the road. He wasn't listening, but he couldn't help but hear.

"Mr. Talbot?" Mike said. "I wanted to let you know that I'm sorry, but something's come up and I won't be able to keep an eye on her tonight."

The screaming from the phone was so loud that Mike held it away from his ear. His cheeks grew flushed. When the noise died down, Mike put the phone back up to his mouth.

"Mr. Talbot, I understand completely," he said in a hushed voice, "and I wouldn't expect you to pay me. I'm sorry."

The screaming began again. Mike snapped the phone shut.

"Everything okay?" Tom asked, glancing over.

"Yeah, fine," Mike said.

They drove for a time in silence. The road over a bridge thumped past. Tom looked over at his friend. The ghostly green reflection from the mile markers flickered across Mike's face. Tom looked at his watch. 28:17:55.

"I appreciate your coming," Tom said, turning his eyes back to the road.

"Don't even say that," Mike said.

"Not the first time you've been the knight in shining armor, huh?" Tom said, glancing at him.

Mike smiled grimly.

"Let's see," Tom said, removing his hand from the wheel and ticking off fingers. "There was the time she took Ellen's car out joyriding and ran out of gas. Then when she broke up with that jackass with the bald head in college and you had to pay him a visit. The money when she wrecked her friend's car. And Chicago. And that's just the things I know."

"You knew about Chicago?"

"Not until after you brought her back, I didn't," Tom said. "Are you kidding?"

Mike smiled and shook his head. Looking straight ahead and speaking in a quiet voice, he said, "I'd do anything for you, Tom. I'd do anything for her."

Tom twisted his lips and nodded that he knew.

"I'd probably be dead now," Mike said. "Or at least in jail."

"No," Tom said, "that was self-defense. Any halfway decent lawyer could have beaten that rap."

"Yeah, but that wouldn't have been the end of it for me," Mike said. "I saw it all around me. First you're just a gang member riding around with a leather vest. Then you run contraband. Next you get in on some action somewhere and you either start dealing or you're a soldier."

"You were a soldier, weren't you?" Tom said.

"Yeah," Mike said, "and that's how I ended up shooting that guy. Believe me, he wouldn't have been the last."

"Remember the first time we met?" Mike asked.

"That orange jumpsuit," Tom said, shaking his head. "God."

"Yeah, I couldn't even button up the front, and you walked in there with your nice suit on and you still called me Mike."

Tom glanced over at him.

"So?"

"Didn't you ever know?"

"What?"

"What that meant to me?"

"No. What do you mean?"

"My whole life, people called me Tubbs."

"Well, that's your name, Mike," Tom said.

"Not to you. Not to Ellen. The first time I met her too," Mike said. He was massaging his right forearm with his left hand. "It was Mike this and Mike that and if she ever got mad at me, she called me Michael. Sometimes I'd do stuff to bug her just to hear her call me that . . .

"Man, I was Tub-o'-Lard or Tub-o'-Guts or Tub Ass or Tubby my whole damn life until you guys. Hell. A fat guy named Tubbs."

"You're not fat, Mike," Tom said. "You're just big. I am too."

"You're in shape, though, man. Like a block of concrete."

"You're getting there."

Mike angled his head away. He kept talking, keeping it all light.

Tom stopped listening. He could think of little else but his daughter.

Tom glanced into his rearview mirror. He'd seen Ellen there once, in the back of the truck's cab. But tonight it was only the blur of taillights heading the other way.

He checked the speedometer. Eighty-seven and still smooth. 27:51:02 on his watch. He massaged the inside corners of his eyes and squinted them hard. His stomach was empty and tight.

He looked at the speedometer again and pressed harder on the gas.

Mike shook his arm.

"Yeah?"

"I said, 'It's gonna be all right.'"

CHAPTER 16

The F-350 was rattling and wheezing and when Tom crashed up over the curb, the frame shuddered. He cut the engine with both front wheels resting at angles on the sidewalk. The radiator emitted a steady steam that leaked out through the seams of the hood and the motor continued to knock for nearly twenty seconds.

He crawled out of the cab and jiggled his legs, flexing his toes against the leather of his Wolverine boots. Mike bounced on the toes of his sneakers and twisted his torso back and forth. The night air was still warm. A crescent moon shone through the haze. Trees lining the street whispered softly. Leaning against the stone railing of the steps that led up to the brownstone where Jane lived was a young man in a black and white herringbone blazer with a white dress shirt open at the collar.

During the drive, Tom had received a call from the lieutenant in charge of the case saying that a Detective Peters would be meeting him at the apartment. Tom saw the bulge of a gun under the man's arm and the glint of a badge on his belt. Peters' hair was slicked back. His entire face, especially his big round nose, was red and glazed with sweat. Spots of acne lurked beneath his jawline. He was talking on the phone.

Tom walked over to him, offered his right hand, and with his left pulled the cell phone away from the man's ear and pushed the off button.

"I'm Tom Redmon," he said. "This is my partner, Mike Tubbs. We're here to find my daughter."

"Sir, could you please step back for a moment?" Peters said. Tom saw he was red-faced and sweating. "And can I have my phone back?"

"Have you spoken to the senator?"

"Sir?"

"Gleason," Tom said. "The senator. What did he say?"

"Mr. Redmon," the young cop said. "I don't know. I was asked to meet you here so you could see your daughter's apartment, sir. I do know that I'm supposed to tell you that so far, nothing has turned up that makes any of us think your daughter's been hurt. This may just be a burglary."

"But she's gone," Tom said. "Who can I talk to about Gleason? When I spoke to the lieutenant on the way down here, he said he was sending someone over there."

"Sir, why don't we go inside," Peters said. "You can look around like you asked, and then I can take you back to the station or to a hotel where you can get some rest."

"Son," Tom said, holding up his Ironman watch and illuminating the digital face. "Do you see that?"

"Yeah."

"Would you mind telling me what it says?"

"24:14:11?"

"That's right," Tom said. "And I got a call last night at twelve twenty-three that may have been my daughter in trouble. That

77

means we've got twenty-four hours fourteen minutes and eleven seconds before the first forty-eight is by the boards. They still teach you about that these days, right?"

"Yes sir."

"So of course I'll be joining you at the station after this," Tom said, mounting the stairs.

Mike fell in behind him, and Peters behind him.

"Any of the neighbors see or hear anything?" Tom asked.

"No sir," Peters said. His hands were in his pockets. "I talked to them all."

Tom pushed open the front door. Mike did a quick check of the lock, feeling it, then putting his nose right up to it.

Tom walked down the hallway to the apartment in the back. Three bands of yellow tape were stretched across Jane's door. Tom yanked them down and went in. The sight hit him in the gut.

In the kitchen, glasses, bowls, plates, and platters lay smashed in a jumble on the granite floor. The coffeemaker had been dumped too, and its used-up grounds were splattered over the broken dishware like bird crap. The heavy scent of Starbucks was in the air.

The living room was worse. Cushions had been torn open. The computer monitor on the desk lay crooked and smashed. Its broken glass was scrambled on the floor with the tipped-out contents of Jane's potted plants; the musk of raw earth filled his nose. Tom picked through the rubble on the desktop and found nothing.

He looked back into the kitchen to see Mike remove a photo from beneath a magnet on the refrigerator and slip it into his pocket.

"I looked real close," Peters said. Glass crunched under his feet. "So did the patrolman who responded. Guy named Forbes. Good cop. We're both thinking maybe they were looking for jewelry."

"Like a leather bracelet?" Tom said.

He moved about the room. He picked up an inlaid wooden box. A gift from Ellen. He lifted the lid and sniffed at the potpourri inside. On the coffee table was an Ace Atkins book. *Dirty South.* On the floor was *The History of Art.* But no papers. No notes. Nothing to suggest the story she had been working on. Mike checked the sliding glass door. He stepped out onto the wrought-iron terrace that led down to the alleyway in back of the building.

Tom crept into the bedroom. The sheets and pillows on the bed had been dumped over with the mattress. Clothes spilled from the open drawers. Framed prints of paintings hung crooked on the textured plaster walls. Monet. Seurat. Turner. Renoir. Tom felt a pang. Jane's hair glistening in the sunshine outside the Met. The broad stone stairs. Fall leaves rattling along the sidewalk. Her smile.

In the bathroom, vials and tubes and jars of every imaginable thing were spilled out onto the floor. A broken bottle of Aromatics filled the air. Jane's favorite. The scent so powerful that Tom screwed up his nose. His stomach suddenly shifted, and he leaned toward the toilet. Mike appeared in the doorway, inhaling deeply.

"She wouldn't have left it unlocked, right?" Mike said.

Tom straightened and shook his head.

"Well," Mike said, "the place is a mess, but there's no sign of a struggle. It's just dumped. I think this guy may be right."

"No," Tom said. "He's not. 'Man will occasionally stumble

79

over the truth, but most of the time he will pick himself up and continue on.'"

"Sun Tzu?"

"Churchill."

Peters was in the living room, examining a broken picture frame. Jane and her best friend from college hugging in front of the Louvre. He put it down quickly and turned around.

"All set?"

"Who talked with Gleason?"

"The lieutenant sent Filbert and Swain out," Peters said. "They're with the dignitary protection unit, so they're used to dealing with senators and such."

"Where are they?"

Peters shrugged. He looked at his watch and yawned.

"Station, maybe."

Tom put the big white truck kitty-corner in a handicap spot. Peters walked up shaking his head.

"I don't think—"

Tom held up his watch and pushed the light.

"23:14:42, son."

Peters put his hands in his pockets and led them inside. The halls were quiet. A uniform went by. Two suits. Peters nodded to them. The heels of his shoes clicked off the linoleum. Mike's sneakers squeaked.

Filbert and Swain were at their desks in the nearly empty squad room. Peters pointed them out. They wore nice suits. Short hair. Silk ties. Filbert, gaunt and pale, was on the phone. He smiled at them and held up one finger. Swain, black and handsome, was typing and never looked up. A fan stood in the corner, pushing dead air.

Tom listened for about ten seconds to Filbert's conversation with his bookie before he pushed the receiver button down, disconnecting the phone.

"Who the hell are you?"

"I'm Tom Redmon. I'm here to find my daughter. You two spoke to Senator Gleason?"

"Who the fuck is this guy?" Filbert said to Peters. He looked over at Swain, who had stopped typing.

"He's the dad. He used to be a cop," Peters said.

"Oh," Filbert said.

"We talked to him," Swain said, "but he didn't talk to us."

"He what?" Mike said.

"He will," Filbert said. "Tomorrow."

"With his lawyer," Swain said. "We've got a meeting at his office at four."

Mike made a grunting noise and said, "Doesn't that mean—"

Tom held up his hand, and Mike stopped.

"Thank you," Tom said. "I'm sorry about your phone call. It's just that I'm upset about my daughter."

"That's okay," Filbert said, his finger stabbing at the phone's number pad. "She's probably fine, you know."

"I sometimes overreact," Tom said. He took Mike by the arm and started to move him toward the door of the squad room. He thanked Peters and exchanged cards with cell phone numbers.

"You should get some sleep," Peters said, his own eyes red from rubbing. "She'll probably turn up tomorrow . . ."

Mike followed him into the parking lot.

"I don't understand it, Tom," he said, his hands in the air. "You heard those jerk-offs. He asked for his friggin' lawyer."

"'When frying small fish, disrupt them little.'" Tom said.

81

"Confucius," Mike said.

"Excellent."

"So what are we doing?" Mike asked.

"We're going to talk to that son of a bitch Gleason ourselves," Tom said. "The only problem is that we don't know where he lives."

"No, that's easy," Mike said. "That's where I earn my keep."

CHAPTER 17

They sat in a little cove at a Starbucks on Pennsylvania Avenue. Open twenty-four seven. The place was next to this McDonald's where Clinton used to get his Big Macs, or so they were told by the espresso guy. They just wanted a couple of black coffees with no hazelnut or vanilla, just the caffeine. And a place for Tubbs to plug in his Dell.

Mike removed the thin laptop from his briefcase. He sat down on the couch, made some room on the coffee table, and plugged the ISDN line into his computer. On the top of the case he'd pasted a *Lord of the Rings* sticker with the dwarf warrior holding an ax.

"What's Gleason's middle name, do you know?" he asked after logging on to the Internet.

"No," Tom said. "Why?"

"Not a problem," Mike said. "I'll find him. AutoTrak. Just like a deadbeat dad. It's just that without the middle name it'll probably spit out a couple hundred Michael Gleasons at you. The Senate will have it on their Web site—hang on. . . . The phone line takes so damn long.

"There it is. Sherman."

Mike began typing again, his stubby fingers running the keys like a prodigy.

"Only three of those," he said after a few minutes. "A nineteen-year-old in Chevy Chase. A sixty-eight-year-old in Arlington . . . Is he that old?"

"No," Tom said, "in his fifties."

"Here it is," Mike said. "Massachusetts Avenue. Let's check. The vice president lives somewhere there. It's called the Naval Observatory or something."

Mike tapped and moved his fingers. Tom leaned over his shoulder and watched the maps change, zooming in, then out, then in again.

"Yeah," Mike said, "this number isn't far from that. Come on."

No matter how much Tom fretted over it, time bled away. Most of the residences in that section of Massachusetts Avenue weren't numbered. Finally, after their third time past a large French Revival home, Mike spotted a barely discernible number on its massive gatepost. They counted backward from that and determined Gleason's home to be a Federalist mansion. Red bricks. Surrounded by lush greenery. Towering blue spruce. Broad pin oaks and several sturdy elms.

An aging brick wall guarded the property's boundaries. Ornate wrought-iron gates gave them a brief view of the circular drive and a flower garden. Mike gazed at the wall.

"They'll have a gardener's gate in the back or on the side," he said. "If we can get close to the house we can either go right up to the door or maybe get him when he comes out to get in his car. Most of these guys have drivers."

"'We must one-time the enemy,'" Tom said, gazing ahead. Eyes glassy. "'Hit him quickly and directly as possible.'"

"MacArthur?"

"Musashi."

They parked the Suburban halfway down the nearest side street and walked back up the sidewalk toward the senator's mansion. Tom looked at his watch. 20:02:29. Up over Massachusetts Avenue, the first hint of dawn, a smoky yellow glow, had crept into the eastern fringe of the sky. The air had cooled and cleared. Great charcoal smudges of cloud hung fixed beneath the purple ball of a moon, whose thin brilliant crescent was almost too bright to look at. The birds began to twitter. The air was fresh and felt cool beneath the towering trees. Other houses rose up like sleeping giants, staring down at them through the leaves and branches with bleary yellow eyes.

"There," Mike said, pointing to a narrow service road that ran between the hedgerows of two homes.

They both scanned the area. There was no sign of anyone. They looked briefly at each other and then set off up the drive. Tom felt his heaviness melting away. Adrenaline began to flow through his veins, clear and keen. The image of crisp early morning police raids from so many years ago filled his mind. This was the best time of day to grab an unsuspecting criminal. The comparison left him feeling for the snub nose on his ankle. Mike had taken a big Taurus 454 Raging Bull out of his bag. A .45-caliber revolver with stopping power.

Tom reminded himself that he didn't even need his gun. He flexed his fingers, then balled his fists. He threw a Shuto chop into the air.

They soon came to the brick wall that surrounded the senator's mansion. There was a walk-through gate. It was rusted and unused and partially blocked by a thick tangle of forsythia. Mike dipped down without hesitation and barreled through the thinnest part of the foliage, snapping branches. He took a tool from his pocket—Tom couldn't make out what it was in the dim light—and went to work on the lock.

After a couple grinding squeaks, the gate swung open and they slipped inside the wall. They eased their way through a small stand of thick red pines and came to the edge of a broad carpet of grass. The scent of needles mixed with that of the cut grass. The lawn stretched for several acres. In its center was a white gazebo with a tall pointed roof and gingerbread trim.

Although the corners of the grounds were still dark, the early dawn had begun to transform the blackness to dark blue. Only a few stars remained above them, and the occasional call of the birds had risen to a chattering. Beyond the lawn another garden bloomed. It was bordered by a fieldstone wall, which separated it from a large rectangular pool. Finally, the massive brick house loomed, with its fluted columns, white shutters, and slate roof.

Tom heard something. He looked around for Ellen, but it was only her voice. He looked to see if Mike had heard, but he was silently studying the house and the grounds. Tom felt a sneer building up along the lines of his mouth.

"This way," Mike said in a low tone. He was moving to the right, keeping inside the fringe of trees and moving silently over the warm sweet-smelling carpet of needles. They reached the adjacent side of the brick wall and kept close to it, shielded from the house by a long wild hedge of lilacs. When they drew even with the pool, Mike thrust his meaty palm into Tom's chest, stopping him in his tracks.

"Shhh," he said. His finger was jammed up against his lips. He stared at the house. His eyes narrowed.

Tom strained to see through the web of lilacs. He saw movement. An icy coldness seized his insides. A light shone in the lower level of the house. Someone had opened a sliding door. A figure in a white robe was making his way toward the pool. It was Gleason.

Without hesitation, the senator mounted the diving board and let the robe fall away. A volcano of purple flesh bulged from where his appendix had once been. Although his arms were tan and lean, the slats of his ribs shone through his skin and his pale chest drooped. He plunged into the water and began a slow steady stroke in the half-light. The curtains inside the open sliding door wafted gently in the light breeze, but otherwise there was no movement to be seen in the house.

Tom followed Mike slowly to the end of the hedge. The space opened onto a side yard dominated by old hardwoods and a thin blanket of wispy grass. From that spot, they could see the driveway that encircled the colorful garden in front. Mike was right: A black Town Car sat there, idling. Tom could see the driver in his dark suit, illuminated by the dome light. He was reading the paper, ready and waiting to take the senator into his offices.

Tom stepped from behind the hedge and started toward the pool.

"Tom," Mike said in an urgent hiss.

"'Opportunities multiply as they are seized,'" Tom said, looking straight ahead.

"Sun Tzu," Mike said, whispering.

Tom nodded and mounted the cobblestone steps up onto the terrace surrounding the pool. He wove his way through half a dozen wrought-iron tables and their chairs to the edge of the deep end near the board. He sensed Mike's heavy breathing right behind him.

The senator was oblivious. He swam their way with smooth

steady strokes. When he reached the wall to turn, Tom squatted down and grabbed him by the arm. He was surprised at the ease with which he was able to snatch Gleason out of the water. The senator twisted and writhed in a panic, splashing like a speared fish. A cry, strangled by a mouthful of water, escaped his throat.

"Senator Gleason," Tom said through gritted teeth. "You and I have to talk."

"Who the hell are you!" Gleason said. As he struggled to free himself water cascaded off him and all over Tom's pants. "Let go of me, you son of a bitch!"

"Where's Jane?" Tom said. He tightened his grip on Gleason's arm. "I want to know. Right now. She interviewed you about things you'd done. Things that would get you in trouble.

"Don't fight me," Tom said. He felt his face contorting. There was a dull throb in his brain. His ears were filled with an intensifying hollow echo. "I'd just as soon rip your arm right out of its fucking socket or make you eat your own ear."

Gleason stopped struggling and swallowed. His eyes flickered toward the house, but no one came.

"I'm Jane's father," Tom said. He yanked Gleason's arm, then pushed him back. Tom was shaking.

Gleason's reaction was like a smashing blow. Instead of crying out in protest, or flooding with concern, the senator's face glowed briefly with relief and what looked almost like delight, as if he had feared something worse than the father of a missing girl.

Tom felt his knees go weak. The knowing smirk faded slowly from Gleason's face. His eyebrows arched and drew to a point above his nose. His nostrils flared, and his face began to redden.

She was dead.

Gleason snatched his arm free. He began backing carefully away from them, his dark eyes blazing. "You're insane."

He turned and bolted toward the house. Mike Tubbs sprang forward so quickly that it made Tom blink. The big .45 was out in his hand and he whipped it down on the back of Gleason's head with a sharp crack.

The senator crumpled to the stone in a lifeless heap.

"*The Fire Book,*" Tubbs said, citing Musashi's martial arts classic. "Isn't it essential to crush your enemy all at once if you consider him weak?"

Tom nodded, eyebrows raised.

"Come on," Mike said, stuffing the gun underneath his shirt and into the waist of his pants. He bent over and scooped up Gleason like a bag of trash, tossing the inert body over his shoulder.

"Mike?" Tom said. As he hurried after the enormous younger man, he stole a glance at the house. Other than the gentle wave of the curtain, there was nothing.

Mike retraced the steps they'd taken on their way in, keeping behind the cover of the lilacs and deep inside the stand of red pines. He took short sharp steps, with his legs perpetually bent. At the gate, he tossed Gleason down on the ground and stood with his hands on his knees, straining for air.

"This bastard knows," Mike said between gasps. "You go get the truck. Bring it up here. Hurry."

"He knows the story," Tom said.

"He is the story," he said. "An open book."

Tom backed through the gate, then turned and stumbled down the path, moving faster with each step until he was in a full sprint.

CHAPTER 18

By the time Mike took his hands off his knees, he heard Tom's truck bouncing up the lane. The truck stopped in a cloud of dust. Mike took a *Battlestar Galactica* T-shirt from his bag and tore it into strips. He bound Gleason's hands and feet. Then he wadded another strip into a ball and crammed it between the senator's teeth. After he finished tying a gag around Gleason's face, Mike opened the barn doors of the camper top in the back and loaded the senator inside, bracing him against the wheel well with an old tire.

Gleason was starting to come out of it, and his eyes bulged as Mike pulled a musty army blanket over the top of him.

"Let me drive," Mike said. "You just drove six hours straight and we need to get out of town."

Tom realized he was just standing there, watching, his hands hanging limp at his sides.

"I can," Tom said.

"If you don't mind," Mike said, "I will."

Tom rounded the truck and climbed into the passenger seat. "Be easy on the gal, she has a temperamental soul."

Mike moved the seat back and wedged himself behind the

wheel. He turned on the old silver AM radio, some Guns N' Roses. "Sweet Child of Mine." He turned it up, unwrapped a stick of Big Red, and began to chew. He tapped the wheel as he backed down the service road and out onto the street.

Tom scanned the neighborhood.

"Not too fast," he said.

Mike nodded and backed off on the gas.

"Where are we going?" Tom asked.

"Frederick, Maryland," Mike said. "A place no one will go, where no one can hear him . . ."

"When were you in Frederick?"

Mike glanced over at him and turned down the radio. He offered over the red pack of gum.

"No thanks," Tom said. He could smell the cinnamon.

"Drug deal," Mike said. "I was riding shotgun for a guy named Hacksaw. He was buying a truckload of meth. We met at this old abandoned amusement park in Frederick."

"Maybe I will have a stick of that," Tom said, picking up the pack of gum off the seat.

He tucked the gum under his tongue, and his eyes began to flutter.

"You should close your eyes for a few minutes," Mike said.

"What?" Tom asked, snapping up straight.

"It's okay," Mike said. "It's been a long night. I slept all day yesterday."

"He knows," Tom said.

"She's okay," Mike said. "She's always okay."

Tom didn't speak.

Mike pulled the gun out of his waistband and pointed it at Tom.

"By the way," he said. "I'm going to kill you if you don't just sit there and be quiet."

"What the hell are you talking about?"

Mike smiled and put the gun down on the seat between them.

"Now," he said, the streetlights scattering across his face in the darkness. "If anything goes wrong . . . it was all me. I took him. I forced you at gunpoint, held you both hostage, and tortured the information out of him."

He looked over at Tom again. He was grinning hard.

"You like that?" he asked.

"Clever," Tom said. "But I can't let you. If things go bad, I'm the one who takes the fall. I'm not afraid of what we're doing. Remember: 'All that is necessary for the triumph of evil is that good men do nothing.'"

Mike snapped his gum. "Edmund Burke."

Tom reached down to his ankle and removed the .38, pointing it at Tubbs.

"So I say to you: Just drive or I'll kill you. Do what I say and . . . or . . . you get the idea."

"Imitation is the highest form of compliment."

"Who said that?" Tom asked.

"Just me."

"Torture?" Tom said.

"We have to make him talk."

Tom looked back through the cracked windshield of the truck and into the hard cover of his camper. Gleason had wormed his way out from under the blanket but didn't appear to be going anywhere. His head was snaking around under its thatch of damp bleached hair.

"This isn't Friendly's Ice Cream," Tom said. "This is the real thing."

"I know," Mike said. "I'm with you."

"What kind of an asshole wears an army coat into an ice cream store in the middle of July?" Tom said.

Mike shrugged and said, "You're right."

Tom flicked open the cylinder of his snub nose and spun the rounds. "I'll do whatever I have to with this guy," he said.

"Not yet," Tubbs said. "There's a method to this."

"How do you know?"

"Ah, there was this guy from the Pharaohs who tried to open up on a street corner over in Jamestown," Mike said, "and we had to grab his younger brother and hang on to him for a while. I was working with an old-time biker. He'd grabbed dozens of people; he knew the deal. Man, that guy was good. He'd put a Super Ball in their mouths to keep them quiet. He was pretty smart, for what he did."

"That was to keep them quiet," Tom said. "We need Gleason to talk."

Mike rolled down the window, spit out his gum, and said, "I know. That old-timer knew how to make 'em talk when he had to do that, too. I'm going to get a blowtorch at Home Depot, and if he needs it . . . I'll do what the old-timer did. Put his feet to the fire."

CHAPTER 19

Tom paid at the Home Depot with cash.

"You have a sunshine day," the woman behind the counter said to him, with a bright smile and an orange apron around her neck.

"Thank you," Tom said with a slight bow. "I will."

As he crossed the parking lot, the first rays of sunshine peeked up over the rooftops of the apartment complex to the east. Mike had parked on the far side of the lot by some trees and away from the early morning stream of pickups and vans. Tom looked down into his plastic bag, rattling off the things Mike had asked for.

The blowtorch. A flint starter. Pliers. Twenty-five feet of rope. Two rolls of duct tape. Garbage bags. Lighter fluid. A fifty-page spiral notebook. A Sponge Bob pen. A rubber ball from the pet section.

Trick or treat.

Two exits down the road, Mike got onto a secondary highway and they drove for nearly ten minutes without seeing anything more than small scattered farmhouses in need of paint. Then a field opened up suddenly on the right-hand side. A tattered chain-link fence sagged along its border for a quarter mile before they came to the entrance. The enormous faded sign arched over the opening in the rusted fence announced SUBURBAN PARK, the letters spelled out in empty light sockets.

"Welcome to 1955," Mike said, unwrapping another piece of gum.

"That's when I was born."

"I know."

The parking lot beyond was scattered with broken glass and waist-high weeds. Off in the distance, decrepit midway rides rose up, faded and broken in the fields of scrub brush and refuse.

Glass crunched and popped under their tires. Halfway across the overgrown parking lot, the truck bounced over the top of an old railroad tie with a jolt.

"Sorry," Mike said. He slowed down.

They were headed toward the old midway, a wide strip of broken pavement between two long rows of broken attractions.

There was an old Ferris wheel, partially disassembled. Only one of the cars remained, and it hung at an odd forlorn angle in the midst of the rusty skeleton. Brambles choked a row of concession stands, their roofs sagging under the weight of their years. The truck kicked up a gang of crows picking over the carcass of a small animal that thumped beneath their tire as they went. The crows screamed with rage.

Halfway down the midway, just past a horseless merry-go-round, was the largest remaining structure in the park. The faded faces of two clowns wearing pointed hats and bow ties laughed on either side of a sign whose letters were made from the nubs of broken lightbulbs.

FUN HOUSE.

"There," said Mike, pointing at the huge faces, frozen in mirth. The clown on the right had a board missing from his eye, which oozed with the disheveled remains of a bird's nest. Mike stopped the truck and killed the engine. It rumbled, kicked twice, then sat still.

Mike took out his gun and opened the barn door in the back of the truck. Gleason was wriggling in the blanket. Blood ran from his wrists where he'd struggled against his bonds, and its sweet smell floated up in the warm close air. Gleason squirmed up against the wheel well area like a frantic crab. He was shivering in the heat, naked except for his damp suit. Under the harsh white bulb in the ceiling of the camper, his pale scarred torso glimmered with sweat. Mike stuck the big black pistol right in the senator's face.

Gleason froze. His eyes grew large.

"I'm going to take you out of there," Mike said gently. "If you fuck with me, if you squirm or kick or fuss, I'll beat the shit out of you. If you behave, I'll be nice. You understand that?"

Gleason nodded that he did.

"Good," Mike said. He grabbed Gleason by one ankle and slowly began to drag him out. When he had him at the edge, he stuffed the gun back in his pants and lifted Gleason up under the arms, setting him onto the warm broken pavement. Mike took a knife out of the side pocket of his pants and bent down, flicking the blade across the rag binding Gleason's feet.

Beneath the arched sign was a third clown, bigger than the other two, less faded, but blemished with mold and bearded with scrub brush. Its gaping mouth was the entrance to the Fun House. Mike grabbed Gleason by the arm and shoved him up the steps and inside the dank building. Vandals had smashed most of the glass in the vast maze, and the mirror shards scattered across the floor created the impression of a vast gleaming pincushion. Gleason high-stepped through the glass, his feet bleeding now too.

The light was dim, but as his eyes adjusted, Tom could make out the crushed and empty beer cans that lay scattered amid the refuse, remnants from teenage parties. Jane had done things like that.

Tom felt a surge of hatred well up inside him. He reached past Mike, grabbed hold of Gleason, and rammed him face-first into the glinting wall. The senator spilled to the floor, and when he wormed himself into an upright sitting position, blood was streaming down his face.

"Do you know me now?" Tom said. The blood only made him hotter. He tore at the gag, ripping it up over Gleason's nose, drawing more blood, more heat.

Gleason spit the rag out of his mouth, choking.

"I'm a United States senator!" he screamed. White flecks of spittle stuck to Tom's work pants. Gleason's face turned scarlet. "I sit on two FBI committees, you fucking psychos."

"Yeah, but now you're just some old creep in a wet Speedo with a shrunken willie."

Tom kicked him in the ribs with his steel-toed Wolverines. He bent down and put his thumb into the nerve in Gleason's neck. The senator began to scream and thrash his feet. Glass tinkled.

"Tom!" Mike yelled.

Tom felt Mike's arms wrap around his chest. His feet losing touch with the floor. Gleason huffed and made small animal noises, writhing in the glinting shards. Tom was breathing hard. Mike set him down.

"'If you attack destructively and take a nation by force, that is a lesser accomplishment,'" Mike said, catching his breath.

"That's all this bastard understands," Tom said. He put his face up to Gleason's. "Do you remember Sook Min, you son of a bitch? Now do you remember me?"

"Easy," Mike said. "Just hold him, will you?"

Mike took the pliers from the bag and put a friendly hand on Gleason's shoulder.

"What are you doing?" Gleason said, his screeching voice was almost unintelligible. He was struggling against Tom's vice grip, shaking his head no, walking the tightrope of hysteria. Tom could feel the bones beneath his flesh. He wanted to snap them one at a time.

"I am a United States senator."

Mike held up the pliers. "I know. I voted for you. But that was before I knew you were a piece of shit. Now here's how this works. . . ."

Mike grabbed the senator by the back of his hair, twining his fingers. Twisting them tight. He snatched up a patch of skin on Gleason's saggy chest in the teeth of the pliers.

"I want you to stop making so much noise," Mike said quietly. "It makes my head hurt. Tom's going to put a ball in your mouth. You can breathe with it okay, but you'll be quiet. If you do good, I won't play Mr. Fixit.

"If you do good," Mike said, "this will be easy."

Gleason nodded frantically. He was twitching, and his eyes were riveted on the pliers.

"Good," Mike said. He turned to Tom. "Okay?"

Tom fished the rubber ball out of the bag. Beads of sweat

broke out on Gleason's forehead. Gleason parted his lips an eighth of an inch at a time. Tom got tired of waiting. He stuck his finger in Gleason's larynx, gagging him, and jammed the ball in.

He looked at Gleason's empty face, his shaking body. Tom felt nothing for him. He remembered the young DA he'd been, the life of the woman Gleason had ruined, and the arrogance and pure evil of taking his daughter.

"Now tape that in there," Mike said.

When Tom's gray band of duct tape encircled his head, Mike said to Gleason, "Good, you did good. Now I'm going to give you the notebook here and this pen and you can write down for us where to find Jane. That's the next thing . . ."

CHAPTER 20

Mike tugged a fresh piece of Big Red from his pack and stuffed it into his mouth. He offered Tom a piece. Tom shook his head. Chewing, Mike dug into the bag. A sheen of sweat was on his brow and it glimmered in the low light. His ginger hair curled softly around his brow like smoke. His eyes had grown larger in the darkness.

Mike handed the paper and pen to Gleason. He snapped his gum and said to him, "I want you to please write down for us where Jane is . . ."

Gleason sucked air through his nose and made a wicked little snarling noise. He scribbled something on the paper. Mike leaned over. He squinted. The letters were wavy, broken, and uneven in the murky light.

I DON'T KNOW

"Bullshit!" Tom said, crashing his fist into Gleason's face, ripping the tape free from his mouth.

"I'll crush your nuts!" Gleason screamed, his eyes bugging.

"Tell us!" Tom yelled. He punched his thumb into the neck

nerve again and ground it down with all his might. Gleason's eyes rolled back in his head. A low squealing noise whistled through his nose, filling the dank space with the sound of a dying animal. He lurched up and butted his head under Tom's chin.

Tom threw a short punch, and Gleason's nose popped. Then he dug right in again on the nerve.

"Tom," Mike said, trying to pull him off. "Tom, let him write it. Tom! You must think large. You must think larger than this!"

Mike tugged harder and harder. The sound of agony pierced the stillness of the warm damp space.

"Think of what Master Musashi would do," Mike said.

Finally, he locked both hands on Tom's shoulders and threw his weight straight back. Tom caught his balance just before he fell. He was off.

"I see. I see it's larger," Tom said. "I must be. I must be a larger warrior. I must connect."

"Please," Mike said.

Tom was breathing hard, but he nodded and looked away. Mike gave Gleason's face a gentle series of slaps. He propped him up and put the paper and pen back into his hands. Gleason looked up at Tom out of blood red half-lidded eyes.

"You . . . ," Gleason said in a barely audible mutter, "want me . . . tell . . ."

His hand shook, but he was writing. Mike leaned over to read.

"Shit," Mike said, shaking his head slowly.

"What?" Tom asked, craning for a glimpse of the paper.

FUCK YOU

Mike said nothing. He picked up the roll of tape off the floor where Tom had set it and began wrapping Gleason from the ankles up. Gleason cackled softly, but soon he was ensconced in his sitting position in a shiny gray cocoon. Mike took out the rope and secured him to a beam.

He put the ball in front of Gleason's face. Gleason snarled and turned his head from side to side, avoiding the ball. Mike picked up the pliers off the floor and locked them onto a hunk of Gleason's flesh. The senator's eyes popped. His mouth flew open in a scream. Mike jammed the ball in and then taped it shut.

Mike took the starter and the propane torch from the bag, holding them up for Gleason to see as he knelt down on one knee. Mike was concentrating. Only the raspy scratch of the starter interrupted his heavy breathing. Its sparks flickered, then spilled down onto the floor. Fireworks in the broken shards of mirror that littered the ground and the walls.

"During the Middle Ages," Tom said in a whisper, "kingdoms used vats of scalding hot oil to dump down upon their enemies during battle. Cauldronsful."

Gleason began to blubber.

"His soul is frail," Mike said without looking up. He braced the propane bottle against his leg and opened the valve. The steady hollow hiss of gas was added to the scratching of the starter. When he brought the two of them together, a triangular blue flame popped to life.

"He's not a warrior," Tom said, now pacing, his hands tucked behind his back like a general. "He's a politician who uses others to beat us."

Mike fidgeted with the knob on the torch, expanding and contracting the flame until he had it just right. Tom stopped and stared. He felt his mouth fall open. All around him he saw a thousand reflected flames. He touched Mike's shoulder.

Mike put his hand behind his head for a moment, then eased the torch toward Gleason's bare feet. The senator's eyes rolled, and he flailed futilely against his bonds. Mike let the tip of the flame lick the arch of his foot. He put his other hand on Gleason's heel and moved the flame closer.

A whistling noise escaped Gleason's nose.

Tom winced.

A single thin ribbon of smoke and a burning stink curled up into the air.

CHAPTER 21

Gleason's muffled scream threatened to tear a hole in his throat. His body shuddered and twisted. Mike pinned his legs with one knee.

Tom looked at his watch. 17:28:09. Less than seventeen and a half hours.

It was just three seconds before Mike removed the flame. 17:28:06. Tom blinked and checked his watch again, shaking it. He looked at his friend. Sweat was dripping down Mike's face now. Tom smelled urine. Beneath the senator was a small dark puddle.

"You want to tell us something now?" Mike asked, his voice still soft.

Gleason's head went around and around. Yes. No. Yes. No.

"I guess I don't understand if that's yes or no," Mike said. He looked away from Gleason and began to flick the starter again. The flame popped to life. He moved it toward Gleason's foot. Gleason's muffled keening mixed with the lingering stench of burned flesh. Mike held the flame between them and stared at him. This time when Mike asked if he wanted to talk, Gleason nodded unmistakably that he did.

Mike took out a pocketknife and sawed through the tape pinning Gleason's right arm to his body, then put the pen in his hand and held the notebook up for him to write. Gleason's hand was shaking so hard that it was difficult to read. Mike snatched it away from him. Gibberish.

"I don't want you to write another word that doesn't tell us where she is," Mike said. "You're doing bad and Mr. Fixit is going to have to repair your soul. Now, I'm going to let you write one more word and it better tell me where she is or else I'm going to have to hurt you some more, only this time it's going to have to last. I'm being very nice to you, but being nice isn't working . . ."

Mike put the notebook in front of the senator. Gleason began to write again, trembling.

THORNE

"What's Thorne?" Tom said, reaching for Gleason's neck with hooked fingers. "Is that who got her?"

Gleason shook his head yes.

"Thorne. Thorne who?" Mike asked.

Gleason wrote: CAN I TALK

Mike looked at him intently. He stroked his neat little beard and said, "If you make any noise, I'm going to chicken fry your little piggies. Do you understand? I won't be happy if you do anything but talk."

Mike struggled to his feet, then bent over and ripped the tape off Gleason's face. He removed the rubber ball and the senator gasped desperately.

"Where is she?" Mike said.

"I didn't tell him to kill her," Gleason said. He sobbed and shook. His voice was tattered.

Tom felt the world tilt. A deep pit of hatred opened in his heart.

"Who?" Mike said.

"Thorne. Bob Thorne," Gleason said, quavering, bawling softly. "He's CIA. They gave me his name—I did a favor. I never saw him. 'Just get my credit card bill. That's it.' She was going to write the story. I told him not to hurt her . . ."

"Where *is* she?" Tom said.

"I don't know, really I don't," Gleason said. He shut his eyes and tears fell in the wrinkles. His whole body shook. "I swear, I don't know! I didn't do anything. 'Just my credit card bill.' You can ask Thorne."

"Where's he?" Mike asked.

"I don't know."

Tom growled low and punched him in the nose. A sharp jab with weight behind it. Gleason coughed and choked. Blood spilled down his face.

"Oh, God. I have a phone number," Gleason said, whining, "that's all. Please."

"Where?" Mike said.

Gleason told him the number and Mike repeated it back to him. Gleason nodded weakly.

"Where is that?" Tom asked.

"Close. Western Maryland. I don't know exactly. I don't know. . . ."

"I believe you," Mike said, plucking the Super Ball up off the floor. "Time for your medicine."

"What?" Gleason said. He started to moan.

Mike jammed the ball back into his mouth. He bound the

senator's face up with fresh tape. Then he lifted him out of his puddle.

"I'll get his legs," Tom said.

Gleason's eyelids fluttered. His legs were clammy. They carried him out and down the stairs like a dresser and dumped him into the back of the truck. Tom covered him up with the blanket. He had wondered what Mike wanted with the garbage bags, and now he knew.

Mike was carefully taping the dark plastic to the inside of the barn door windows. He checked them from the outside, then slammed the camper door shut. Tom nodded his approval.

Mike disappeared briefly back into the Fun House. When he returned, he had the Home Depot bag in one hand. With the other, he was dousing the doorway with the can of lighter fluid. When it was empty, Mike shook it and tossed it back into the clown's gaping mouth. He flicked the starter and lit the propane torch again. When he reached the top of the stairs, he turned and rolled the flaming canister back toward the entrance. The puddle of fluid ignited with a thud. Mike jogged down the stairs.

"Motorcycle Gang 101," he said as he climbed into the cab. "When in doubt, burn all evidence."

In the silence, the faintest of sounds could be heard from inside the truck. Gleason moaning.

Tom sighed and said, "Jesus, Mike, he deserves it, but we burned the man."

Mike raised his eyebrows and shook his head.

"Not really," he said, drawing out a fresh stick of gum.

"Mike, I smelled it."

"That was my hair."

"What?"

"My hair," Mike said. "Smells just like burning flesh. Powerful suggestion. I pulled a couple hairs out of my head, let him feel the warmth of the flame and smell the stink. You did more damage punching him."

"I could have done worse," Tom said. "I wanted to."

"He's fine," Mike said. "I don't know what the hell we do with him now, though."

"We can decide after we find Thorne," Tom said. "'Keep your friends close and your enemies closer.'"

"Should we put him someplace?" Mike asked.

"Right back there is probably the best place to keep him," Tom said, firing up the big diesel engine. "Your truck is like your home. The cops can't search it without a warrant."

"Good. Now if we can get an ISDN or a phone line somewhere," Mike said, "I can reverse-directory for that phone number and get an address. It's a Maryland area code so it can't be too far."

Tom looked at his watch. 17:17:09. He showed Mike his wrist.

"Seventeen hours and change, Mike," he said, glancing in his side mirror at the black billows of smoke surging up into the morning sky behind them.

"I know," Mike said, "but the last six have been pretty goddamn productive. We keep going like this and we'll have her back by dinner."

CHAPTER 22

Tom drove them onto the highway and went west for two exits to a Budget Host motel. Tom went in and got a room in back for thirty-nine dollars in cash. They parked just outside their door and left Gleason in the back of the truck. Mike pulled the phone line out of the phone and snapped it into the back of his computer.

Tom watched him do a reverse-directory search on the number. The address that came up was 1771 Edinger Road. Old-town, Maryland. Mike searched MapQuest. Bob Thorne lived in a rural part of western Maryland. It was the narrow arm of the state, squeezed in between West Virginia and Virginia under the shadows of the Buchanan National Forest.

They got on Route 70 and headed west to 68.

Tom checked his Ironman: 16:24:12. But they were already driving along a country road, looking through the trees, seeing glimpses of a twelve-foot chain-link fence that apparently surrounded Thorne's property. When they got to the driveway and the gate, Tom stopped the truck and stared. It was topped with concertina wire.

"Go up there, okay?" Mike said.

Tom drove another thousand feet up the road and pulled over at the corner of the fence. Mike leaned over the seat and fished around in his bag until he came up with a pair of binoculars.

"I've got an idea," Mike said. The truck door squeaked as he opened it. "I think I know what this is, but I want to be sure. Come on."

Tom got out and followed him through the trees. The sunlight glared down, baking them, even through the canopy of leaves. The air was still. Stifling. They came to an opening. Beside the fence, wild grasses sprouted knee-high, still damp with warm dew and shedding ripe seeds down the legs of their pants. They walked along the perimeter of the fence until they came to a high spot where they could see a house and a detached garage through the trees. The buzz of a locust pierced the stillness. Mike put the binoculars to his face and studied.

"Hmm."

"What?" Tom asked.

"There's no furniture," Mike said, handing the binoculars to Tom. "It's a safe house."

"A safe house?" Tom said.

"He said CIA . . . ," Mike said. "I staked one of these out about four years ago. Some rich lady from Westchester. Old money. She married this diplomat; they met in Paris or something. Anyway, he was a spook and he had a little thing on the side and he took her to a place just like this out in Bergen County. Weird. I had no idea what the hell was going on. Fence like this one. Vibration sensors. Motion detectors. The fucking works.

"I thought, No problem," Mike said. "I could shoot them with a telephoto through the window. Then they go into this place and disappear. There was nothing in there."

"So how'd you find out about it?" Tom asked.

Mike grinned at him and said, "I waited until they left and I cut the power at the pole. Then I strolled in there and checked it out. Everything was underground. Red satin sheets. Movies. Leather shit. I planted a camera in there and three weeks later, voilà. Instant divorce."

Mike spit his gum into the grass and pulled another stick out of his pocket.

"The guy told me all about it," he said, chewing. "I ran into him the night after the proceedings in a little Irish pub in White Plains. He was drunk, and I wasn't feeling too bad either. He recognized me from the courtroom and came right up and asked me how I got in. I told him and asked him some questions. He blabbed his head off. It was pretty educational; I actually got lucky. They have backup generators. The one at this place just malfunctioned. Anyway, these things are like rabbit holes—there's always a second way out."

Tom turned and started back for the truck.

"Tom?" Mike said. "What are you doing?"

Tom had heard enough. He stopped and looked at Mike.

"'Take time to deliberate but when time for action has arrived, stop thinking and go in,'" Tom said.

"Churchill?"

"Napoleon," Tom said. "I'm taking the truck right through that gate."

Chapter 23

Sticks snapped under Tom's feet, sending tree dust and the smell of the woods into the warming air.

"Tom, wait," Mike said, breathing hard and putting his hand on Tom's shoulder. His stomach shook as he ran with his little legs.

Tom stopped and drew the back of his hand across his face, wiping the sweat.

"'Force him to reveal himself, so as to find out his vulnerable spots,'" Mike said.

"Sun Tzu."

"Yes," Mike said. "Maybe we can get him to come to us."

"She could be in there right now," Tom said, pointing.

"I know that, but we've got to be careful," Mike said. "It's not going to do anyone any good if we don't do this right."

"It worked for the Ithaca Police," Tom said, raising his jaw. "Storm the gates. That's how we always did it."

Tom had taught Mike too well to question the authority of his old unit. The tactics of the Ithaca Police, Tom's old force, was beyond even Sun Tzu.

"What about a compromise?" Mike said.

"What?" Tom said.

"Let me find the rabbit hole," Mike said, speaking fast. "The escape hatch. The tunnel. If I'm right, there'll be one. Give me . . . thirty minutes. Then you bust in there. Like when the ferret goes down the main hole and the rabbit comes out the back—I'll be waiting. Do you have cell reception?"

Tom took his phone from his pants pocket.

"Two lines," he said.

"Me too," Mike said, holding up his own phone. "Give me a little bit. I'll find it and I'll call you. Okay?"

"Okay," Tom said. "Thirty minutes. That's it."

Tom reached for the door handle of the truck.

"Wait," Mike said. He opened the back door, leaned in, and fished a short-barreled shotgun with a black synthetic pistol grip out of his bag. He handed Tom the gun along with three slim boxes of hollow-point slugs. "Here. Nothing against your .38, but this has a little more oomph."

"Thanks," Tom said. He loaded the gun and popped one into the chamber with that slick metallic crackle that distinguishes a shotgun from all other weapons.

Tom climbed in and waited. Not a single car came down the road. The air grew close. Tom looked at his watch. 15:59:59. He started the truck and put the AC on. At 15:57:03, his phone rang.

"I got it," Mike said. He was breathing hard into the phone. "Any more ideas about this safe house thing?"

"Look for a basement door," Mike said. "In the kitchen or the garage or underneath the stairs going to the second floor. Bring some extra shells and use the shotgun on the lock. There will be a lock. Keep your phone on."

Tom put the truck into gear.

He reached the gate and backed up across the road, facing the glimmering galvanized metal. He revved the engine. One foot on the gas, the other on the brake.

The truck howled, straining against the brake, rising up. He let go with his foot and shot forward, rocketing across the road and down the short gravel drive, smashing full force into the gates. The air bag exploded in Tom's face. The truck bucked up. The gate shivered and snapped, up and over the top of the truck, raking it. Metal shrieked. Tom's foot went instinctively to the brake and he slid to a stop in a dusty cloud.

He blinked his eyes and coughed and wiped the white powder from the air bag off his face as the bag slowly deflated. When he could see again, he punched his foot all the way to the floor and shot straight down the drive. The imagined sound of the alarm inside the house was ringing in his head.

He sped toward the side door that led out to the detached garage, skidding to a stop, showering the side of the house with gravel. When he hopped out he had the shotgun pinned tightly to his leg. The contours of the pistol grip felt good in his hand. He reared back and kicked in the door. Splinters exploded from the frame and the door sagged there. He kicked it again. It burst inward this time and Tom barged in, shotgun leveled. There really was nothing there. No furniture. No rugs. No knickknacks.

On the other side of the kitchen, Tom saw a metal door, painted white like the walls. He peered down the hall. It was beneath the stairs that led to the second floor. He tried the handle. Locked. This was it. In its center, at eye level, was a fish-eye peephole. He stepped back and fired a blast from the shotgun, punching a nickel-sized hole in the door just beside the lock. He gave it a kick.

Nothing.

Tom fired again and again, emptying the chamber. The air was blue with smoke and tangy with the taste of powder. A tight cluster of holes gaped in the door between the handle and the jam. Tom kicked again. This time it gave, but sprang back at him. Something was holding the upper corner. A dead bolt. Tom reloaded the shotgun.

He kicked the door harder, higher this time. Once. Twice. On the third time, it banged open. He lumbered down the stairs, the gun raised at eye level. He hit the floor below flat-footed, spinning in a circle, searching for a target. His eyes drank in the sight. Rows of books. A table. A desk. A bed. A chair. He stalked slowly toward the back. His eyes skittered across every possible place that Jane might be. Tied up. Wide-eyed. Waiting for him to rescue her. His chest felt as if it were about to burst.

He found the bathroom. Empty. Here was a small kitchen. Empty. Beside it, another closet door and a pantry lined to the ceiling with what looked like cans of food and plastic jugs of water. Empty. The place was absolutely deserted.

But as his eyes adjusted to the gloom of the pantry, he noticed that in the back the shelves protruded at a funny angle. Tom walked in. Quietly. He reached out and grasped the edge of the shelving with his left hand. In his right was the shotgun. He slid the barrel into the dark crack on its edge and eased the entire shelf back toward him.

The rabbit hole.

He crouched. Ready to fire. Ready to be fired at.

CHAPTER 24

Just a storm sewer. That's what most people would think. But it was too big and it was bone-dry and it ran in a straight line from where Mike knew the safe house was. Six feet in diameter and emptying out into the side of a natural gully, the tunnel had an iron grille locked across its front. A Master lock. Not faded with rust, but shiny, even under the shadow of the gully's broken lip.

Mike knew that when Thorne came out, he would have to pause to unlock the grating. Both hands would be occupied. Mike could press himself against the bank and wait unseen beside the neck of the pipe. When the time was right, he'd slip out in front, his gun aimed for a kill shot if need be. His heart began to pump hard, not so much from the effort of hustling through the woods looking for the escape route, but from nerves.

Perspiration ran down his temples and he wiped his face on his shirtsleeve, leaving a stain to complement the ones that had already soaked through from his armpits. He took out the Taurus 454 Raging Bull from the waist of his pants and checked the load the right way. The way Tom had always taught him. He tucked himself in beside the massive pipe, plastering his back to the dirt bank. Feeling its cool dampness on the back of his head. Dappled sunlight fell down from above. A red squirrel chattered angrily somewhere above. A chickadee scolded back.

The quiet woods were suddenly disrupted by the distant crash of metal. The green veins in the back of Mike's shooting hand grew shadows. His fingers were tight. His eyes darted toward some movement. A frog, launching itself from the bank of the creek, plopped into a murky pool. The ripples spent themselves completely, and the frog's head popped up on the far side of the milky brown water. Then came the gunshots, muted, but echoing through the woods. One, then several in a row. The silence grew back. Mike licked salty sweat from his upper lip, his breathing shallow.

Then he heard it: the soft shuffling of feet across the bottom of the concrete sewer pipe. Faint. His heart pounded so hard that the surge of blood filled his ears. His fingers were cramped and tight. He loosened his grip on the gun, wiped his hand on his pants, then grasped the weapon tight again. He crouched a little to take the strain off his knees. The shuffling was no longer a whisper, but the raspy scratch of leather against the dried silt in the bottom of the pipe. Then it stopped. Mike could feel the presence of another human being, could sense him scanning the thick foliage of the woods and the lush tendrils of vines that draped the gully's sides. The creek trickled softly over the round stones in its bed.

Mike strained for the hint of Jane's presence—a moan, a soft gasp. All he heard was the clink of the lock as it was twisted against the latch. The grate groaned as it swung open.

Mike sucked in a quick breath and stepped out in front of the pipe, aiming for the kill. Confusion struck him. Bob Thorne looked like his grandpa. Mike faltered under the steely gray eyes, the plastic glasses, and the white slicked-back hair that barely hid the liver spots on his pink scalp. Mike's eyes flickered for a sign of Jane. Thorne was alone.

"Don't move," Mike said. His voice trailed off down the pipe.

Thorne's hand was already inside his jacket, wrapped around the handle of his gun.

"Take it out slow or I'll paint the inside of that pipe with your brains," Mike said. "Now drop it."

Thorne did as he was told and the gun, a small .22-caliber pistol with a nasty little silencer, clattered off the concrete. Mike was in control, but for some reason he found Thorne's smooth compliance unsettling.

"You shouldn't do it," Thorne said to him.

"What are you talking about?" Mike said. Through the pipe, he could hear Tom's footsteps, in the distance, sprinting toward them.

"Terminate me," Thorne said. "I'm you. You're me. I was afraid of this: After all these years, instead of the payout, you show up. I was always afraid they'd cross me in the end. But I thought, If they do, and I can talk to him . . ."

"Who do you think I am?" Mike said.

Thorne snorted through his nose.

"I know you're from the company," he said. "How would you know about this culvert?"

"Did you kill the girl?" Mike said, nearly choking on the words. Tom's footsteps were growing louder. When he burst out from the end of the pipe, the game would be up.

"Is that why they sent you now?" Thorne said, glaring at Mike. "I've lost my usefulness? My record is unblemished. Perfect. And I didn't fail this time, either . . ."

CHAPTER 25

Mike swallowed, but his mouth was dry. He could hear Tom. Running. Breathing hard.

"What?" Mike said, the word escaping him, more a guttural sound from his throat than a word.

"It wasn't my fault," Thorne was saying. "She was gone. Someone got her before I did. If they can do this to me, they can do it to you. We're the same. It's against every protocol."

Thorne glanced over his shoulder. Tom's form materialized, hunched over in the throat of the black hole.

In a blink, Thorne dropped down and whipped a second gun from under his arm. Mike let out a shout, but Tom didn't need it.

Tom dropped and fired, just as Thorne's gun licked a flame into the tunnel that roared noisily down its length. Thorne's head hit the bottom of the culvert with a crack, and he lay still. Blood trickled from his ear.

Tom gathered himself up off the bottom of the culvert pipe. He stumbled toward the light, plucked Thorne up by the collar, and angled his face toward the light.

"Is he dead?" Mike asked.

"Where's Jane?" Tom said, his voice broken. Red welts

striped his face, and the corner of his mouth was split and bleeding.

"He was alone," Mike said.

Tom shook the old man's limp form, growling.

"He didn't get her, Tom," Mike said.

Tom's eyes narrowed, and he glared at Mike.

"He thought we were with the Agency," Mike said. "That they sent us to kill him. He said when he got there, she was gone."

"Gone?" Tom said. "Gone from where?"

"I don't know," Mike said. "Her apartment? He didn't say if it was him who dumped it or not. But he said someone else got her first."

"Someone else . . ."

Tom let Thorne fall. He hopped down out of the pipe, climbed the bank of the gully, and marched toward the fence.

Mike followed close behind, running quickly. Out of breath.

"Where?" Mike gasped. "Are we going?"

"Her apartment," Tom said, turning. "Do you think he told the truth?"

"I . . . think."

"Then we start over. And don't look like that."

"What?"

"Your face. We have to believe," Tom said, staring intently at him. He was breathing hard. There were bags beneath his eyes now and they were beginning to droop. A gray stubble that matched his short stiff hair had broken out on his face. His tan work pants were stained and grubby. The collar of his polo shirt was wrinkled and bent at an awkward angle that left Mike wanting to straighten it.

"Somewhere," Tom said. "She's somewhere and she's okay."

Tom turned and started off down along the fence line. Mike let his eyes slip away. He looked at his own watch. A Harley-Davidson Special Edition Seiko with a sticky brown leather strap. Nine o'clock.

Time.

According to Tom's theory, they were nearly out of it.

CHAPTER 26

Little Galloo Island's two thousand skinny feet reflected on the calm black sheet of Lake Ontario. Even in the height of summer there wasn't a single dab of color to be seen. The only hint that it had ever been anything but an island of guano and shrieking birds were the black skeletons of trees straining toward the pale blue sky. The three-hundred-acre island looked as if it had been hit by a nuclear bomb after being ravaged by thousands of cormorants.

Mark Allen awoke. A cool dew had settled in on the boat and all its rigging. The air smelled of diesel, and a dull throbbing engine pulsed. The sun cast its first yellow spears of light over the tops of the trees back on the shore, taking the blue out of the sky.

Dave was at the wheel of the refurbished coast guard patrol boat. When they pulled into the old station on Big Galloo, Mark ignored Dave's glare. He looped the shoulder strap of his briefcase around his neck and hopped ashore without bothering to help moor the boat. His shoes scraped divots in the lichen that infested the crumbling concrete pier as he jumped into one of the jeeps. The engine started right up, but the only reward for his jouncing trip halfway across the island was a protracted wait. The door to Carson's office was closed tight. Mark knew what that meant.

He put his ear to the door and listened.

"Find a goddamned engineering firm that'll give you the results you need. Do I have to tell you Brits everything? They do a goddamned sampling, for Christ's sake. Find someone who takes the samples in the right goddamned places. Have you ever dug up a fucking streambed? It never fucking ends. We dig that up and you can forget making your numbers for the year, forget about the quarter . . ."

Mark sighed and walked down the hall to the next set of stairs. His rooms were on the third floor. He went there, set his briefcase beside his desk, and put in a call to the office.

"Get me Slovanich, will you?" he said to his secretary.

When he heard the gruff Ukrainian's voice, he said, "It's me. Where do things stand?"

"Everything is ready," Slovanich said.

"For next week?" Mark said.

"No. Is for today."

"I said next week."

"They say you back today. I like to work before deadline," Slovanich said. "This I learn from many years communists."

"Where is it?" Mark asked.

"I no leave this for people find," Slovanich said. "I put in lab truck. Security truck. Sixty-gallon drum. Black. Truck wait for you at dock. Only just for you I tell man. Just like you say."

"It's just sitting there?"

"This what you ask. Everything is good. Every test, she pass."

Mark stopped pressing the Ukrainian because he knew better. It was like a house of mirrors, only with words. He got off with Slovanich and called Rusty at the docks.

"Bronco's right out front. I got the keys in my desk drawer," Rusty said. "The Russian dropped it off and said you'd be coming."

Mark got off the phone and returned to the door outside Carson's office. For a while he paced up and down on the heavy carpet, past the suits of armor and beneath the maces and battle-axes that hung crossed on the wall. Behind the thick carved-oak door, he could hear the ebb and flow of Carson's voice. Now was when he made his morning calls to their European division, where it was already afternoon. He rested his head against the door.

Mark made a fist and poised it just in front of the door, ready to knock. Then he thought better of it. It had been a long time since he'd done something undisciplined. It was years since Carson had beaten him, but the sensation was palpable even today. He felt a boiling sensation churning his gut that left him vaguely thirsty.

Instead, he turned and let himself out at the end of the hall, onto the battlement that covered the driveway. At least Carson would be able to see him waiting dutifully from the office window. In order to give the appearance that he wasn't upset, Mark pulled up a deck chair, leaned back, and braced his feet on the battlement.

Overhead, a pair of golden eagles circled and dove in the blue sky. Their mating screech pierced the morning's unusual stillness. Their dark shapes soared, then met, twisted together and plummeted toward the earth. Beyond the carpet of trees, the big lake stretched on forever, still flat and dark. Insects droned in the meadow below.

It was a glorious day, actually, with the bright sun baking away the last pockets of damp coolness that invaded the island night after night no matter what the season. Mark heard Carson's voice rise and then ebb. He gazed up at the stone tower that rose from the northwest corner of the house. To him, it was a house. To clients and executives, however, it was the Galloo Island Hunt Club.

A Romanesque Revival home, it had been built in England in 1757 and taken to America, stone by stone, in 1867. Its owner, Tibernius Smith, a munitions manufacturer who made his fortune during the Civil War, had visions of other American aristocrats building similar homes throughout the Henderson Bay area. They did not.

Instead, the house fell into disuse and disrepair until Carson Kale purchased it along with the entire six-mile island in 1983 for a mere $1.4 million. In the interim, the island had become the home of a waning hunt club that catered to duck hunters from both sides of the U.S.-Canadian border. During the huge growth of Kale Labs, Carson continued to pour money into the house, refurbishing it to its original grandeur and writing off every penny of it as a business venture.

Mark closed his eyes and remembered the sweat and the dusty film that would stick to his skin. No one had been immune to Carson's zealous determination to restore the house. Like the hunting guides who worked the island, and like Dave, the former army officer who commanded them, Mark had done his fair share of sanding and scrubbing to help with the effort. Most of the time, Mark had lived and gone to school in Watertown, not far from Kale Labs' massive pharmaceutical plant and corporate headquarters. But nearly every weekend and for the entirety of every summer vacation, home for Mark

Allen had been this old stone mansion that Carson had renamed the Galloo Island Hunt Club.

"Long night?"

Mark jumped from his chair and turned to face his guardian. Carson wore jeans and a light flannel shirt with the sleeves rolled up to his elbows.

"Just resting my eyes," Mark said, offering a firm handshake, the way he'd been taught. "It's good to be home."

"You've been down there how long?" Carson said. "Two months?"

"Everything is ready now, though," Mark said, standing tall.

"Is it?" Carson said, raising an eyebrow and crossing the balcony to stand at the battlement's edge with his hands clasped behind his back. His wavy hair was longer than it used to be. Silver instead of black.

"I tried to tell Dave," Mark said, "that . . . that . . ."

The words "son of a bitch" were on his tongue, but Carson deplored swearing.

". . . but he wouldn't listen," Mark said. "Nothing new there."

"Of course he didn't listen," Carson said, his back growing even more rigid. "He was obeying *my* orders."

"I forgot," Mark said.

"Well don't."

"Or else I end up like my mother?" Mark said.

Carson narrowed his dark eyes and said, "She was a whore and she wasn't your mother."

"Because she didn't obey your orders?"

"Because she flaunted herself around here in those slutty bathing suits, trying to get a rise out of anyone within fifty miles of here, including you," Carson said.

"How the hell can you say that?" Mark said.

Carson angled his head. The left half of his face was pulled down tight toward his collarbone. Tendons sprang from his neck.

"Because this is my world," he said. "And I let you live in it."

Carson turned his back on Mark with his hands clasped behind him.

"I'm sorry," Mark said after a while, "but what am I supposed to tell her when she wakes up?"

The rhythm of Carson's breathing slowed, and he turned to face him.

"I hope you're kidding," Carson said.

"I . . . don't know."

Carson blasted a sigh.

"If the girl had written her story and it went to press, then, yes," Carson said, "But now? Think . . .

"She's already working on it," Carson said. "The editors know about it. Now what happens when she disappears? How long before Gleason is being investigated? You can leak this Thorne's name to another reporter. How long will it take for Gleason's numbers to drop like a stone? He'll be finished. Our candidate's numbers aren't bad as it is."

"But her article will do the same thing," Mark said, fighting to keep his voice even.

"Maybe," Carson said. "Maybe not. And it certainly won't resonate the way this will. A young journalist missing under strange circumstances? The media will do our work for us. Actually, I'm disappointed you didn't think of it. Sometimes your failure to understand that next level disturbs me."

"But you'll have to keep her . . . The election is more than three months away," Mark said. "She'll never . . . That's kidnapping."

"Oh, but you're wrong again," Carson said, a faint smile curling the corners of his lips. "There's another way."

Mark bit the inside of his cheek and said, "You know I don't like to play your guessing games."

Carson's smile melted.

"Then I'll spell it out," he said. "Think like war. This company is fighting for survival. Everything I've worked for. The economy of this entire area depends on Kale Labs. Thousands of people. Families. You need a gut check, boy. In this world, people have to make sacrifices . . ."

In the silence, Mark heard the eagle's scream. Carson's tone cut him. The word "boy" rang in his ears.

"Versed," Carson said, cutting off his thoughts. "She won't remember last night. We'll keep her in isolation, and then put her back where we found her. No one will know. You never learned that in Military Intelligence? God damn . . ."

Versed was an amnesiac, given to people who woke up during surgery. They never remembered a thing. If the dosage was strong enough, it could wipe out days of memory.

"Why do you look at me like that?" Carson asked. "So indignant? So . . . offended?"

Mark tried to quell the tremble in his voice.

"She trusted me," he said. "I learned *that* in MI."

"Good. She trusted you. I just don't want you going sweet on me. I've got a plant manager in Manchester who's sweet and he almost cost me ten million dollars."

"Was I sweet in Malaysia when I shot that union organizer?"

"That was practically self-defense," Carson said. "I'm talking about making calculations without getting emotional."

"Maybe I'll surprise you one of these days, Carson," Mark said. "Maybe I'll live up to your ideal . . ."

"I hope you will."

"In the meantime, I don't want Dave and his thugs *touching* her," Mark said. "Let them save it for their whores up in Kingston."

Carson looked him over and said, "You're sweating and your fists are tight."

"I know."

"Remember, when you first came to me, that little shih tzu mutt you brought home?" Carson said, smiling warmly. "That thing slept in your bed, even though I told you not to. Remember?"

Carson's smile twisted into a perverse line.

"And I told you and told you it wasn't good for you. Then finally, you brought her out here for the summer," he said. "And she disappeared . . ."

"I know," Mark said. "You told me about the coyotes and I didn't listen. That was a long—"

"No, you didn't listen," Carson said, "and that's been a theme with you. And as well as you've done in some ways, sometimes you still don't listen. But I'm not asking you this time. I'm taking care of things, and I'll take care of the girl. She's not your problem anymore. She belongs to me . . ."

CHAPTER 27

Jane opened her eyes and saw nothing.

She jerked herself upward, striking her nose. Pain exploded in her head but went almost unnoticed amid her panic. Her hands felt the smooth wood only inches from her face. A coffin? Had they buried her alive?

A desperate sound escaped her, a muffled shriek that faded to a whine. She groped frantically to one side. More wood. She groped the other way, felt a blessed empty space, and threw herself toward it. She fell a good distance, thumping onto the wooden floor below, then scrambled to her feet. She bumped her head again, and this time the pain made her kneel down. She held her throbbing head tight, careful to avoid the swollen knot just above the hairline.

In the darkness, she breathed deep, gathering her wits, trying to put the pieces of what happened back together. A dream within a dream.

She remembered back to her story. Writer's block. The rain. She'd gone for a jog. A car drove past. The man following her through the park. Running through the trees and then nothing until she awoke the first time with his face hovering over her. Him, Mark Allen.

He had smiled at her. Her head had throbbed. There had been dried crust around the edges of her nostrils. Blood. She'd been on a low black leather couch. His couch.

There was a coffee table with a single can of Sprite, a TV, and nothing else until the table and chairs in the dining area. The walls were bare. No magazines. No books. No rugs. Muddy footprints on the light-colored hardwood floor. A single globe of light on the ceiling. The smell of dry dust.

"Where am I?" she had asked.

"It's okay," he said. He sat on the edge of the couch at her knees. "You're safe."

"Where the hell am I?"

She swung her legs free and sprang to her feet. Her head swam. A flurry of comets streaked across her vision.

"My apartment," he said. "They're trying to kill you."

"What?" she said, backing a step toward the door.

"The man in the park. Gleason sent him. A professional. CIA. Bob Thorne. He's called a cleaner."

"How do you know that?"

Mark had looked away, then back at her, smiling. "Same way I got everything else. Gleason's office . . . I tapped it."

He reached out and put his hand on her arm. She almost snatched it away. His grip was strong, and she could feel its warmth through the wet nylon shell. She was suddenly filled with an intuition so powerful that her face relaxed.

"Shit," she said, shrugging him off.

"Don't worry," he said. "You're safe."

The chiseled lines of his face softened.

She accepted his clean dry T-shirt and a sweat jacket; her own had been spattered with blood from her nose. She changed in the bathroom, locking the door, then sat at his small round table in her damp running shorts, drank his tea, and listened to his explanation of how he'd listened to the wiretap and thought he might have been too late.

"I record everything on a CD and listen when I can. I didn't get to it until about ten. He called this guy Thorne and basically told him to kill you. I took off and got lucky, really. I was going toward your apartment and I saw you running into the park. Then I saw someone, Thorne I'm sure, get out of his car and follow you.

"I don't know how many others there are, but I got you out, and I've got help coming. He was an army officer. He works for my . . . my father."

Before she could ask anything, there was a heavy knock at the door. Mark got up to open it. The man waiting there was so large he had to duck his head to get through the doorway. A big brown beard hid his mouth. He turned his milky green eyes on her. They were empty.

He gave her a nod and began talking to Mark in whispers. In the waist of his pants, Jane caught a glimpse of a shiny nickel-plated pistol with a pearl handle. It looked like the .45 George C. Scott carried in the movie *Patton*. Jane shifted in her seat and thought about getting up, sensing danger.

But she didn't.

Mark sat back down and the next thing she knew, the big man was behind her. When she turned her head, he clamped a strange-smelling rag over her face.

Then blackness again until now. Waking up in the coffinlike space and falling to the floor. She could still taste the nasty smell of that rag.

A knot of pain lingered directly behind her eyeballs.

She felt carefully around the confines of her prison, letting her senses confirm for her that she was in the here and now. The walls were curved and triangular. The floor was cool against her feet. She felt off balance, but realized it was the floor that was unsteady, not her.

She was on a boat.

Her hand explored a strange narrow window, lozenge-shaped and lying on its side. She tried it, but it was jammed shut and no light came in. She figured she must be in a cabin in the bow of the boat. She had no idea how long she'd been unconscious. It might have been days. She could be halfway across the world. Her heart began to hammer again.

She groped with her hands over every available surface, swallowing fast to keep from getting sick. Her fingers found a metal ring. The handle to the cabin door. She yanked at it. Nothing. She threw her shoulder against it again and again, pounding it with all her might.

Slivers of light appeared at the edges of the door's frame as she hammered. The wood cracked.

From somewhere outside she heard the muffled shouts of a man, maybe two. Then she heard the thuds of running, then the clump of steps on a nearby stair. They were coming for her.

CHAPTER 28

Tom was behind the wheel, signaling his lane changes as he drove through the traffic on 70. His throat was dusty. He needed a cool drink and a splash of Knob Creek. He pressed his lips together and swallowed down something unpleasant that had crawled up from the back of his throat.

Above them, wispy brush strokes of white cloud did their best to cloak the burning sun. Tom's eyes ached from squinting. He fished for sunglasses under the seat and came up with nothing more than a dusty old pair of wire-rimmed Ray•Bans. One-handed, he bent them to fit his face.

A glance in the mirror confirmed that the glasses were ridiculously outdated. That didn't bother him as much as the sagging jowls and the drooping lines of his forehead. It was all right for his body to be tired, as long as it didn't infect his spirit. He picked up his tennis ball and began to squeeze as if he could manually pump some vitality into his system.

"You think they're looking for him yet?" Mike asked, his head flicking quickly toward the back of the truck.

"He's a U.S. senator," Tom said. "I can't imagine going too

long without someone pushing the panic button, especially since the police paid him a visit yesterday."

"Maybe they'll think he's avoiding them," Mike asked.

"Maybe. Or maybe that someone grabbed him," Tom said.

"Us?"

"After a while," Tom said, "even a greenhorn like Peters is going to start putting things together, and we'll be pretty high on his list."

"What if someone saw us?"

"If that happened, then we'll get to see our faces on the news at the top of the hour."

"Even if they didn't see us. If someone saw this truck down that side street . . . ," Mike said.

"It'll be a while before they get that far, though," Tom said. "They're not fools, but they are cops."

"You were a cop."

"But then I was a lawyer. Cops catch the bad guys, but it's the lawyers who put them away. Besides, how logical is it that the father of a missing girl would grab a U.S. senator out of his own home and then drive around with him in the back of his truck?"

"That would be totally insane," Mike said with a smile.

"I rest my case."

After a while, Mike began to shift in his seat. He cleared his throat a few times until Tom said, "What's up?"

"Nothing."

"What? You need to stop?"

"If you do."

Tom pulled off the highway at the next exit. He needed fuel anyway, and there was a Burger King right next door. He parked in the back by a greasy Dumpster beneath a clump of choking willow trees. The grass under the trees was long and thin and sprinkled with garbage. Before the truck had even stopped shaking, Mike was out the door. Once the truck lay still, Tom got out too. There was some banging back in the camper, and he glanced around quickly before circling the truck and opening it.

Gleason stared up at him with wide red eyes. Teardrops glistened on the duct tape. Tom puckered his lips, then said, "You better be quiet."

He shut the door, shaking his head. His words had sounded almost kind. He followed Mike inside, walking briskly. As he reached for the rest room door, Mike was coming out.

"I'll just grab something quick," Mike said. "While you're going. You want anything?"

"A coffee," Tom said. "Maybe get something for Gleason, too."

When Tom came out, Mike was already outside, walking toward the truck with a bag of food in one hand and a bag of drinks in the other.

Tom had backed the F-350 into the lonely spot and when Mike got there, he disappeared behind the truck. By the time Tom got there, Mike had pulled Gleason's tape gag loose. The ball was on the floor. Gleason was venting.

"—to a U.S. senator? You'll fry for this," he said. "They'll wear your asses out in jail, and it won't be any federal prison for you two assholes—you'll go to the state pen. I know every fucking judge between New York and Washington."

Mike stuffed a hunk of sausage sandwich into Gleason's mouth.

"*Bon appétit*, motherfucker," Mike said. He strapped the tape back down over his mouth and slapped the top of his head, ruffling his hair.

"Not in a very good mood, is he?" Tom said.

"Probably just hungry," Mike said.

Despite his state, Gleason was gulping down the hunk of meat like a dog.

"Might be a little low on oxygen, too," Mike said. "You busted his nose up pretty good."

Mike took out a pocketknife and brought it toward Gleason's mouth. The senator cringed and tried to squirm away. Mike got him by the back of the neck and punched a hole in the tape. Then he closed the rear door and jammed the rest of the torn sandwich into his own mouth.

Through the food Mike said, "I figure when the jury finds out we fed him—you know, treated him nice—maybe they'll take four or five years off our sentence."

Mike lifted his Burger King bags off the curb, and they got back into the big white truck.

"Here's your coffee," Mike said, taking a sip from a giant-sized diet Coke.

The food seemed to have lifted Mike's spirits, and Tom wondered again about a drink, even a splash of Baileys in the coffee. A morning pick-me-up.

"Thanks," he said, adding cream to the coffee.

He decided not to mention the Baileys. Instead, he took a sip of coffee and pulled up to the pump. The big truck had two gas tanks. Tom filled one and looked at his watch. 15:04:19. He hopped into the truck. When he hit the highway, he flattened the pedal.

★　　★　　★

Down the street from Jane's they found a parking garage that would take the oversized truck and keep Gleason from baking in the heat. There was no sign of a police car in front of Jane's apartment, and the inside looked the same as when they'd left it.

Mike disappeared immediately into the living room, saying he wanted to check Jane's computer. Tom went to the bedroom. If Jane really had been gone before Bob Thorne arrived, maybe there'd be signs that she packed some things. Maybe there'd be a clue as to where she'd gone. Maybe she'd even left some kind of secret message. Tom dabbed at the fine beads of perspiration that had broken out on his forehead.

He went into the bathroom. Her toothbrush was right there in the ceramic holder beneath the mirror. A leather travel bag loaded with makeup was under the sink. His hands trembled. He started for the closet, digging into his mind to recall a favorite suitcase or duffel bag that might not be there. Next, he'd check the kitchen. She might have a bottle somewhere. At least a beer.

"Tom."

It was Mike from the other room. Tom felt a rush of adrenaline. He burst out into the hall and dashed into the living room. Mike was at his daughter's desk.

"You've got to see this."

CHAPTER 29

When Carson returned to his office, Dave was already there, sitting in one of the crushed velvet chairs that faced his broad desk. Where there weren't shelves of books, old black-and-white photos lined the wood-paneled wall. Grainy pictures from the past. Men and horses moving ice and timber. A hillside of sheep behind a man in a wool jacket with a dog. Tibernius Smith and the Union generals wearing walrus mustaches and standing beside a massive cannon.

Dave had one of his long massive legs slung over the arm of the chair. With his checked flannel shirt and thick lumberjack's beard, it would be hard to guess he had ever served as an officer in the army.

"Well," Dave said, his flat eyes staring at him without a blink, "I got her. Now what, Colonel?"

"Don't call me 'Colonel,' damn it," Carson said. He had been a CEO now for over twenty years. The army was another life.

"Sorry, I forget."

"You have a habit of forgetting certain things, don't you? Like when I tell you to stop running your stolen weapons across the border. I thought you would have learned your lesson at Fort Drum."

Dave had been a supply captain.

"I left the army on my own terms," Dave said, swinging his leg off the arm of the chair.

"Oh?" Carson said. "There wasn't an issue of some ordnance disappearing underneath your command? My sources must have been off."

"I figured as an entrepreneur, you'd respect another man's private ventures," Dave said.

"I don't want to be called 'Colonel,'" Carson said. "I just want you to act like I still am one."

"Like the boy?" Dave said.

Carson sat down and peered at the big man, looking for the hint of sarcasm. But Dave's face was blank. His thick hairy hands were clasped to the chair's wooden arms.

"Did you have to goad him?" Carson said, his words sounding more snappish than he'd intended. He picked up a small replica of a Civil War cannon off the top of his desk and spun the muzzle, stopping it with the click of his academy ring and starting over again. *Click. Click. Click.*

Dave continued to look at him. He opened his mouth and rolled his tongue around.

"He was supposed to stay behind," Dave said. "But he wouldn't listen. Again. So instead of slitting his pretty little throat, I had some fun. I told him there's things I can teach that little girl and then give her your mind drugs to forget, then have fun teaching her all over again. It's not a bad idea, really. . . ."

Carson sighed and set the cannon down, looking at his hands. The knuckles were beginning to swell with arthritis.

"I heard you lying to him out there about that pup," Dave

said, nodding toward the battlement. "Remember that? Me taking that thing out on the lake, bashing in its skull, and dumping it over. You all worried that he'd find out?"

"I was worried for you," he said, snapping his eyes up at Dave.

"I could kill that boy just looking at him."

"That 'boy' is an officer," Carson said, straightening his back. "Just like you. He's got a master's degree. He's the executive vice president of a billion-dollar corporation, David. This isn't boot camp, and it isn't your gang of border pirates."

"You set him up with all that, Colonel. Not him."

Carson dismissed him with a wave. "Let's talk about the girl."

"No one saw us," Dave said. "I drove right out onto the tarmac and loaded her up myself. There wasn't a soul when we landed in Watertown. No one at the docks, either. Clean. Just like you ordered."

"Well, get rid of her."

"Rid?"

"When it's dark. Out deep. I don't want her found."

Dave's long yellow teeth shone out of the heavy mass of beard.

"There's some time between now and dark," he said.

"I don't want any of that," Carson said. "Just do your job."

"Then . . . just like a pup," he said, smacking the palms of his hands together. "Just like a little shih tzu."

CHAPTER 30

Jane was suddenly aware of the stuffy air and the stale smell of moldy cushions. Her breath came in short desperate gasps. Somehow she sensed what was about to happen. They were going to hurt her.

Statistics. A show on Lifetime. Victims and survivors. Abduction equals death. Ninety-five percent.

Her father's lessons in the basement. She could see him, his thick arms pushing the sleeves of his T-shirt up toward his big round shoulders. They stood facing each other on the mats. Above them were the old rough-hewn wooden beams. The tarnished pipes. The shiny ductwork. In the damp cobblestone corner, his own private racks of weights and bars silently enjoying a reprieve from their pounding.

She could smell the sweaty mats, but it was a strain to remember the moves. There were so many. She never should have stopped.

The lock rattled. Jane's fingers curled until her hands were two twisted claws. That she remembered. The door opened. She sprang at his face, tearing, ripping, screeching.

The man was small but well built. He tumbled backward. Jane

sensed a gun dropping to the wooden deck with a thump. He flailed back at her, striking the side of her head. Pain shot through her brain, but still she clawed. She felt the nail of her middle finger digging into the soft flesh around his eyes. A howl shook the narrow space. The pounding stopped.

Jane scrambled over him and up the metal stairs, falling in the process and banging her chin. On deck there was another man, taller, but not as muscular. His face dropped at the sight of her, and he fumbled for the knife on his belt. Jane went right at him, a fury now.

He grabbed her wrists only an instant before the slashing nails found his face. He twisted her arms. She cried out, but at the same time she kicked his groin. She remembered that, too. She heard him suck in a desperate gasp of air. She felt his grip weaken. She twisted her hands in and away from his thumbs. Remarkable how it all came back. She was free.

She dove over the side, aware of nothing more than a pier and a small collection of other boats moored alongside the one she'd just escaped. The water was cold and clear. Fresh. She held her breath and fought to gain distance from the boat. When she came up out of the water, she looked around, not thinking, still reacting. The man she'd kicked was holding the rail of the boat she'd been on, hunched over in pain and talking into a radio.

Jane spun around in the water, kicking hard. A small skiff with an outboard was tied to the pier fifty feet away. Jane dug into the water, swimming hard against the current and the drag of her baggy clothes.

When she reached the skiff, she grasped the gunwale and heaved herself up into the bottom of the boat, scrambling for the motor. A pull cord and a black rubber handle, like their lawn mower growing up. Two desperate pulls and it started.

Someone behind her in the boat yelled, "Stop!"

Jane had the mooring line undone. She looked up. The man she'd kicked. He had a gun now. She opened the throttle wide. The motor's grinding scream filled her ears. The vibration shook her whole body. She ducked instinctively, but neither felt nor heard a shot. Risking a glance back, she saw that the man was now behind the wheel of the big boat.

Beyond the pier was a cluster of grimy white buildings with green metal roofs. Another man in a flannel shirt suddenly bolted out of the biggest building and began to work at the big boat's moorings. Another, holding his eye, came off the boat to help too.

Jane searched ahead, squinting back the yellow rays of the morning sun. She was in a rocky cove. Beyond was open water. Freedom. A rocky spit closed off all but a small entrance to the big water. Mammoth boulders rose up on the shore at either end of the spit. On the side closest to Jane was a small stretch of water riddled with the protruding teeth of jagged stones. At the other end was open water.

Jane looked back. She saw a jeep now, and the big bearded man, Dave, hopping aboard the boat. It pulled away from the dock immediately and headed her way. Along the shore in front of the buildings, the man holding his eye was sprinting for the spit, racing to cut her off.

The black jagged rocks were quickly approaching. She either had to swing away and race the big boat for the opening or risk getting through. Energy flushed her sluggish exhaustion away. Her heart pounded so hard that her chest began to ache. The bow of the boat skittered across the water's surface, and still she twisted at the handle of the outboard, urging more speed from it. It was futile, but the rocks were upon her now anyway. She could see them glaring up at her from their bed of golden brown sand beneath the clear green water.

The sudden impact tossed her over the skiff's middle seat and into the bow, banging her bare knees. The motor shook and bounced and made a horrible grating noise. The hull beneath her shrieked as the jagged rocks tore into its aluminum skin. The force was enough, however, to carry her just over the rocks.

From the bottom of the boat, she looked up. The man holding his eye was now atop the boulder point. He backed up on the massive stone outcrop, took a running start, and launched himself with a shout. With arms and legs pinwheeling, he careened through the air, straight for her boat.

CHAPTER 31

The hard drive had been ripped out of Jane's computer. Mike convinced Tom that she'd have a backup at the paper. Tom knew he could get in.

When they arrived at the *Washington Post*, Tom stepped right up to the security desk, standing straight. He cleared his throat and in the low tone he used for juries plowed through the security guard and got Don Herman to let him up to the newsroom.

They signed in, and the guard gave them blazing yellow visitor badges before directing them to the fourth floor. They rode the elevator in silence with a handful of the paper's employees. The elevator stopped at two and three. Tom flexed his hands and tapped his foot. "We're not criminals, Mike," Tom said.

"I know."

"Don't worry," Tom said. "Did you see *Camelot?*"

"In the Ithaca Playhouse when I was twelve."

"You've got to see the one with Richard Harris," he said. "I saw it when I was a teenager. I didn't want that movie to end."

Mike tilted his head, listening as the elevator shot upward, slowed, and stopped.

"It's all about 'might for right,'" Tom said. "'Might for right.'"

Finally, they reached four. A balding man with kinky auburn hair, a rumpled shirt, and a loud blue tie stood waiting for them.

"I'm Don Herman," he said to Tom, extending his hand. He glanced briefly at Mike. "How are you?"

"Not that good," Tom said. "This is Mike Tubbs. He's a private investigator and my best friend."

Mike moved his shoulders back and smiled at Tom as he shook the editor's hand.

"Why don't you come with me," Don said, leading them through the labyrinth of desks.

Tom noticed the stares they drew. Mike, he realized now, had a spatter of dried blood on his thick upper arm. His thin red hair was tousled and flaming upward. Tom looked down at himself. His shirt and pants were smudged from hitting the deck in the culvert pipe. At least it helped disguise the coffee he'd spilled down the front of his shirt during the drive.

Tom was glad that Don Herman had a place for them to go—a glass-enclosed conference room with black leather swivel chairs and a glossy black table sporting three telephones that filled the center of the room. At one end of the table sat a small man in a silky chocolate brown suit with a yellow bow tie. Beside him on the carpet was a leather briefcase. In front of him were a blank yellow pad and a Mont Blanc pen.

Tom stepped farther inside. He had to push the end chair tight to the table and wedge himself around the corner to make room for Mike. He signaled to Mike to wipe the flaky crumb from the breakfast sandwich out of his beard, but he only stepped back, and when Don Herman tried to shut the door, he banged Mike's foot.

"Ow. Shit," Mike said.

"Sorry," Herman said, finally getting the door to close. There was a narrow sideboard against the wall with two plastic thermoses of coffee, some mugs, and a sweaty pitcher of water.

"Please," the editor said, moving down to the lawyer's end of the table, "sit. Can I get you a coffee?"

"Thanks, but I don't have time to sit or have coffee," Tom said, remaining at his end of the table. "'An inch of time cannot be bought by an inch of gold.'"

"Chinese proverb," Mike said. He wedged himself in beside Tom with his hands on the back of the end chair.

"That's right," Tom said.

"I hope we're all just making more of this than it is," Don Herman said.

The little man in the bow tie covered his mouth and coughed.

"We can't make enough," Tom said. He held out the watch on his wrist for Herman to see.

Don Herman wrinkled his brow and said, "Military time?"

"No," Tom said. "13:57:37. As of right now, I have no idea where she is, and I've got thirteen hours fifty-seven minutes and thirty-seven seconds to find her. Thirty-*five* seconds now."

"Mr. Redmon?" Herman said, arching his eyebrows.

"The first forty-eight," Tom said.

"Of course," Herman said.

The man with the bow tie wrote something down. He looked up, blinking from behind his silver glasses.

"Okay," Tom said as he began ticking things off on his fingers. "I want the last ten people who talked to her in here in the next ten minutes. Anyone she's close with. That Gina woman. I want any notes she might have had. Also, any audio-cassettes she may have dictated. Let's get them transcribed . . ."

"Mr. Redmon," Herman said. "That's quite a list. Now, I know you're anxious, but we've arranged for a suite for you at the Ritz-Carlton in Crystal City right across the river. The police are working quite hard. I think you could use some rest. You look exhausted."

"I want her things," Tom said.

"Of course, and you'll get them if it's necessary," Herman said with a small laugh. "But Jane may be fine. She wouldn't want anyone, even you, going through her work. She might just be upset with the paper. You see, I left her a message the night before last that we were putting a hold on her story. We think she may have been given some erroneous information about Senator Gleason."

"Believe me," Tom said, "her story on Gleason is true. She's gone. Someone took her."

"Excuse me," the little man said, "but how can you be so sure?"

Tom tilted his head and said, "You're the lawyer, right?"

"Foster sits in on a lot of meetings we have with people outside the paper," Don Herman said. "It's not anything out of the ordinary."

"Being a lawyer myself," Tom said, "I know it's pretty safe to presume that when someone brings one to a meeting, it's not to help the other guy."

"We certainly want to help, Mr. Redmon," Herman said, "but this is a very sensitive situation. Senator Gleason is talking about a lawsuit."

"Since you're talking to someone who sued the *New York*

Times," Tom said, "you'll understand why I don't give a rat's ass about that. I can sue you too. You're obstructing justice."

"Mr. Redmon, can I ask why you said you knew she was right about Senator Gleason?" the lawyer said.

"I got a call from her phone, late on the night she disappeared," he said. "I think I heard her . . ."

"Yes . . . ," the little lawyer said. "We know that sometimes you do hear . . . things, Mr. Redmon. The police have asked us to be very careful with how we proceed here."

Tom felt Mike's fingers touching the back of his arm, as if he was getting ready to hold him back.

"I need to know who she was talking to. There were other people," Tom said. "Sources. We need to know who. You can tell me that at least, right?"

Don Herman cleared his throat and said, "This story came together unbelievably fast. I'm the one who knows the most about the story and—"

"And we want to help, Mr. Redmon, give you everything you want," the lawyer said, cutting off the editor. "And we'll do all that. But right now, the best way we can help you is by working with the police."

"They've already contacted Senator Gleason," Herman said. "They're going to talk to him later today. He may be able to help us."

"The hell with the police. You're going to stand there and withhold information from me about my own daughter?" Tom said, clenching his fists.

"What I know isn't going to help you, Mr. Redmon," Don Herman said, holding up his hands. "Let's not get into an altercation here about something that's insignificant in the first place."

"I don't know if it's insignificant until you tell me what the hell it is," Tom said. His voice was raised.

"Tom," Mike said, his mouth close to Tom's ear, his voice insistent, "come on. Let's go. There's nothing here for us. I've got an idea. Come on. Trust me."

Tom allowed Mike to tug him toward the door. He glared at the lawyer. When they were outside the glass office, he turned to Mike and said, "Why?"

"Trust me," Mike said, continuing to tug him along through the desks. "They're giving us that passive-aggressive bullshit, but I've got an idea. You walk with me to the elevator, then I want you to march right back in there and give them hell for about five minutes. That's all I need.

"If they won't help us," Mike said, "I know how we can help ourselves."

CHAPTER 32

Jane dove back into the stern of the skiff.

The motor was still racing, vibrating the entire aluminum shell, but the boat wasn't moving.

The man hit the water close enough so that fat droplets spattered her cheek. As she fumbled with the motor, she made a groaning sound. She could hear him splashing toward her. A hand appeared suddenly on the shivering gunwale, rocking the skiff. At the same time Jane saw what she thought was the lever that would put the outboard motor back in gear. She grabbed hold of it with both hands and with the engine still screaming, pulled it forward as hard as she could.

The transmission popped and the boat jumped forward, veering back toward the boulder point under the lopsided drag of the man, who now had both hands locked on the gunwale. He was heaving himself on board. Jane grabbed an oar from the bottom of the boat, which was taking on water, and swung at the man's head. The crack of board on bone was startling. The boat lurched, suddenly free from his grip. Jane staggered, her arms flailing, and nearly went overboard. She lunged for the outboard's throttle and grabbed hold, saving herself and quickly regaining control of the boat.

On the other side of the spit, the patrol boat was surging for the mouth of the cove, a creamy white foam slipping along its gray hull. Jane pushed a dark string of wet hair off her face and looked ahead. To her right was the patrol boat, now almost invisible in the glare of the rising sun. Ahead, water forever. To her left, a point of land. Beyond that? Maybe something. They would catch her on the open water. She went to the left.

Water bubbled up from the leaky bottom. Jane's sneakers were underwater. She looked back. The big boat was at the mouth of the spit. She twisted the throttle, but it was already as far as it could go.

By the time she reached the point, they were fishing the man she'd clubbed out of the water. She rounded the point and lost sight of them. Ahead was more water. Flat water forever and no sign of another boat. To her left, the shoreline continued. An island? That or a massive peninsula.

Either way, there was no sign of anything but rocks and trees. Jane strained her eyes. Was that an inlet? She could hear the rumble of the big boat's engines as it approached the point. She looked back and saw its bow plowing up the water. She willed her skiff to go faster, but it did the opposite. The water in the bottom now sloshed up over the tops of her ankles, and its added weight was slowing her down.

There *was* an inlet. She could see it clearly now. The small dark opening in the shade of the trees. She craned her neck. A narrow murky stream. The water was dark, soiled by the mud from the small estuary. Jane looked back. She could now make out the forms of the men on the bow of the patrol boat. One of them had what looked like a shotgun. He aimed it at her.

Jane looked back at the stream. She was almost to its mouth. She turned her attention again to the patrol boat and saw the small burst of smoke issue from the shotgun's barrel. A second later, she heard the slug buzzing angrily past her. It struck the stump of a nearby tree with a *thwack*. The man fired again. Jane felt a fresh bolt of fear. She crouched and swerved her boat back and forth. The leaves and branches of the trees snapped and hissed at the passing slugs.

She was at the mouth of the stream now. She shot right in and soon had to duck to avoid random low-hanging branches. The morning light filtered through the heavy canopy of leaves. It filled the cool air with soft brown light. The motor's whine was muted now by the thick foliage and the heavy smell of mud and sulfur and rotting plants. The water's edge was crawling with thorny brambles.

The stream began to bend wildly and she was forced to slow down. Jane puttered on, careful not to entangle her boat in the thickening foliage. Above, the canopy began to diminish, and the cool air was replaced by the burning yellow sun. The stream grew wider. Many of the trees were now dead, bleached by the sun, rent with dark holes, broken and decayed.

Now the motor began belching blue smoke. She was riding too low. The water in the bottom of the skiff was almost to the middle of her shins. She doubted that she could go much farther before she sank. The stream became a swamp, thick with dead trees. Green slime floated atop the water now.

Jane let up on the throttle for a moment to listen. In the silence of the swamp, she could easily hear the distant putter of another outboard motor. It was hard to tell, but she could only presume that they had lowered another skiff from the big boat and were now pursuing her into the swamp. She opened up her outboard again, frantic now for a landfall.

When she saw a grassy finger, she headed directly for it. It wasn't until she was beneath the big dead tree that she realized it was covered with something strange, as if it had endured a snowfall of slick black jelly. Each of its dozen or more dead branches was heavy with whatever it was. She was under the first branch when she saw the loop.

They were snakes. She swung the outboard hard to the right to get away, but the maneuver bumped the stern into the trunk of the decaying tree and the snakes all began to writhe at once. One dropped down into her boat and darted toward her with its teeth bared. Jane shrieked. She jumped up and fell backward over the gunwale, into the slime.

The water's surface boiled with writhing black snakes. Jane splashed toward the grass. Something bit her neck. She screamed. Her feet found the mucky bottom, and she thrashed at the water. Another snake bit her leg. She spun, kicked, and screamed again, throwing herself back into the warm grass. She crabbed backward, kicking at the snakes. Her fingers dug into the sandy dirt, and she flung handfuls of it at the writhing snakes.

Then she blinked, and they were gone. The last flicker of a tail whipped away into the shadows of the tall grass. Jane looked up. The skiff had continued on without her, slogging slowly through the swamp, leaving a dark plume of smoke floating in its wake.

Jane grabbed at the stinging in her neck. Her muddy hand came away with a streak of bright red blood. She gasped and pawed at her leg. Two deep holes oozed blood of their own. Breathing heavily, she unzipped Mark Allen's sweat jacket and pressed the clean white lining against the bleeding bite. How poisonous?

She used the jacket lining to wipe the worst of the pungent slime from her face and rose, trembling, from the grass. She started at the sound of her skiff as the prop clattered noisily against a submerged tree, then ground to an abrupt halt with the violent sound of the snapping of metal. A blue heron flapped noisily up into the sky, startling her with its size.

In the quiet, she could clearly hear now the drone of the approaching motor.

She had lost one of her sneakers in the muck. She thought nothing of it until she felt the nasty prick of thorns as she scrambled across the grass finger and toward the thicker trees.

The ground grew firm beneath her uneven gait and she began to run through the maze of black bark and bright green leaves. She looked up at the sun. It was close to its apex and gave her no sense of the direction she was moving in. She had no idea where she was going. But she knew with the instinct of a wild animal that her hunters were right behind her.

CHAPTER 33

Tom, bleary-eyed, looked like he was sleepwalking. He muttered something under his breath, talking to himself. Or someone else. But Mike had seen him appear this way in the courtroom and then snap out of it to deliver an awe-inspiring closing argument. When they reached the elevators, Mike pulled off his glaring yellow badge and deftly tossed it into the side port of a brass trash can. A soft bell rang and the elevator doors slid open. A thinly bearded young man got off and started past them into the newsroom.

"Excuse me," Mike said. "They sent me up from tech. Mr. Herman called. Some kind of problem with someone's computer, Jane Redmon's."

The man raised one eyebrow and said, "I guess they don't know where she is."

Mike shrugged as if that had nothing to do with him and asked, "Where's her desk?"

"Over here," the man said. "I'll show you."

Mike gave Tom a little shove back toward the conference room and started after the man.

"Go," he said under his breath.

Tom went. Mike watched from the corner of his eye. The two men were still visible inside the glass conference room, and their heads turned in unison when Tom appeared outside the door. Tom went in and slammed it behind him. Mike pursed his lips to keep from grinning. The entire newsroom craned their necks to watch.

"Right here," the young man said, pointing to a simple blue metal desk in the middle of all the other primary colors. He was looking toward the conference room.

"Great, thanks," Mike said. "Freaking viruses, you know?"

He sat immediately and hunched down over the keyboard. The computer was already on. His fingers pounded away at the keys, bridging the gap between his mind and the computer almost seamlessly. The world around him seemed to melt away.

No more than two minutes had gone by before he was aware of people standing at his side. A bead of sweat dripped from his nose and spattered down on the space bar. Whoever they were, they were saying something to him.

Mike ignored them. He was almost into Jane's hard drive. Once he had it, he'd have to download it. The voice of the person next to him broke through his concentration. They were barking at him now to stop. Mike pounded on. He could feel the sweat in his armpits bleeding into his shirt. There were two of them, maybe three. Someone put his hand on Mike's shoulder. Mike spun his head up and snarled.

He shrugged the hand off his shoulder and threw his attention back onto the screen.

"Someone call security."

Mike figured he had two more minutes, and he would need all of that. A small crowd was beginning to gather. His heart fluttered and the air seemed terribly thin. Another bead of sweat fell from his nose.

"Sir," someone said. It was an authoritative voice. "Sir, you have to come with us. Sir."

Mike's fingers pounded. They danced. They sang. He was into the hard drive. He had a link to his E-mail address. He felt two strong hands on either arm. Mike tore free and screamed, "Great souls have wills, feeble ones only wishes!"

He shook them off and pounded a dozen more keys in quick succession. They grabbed him again, harder this time. Mike rose from his seat and roared. People stepped back. They had him good now, two big men. Mike saw the hourglass icon in the middle of the screen. The tiny green light of the hard drive beneath Jane's desk flickered wildly. The whole thing was emptying itself into his E-mail.

He pushed back into the guards and kicked out with his right foot. The computer screen imploded with a rich thud. Blue sparks spilled out onto the desk and cascaded down onto the floor. Someone yelped.

Across the room, Tom burst out of the glass office and came bellowing toward them.

"Let him go!" Tom said.

Don Herman was behind him. The guards looked stupidly at Tom.

"I'll sue you both personally for assault," Tom said with a roar, thrusting his finger at them.

"Let him go," Herman said. "Let him go."

Mike shrugged free.

"You have no business at that computer," Herman said to him. "I want you both out of here. Now. Or I'll call the police."

"Something they might be able to handle," Tom said. "Come on, Mike."

A lane opened as people cleared the way for them. The guards shifted nervously. Mike knew he shouldn't look, but he couldn't help himself. Beneath the desk, the small green light continued to flicker. He had destroyed the monitor, but that wouldn't stop the computer from continuing to download the hard drive.

"What was that all about?" Tom said under his breath as they walked to the elevator.

"Dismantle the bridge shortly after crossing it," Mike said quietly, holding out his pack of Big Red.

.Tom nodded and took one.

Mike glanced back again as he stuffed a stick into his mouth. As long as no one looked closely at it for another ten minutes, he'd have everything they needed.

CHAPTER 34

Mark Allen walked down the back stairs and left the big stone house through the rear door. There was a spruce stand out back that had a winding path through its bed of needles. At the path's end was an outcropping that overlooked the trees and water to the north. From there, everything but the heel of the foot-shaped island was visible, including a portion of the small airstrip and even the notch that marked the beginning of North Pond. The outcrop itself was a massive slab of granite, big enough for a picnic. Somewhere nearby, a balsam tree shed its warm scent. Even without a breeze, the sweet smell reached Mark Allen's nose as he sat atop the sparkling pink stone. He was lost in thought.

The stillness was suddenly ruptured by the distant echo of a shotgun. Mark jumped to his feet. The sound had come from the direction of North Pond and the old coast guard station. The girl.

Another shot echoed past.

Mark turned and ran toward the house, letting himself in through the back door. The gun room was locked. Mark punched in the code and the latch clicked. Inside, he grabbed a gun from the rack lining the wall. A .12-gauge Remington 1187 with a black synthetic stock and a shortened slug barrel. From a drawer he took three boxes of hollow-point slugs, stuffed them in his pocket, then reached for one more. A set of handheld radios were lined up in their charger. Mark took one of those, flipping it on to channel two, and then grabbed one of a dozen small army packs that hung from a set of wooden pegs.

His jeep was still parked in the shade underneath the porte cochere, just below the battlement outside Carson's office. Mark fired it up and took off down the path. Before he rounded the bend, Carson yelled to him from the battlement, asking where he was going, but Mark pretended he hadn't heard.

A brown cloud of dust chased the jeep across the island. The sun bore down, making the wheel hot to the touch. Mark heard the crackle of the radio from the passenger seat. He jammed on the brakes. The dust cloud engulfed him, turning the sun into a passive pale disk. Mark coughed and covered his face with one hand. With the other, he snatched up the radio and brought it to his ear.

"—the boat and there's tracks on the south side of the swamp."

A voice Mark couldn't place. Static. Then nothing.

"Okay, you keep after her. I'll go get the dogs."

It was Dave.

More static. Nothing.

Mark looked around in panic, as if Dave was about to materialize in front of him. He took a couple deep breaths and put the radio down. He was in the widest part of the foot, just past where the road broke off to the west and the airstrip. The swamp was due west of where Mark was now, in the ball of the foot. There was no direct path, but most of the half-mile was a low hill covered with hardwoods that were navigable, even with all the tangled undergrowth of summer.

If Dave was coming for the dogs, he might already be on his way down this road. Mark pulled the jeep off the path and down into the trees where it couldn't be seen from the road. He hoisted the pack onto his back and slung the shotgun over his shoulder. The radio clipped onto his belt.

He started off at a slow jog. Images of West Point. Forced marches and fifty-pound packs. Brambles tore at his pants and branches left thin pink scratch marks on his arms. As he ascended the hill, he stopped under a deer stand to listen. He wiped his brow with a handkerchief, then replaced it in his pocket. A breeze suddenly whispered through the trees, and Mark looked toward the sky. High thin wisps of cloud. Horsetails. The first sign of bad weather to come. The breeze kept up, cooling the sweat that remained on his face.

Otherwise, no sounds. No shots. No shouting. No barking dogs. Yet.

Mark started off again. As he pushed on through the undergrowth, his face tightened. The wind was playing tricks. He knew that's what it was. And still he couldn't stop identifying the sound as the one he'd grown used to as a boy. The low whistle of Carson's belt.

CHAPTER 35

The smell of coffee floated in while Beethoven's Ninth Symphony played from tiny speakers overhead. Still, Tom couldn't calm his mind. Mike was hunched over the coffee table in front of their two stuffed chairs. He had everything they'd gone to the paper for: Jane's entire hard drive; the story on Gleason and her notes, including nearly two dozen sources.

The problem was, except for a couple politicians, the names meant nothing. To them. Tom thought to call Jane's friend Gina. She said she'd be right there.

When Tom saw a middle-aged woman in a beige pants suit and flat shoes with a wild shock of bleached hair, he set down his triple espresso and waved his hand in the air. He stood and offered his chair, taking up a wooden one for himself.

"Can I see the list?" Gina asked as she took Tom's seat.

Mike handed over his laptop, the ISDN line trailing from it like an umbilical cord. Gina laid her index finger along her cheek and covered her mouth. Her lips rustled as her eyes scanned down the screen. She advanced it once, then again. Tom shifted in his seat.

"Mark Allen," she said. "He's the guy you want. Creepy. He used to have Jane meet him in this parking garage."

Tom peeked over Gina's shoulder and scrutinized the name of Mark Allen. There was a cell phone number, the name of a law firm, and the firm's address and telephone number.

"Duffy & McKeen," Tom said with his thumb on the name, turning to Gina. "Heard of them?"

"They're mainly a lobbying firm," Gina said. "Lots of juice."

"Fucking lobbyists," Tom said, wrinkling his nose. "They wouldn't know a deposition from a restraining order. Evil corporate ass-sniffing bastards."

"That office is only about seven blocks from here," Mike said.

Tom stood, shook Gina's hand, and thanked her. She gave him her cell phone number.

"Anything you need," she said.

On the way, they had to pass the parking garage where the Ford 350 was parked deep in a corner spot. Gleason was battened down, but Tom wanted to make sure so they dropped down in and listened for a minute before continuing on. As they walked down 22nd Street, Tom dialed the law office. Mark Allen wasn't in. A secretary directed him to a partner by the name of Bob Kestrel. Tom told the man it was urgent that they talk. He picked up his pace, and by the time they arrived at the stone building on G Street, they were both in a good sweat. He looked at his watch. 12:34:01. When they walked inside, Tom looked up and around. Marble. Crystal chandeliers. Ornate brass fixtures.

Tom tried to walk right past the guard sitting at the desk inside the door, but before he could set foot in the elevator lobby, the guard had raised his voice to a level that made him stop and turn.

"And you are, sir?"

"Tom Redmon and my friend Mike Tubbs. Mr. Kestrel said to go right up to four," Tom said, looking down his nose at the guard, who had stood up behind the desk, a handheld radio in tow.

"Oh, yes," he said, "Mr. Kestrel told me that . . ."

The guard's eyes were glued on Mike's black White Stripes T-shirt.

". . . you'd . . . be coming. Who is this?"

"My friend. Fourth floor, right?"

"Yes," the guard said. He picked up his phone just as the bell on the elevator car rang. "Four."

Tom ran his hand over the bristles of his hair and straightened his collar in the reflection of the brass doors as they rode up to four. There was a waiting area. Four tall wing chairs surrounded a glass coffee table on a deep blue oriental rug. A large plum blossom print hung on the wall. Beneath it was a side table with a large vase of flowers. The sweet scent of tiger lilies hung in the air. The receptionist offered them a seat.

"Thanks," Tom said, smiling, "we've been sitting."

In a moment, a tall blond man in a charcoal suit with a black and gold herringbone tie walked in and did a double take. His eyes shifted behind his delicate gold-rimmed glasses. He extended a tentative handshake.

"Mr. Redmon?" he said. "How can I help you?"

Tom grasped his hand and held on. "We've got to ask you some questions about Mark Allen and my daughter, Jane Redmon. She works for the *Washington Post*."

"You said you were a client of the firm's. What does that have to do with the firm?" he asked, gently trying to draw his hand away, his eyes assessing Mike from top to bottom.

Mike looked at him coolly. Scratching his beard and snapping his gum.

"My daughter is missing," Tom said, not letting go of the man's hand. "I think you people know why. I want to know where the hell Mark Allen is, and I want to know now."

"I have no idea what you're talking about," Kestrel said to Tom, his brow wrinkling, eyebrows knit together now. "Who are you?"

Kestrel backed toward the receptionist's desk, wriggling his hand free.

"Erma," he said to the receptionist. "Would you call Chip, please?"

Tom reached for Kestrel again, but the tall man ducked back behind the desk.

"Where is he?" Tom said, lowering his hips, getting ready to move.

The elevator rang and out came the guard from the lobby.

"Chip," Kestrel said. "This gentleman needs to be escorted outside."

"Sir, you'll have to leave," Chip said.

Two more blue-uniformed guards got off the next car. The three of them cordoned Tom off from the desk. Kestrel opened a side door and disappeared. Mike had Tom by the arm again, tugging him back toward the elevators.

Mike put his lips to Tom's ear and said, "We've got a U.S. senator jammed in the back of your truck. Take it easy here."

"He knows," Tom said, shaking free from Mike, looking at him hard.

"I know," Mike said, tugging him toward the open elevator doors. "But this isn't the way. . . ."

"We'll get him to talk to us," Mike said. "I know how."

CHAPTER 36

Dave cut the engines and bumped the old coast guard boat up against the pier. He jumped out from behind the wheel. Quentin lay stretched out on the deck, soaking wet. Bleeding from his ear. One eye a swollen knot, oozing blood. There was no one else to help, so Dave grabbed a mooring line and leaped off the boat. After tying up, he considered Quentin for a moment. The man needed medical attention, but he could be replaced. Along with the interesting new weapons, high-quality rejects were spit out of Fort Drum almost every week.

Dave ducked down into the cabin and tore the sheet off the bunk where the girl had been. He balled it up and stuffed it under his arm. He grabbed his shotgun as he left the boat, then got into the jeep and took off in a cloud of small clattering stones. The ride was short, but fast, and it left his joints numb. The island was roughly the shape of a right foot, with North Bay between the big and the second toe. The kennel and his operations were just below the little toe. The Hunt Club, all the way to the south on the high ground, was in the heel.

He took a left down the drive and stopped before reaching his lakefront cabin. Before that, on the left was his men's bunkhouse. The dogs were down a slight grade and around a bend from that. Close enough to make it convenient, but far enough away to mask the smell.

He whipped the jeep down around the back of the bunkhouse just in time to see Vern opening one of the kennel's chain-link doors. Dave stopped the jeep and hopped out.

"Don't feed them dogs," he said.

Vern looked up from the Doberman kennels, puzzled. Under his arm was a plastic tray brimming with bloody red scraps of meat.

"No?" Vern said, looking and sounding stupid behind his scraggly beard and broken teeth, even though Dave knew he was not.

"I want 'em hungry," Dave said, striding up to the kennels.

The dogs, which had been howling outrageously for their food, suddenly quieted. Dave looked down at them and narrowed his eyes.

"Let 'em out."

Vern stood aside, gaping as the four Dobermans skulked past the tray of meat without much more than a sniff.

The dogs in the other kennels—retrievers, beagles, and a pair of coonhounds—started up the din again.

"Quiet!" Dave yelled.

The only sound then was a blue jay cawing obscenely. If Dave had had bird shot in his gun, he would have killed it.

"Kennel," he said to the four Dobermans, pointing at the back of his jeep. The dogs poured themselves in. The male whined a bit. Otherwise they spoke only with their longing yellow eyes.

"Coyote hunt?" Vern said, his eyebrows raised. Mostly they ran coyotes in the wintertime.

"Manhunt," Dave said, getting back into the jeep.

"Oh," Vern said.

"You get them other dogs fed and then get going on that roof."

"Yes, sir," Vern said, straightening.

Dave put the vehicle in gear and headed back toward the south end of the island. He stopped well before North Pond and pulled his jeep into the grass. There was an old sheep meadow that butted up to the eastern edge of the swamp. It would be impossible going from there on foot, so he picked up his radio and pressed the talk key.

"Jeb," he said. "You got anything on her?"

"Had some man tracks in the mud here near a den of water snakes," Jeb said through the static, *"but nothing since. We're looking."*

"You leave Curly there and meet me with the boat at the west edge of the swamp near the sheep meadow."

"You want me to leave right now?"

"Yep. I'll probably beat you there as it is."

"I'm on my way."

Dave kept his eyes open as he went. You never knew with something like this what she was going to do. Girl like that, with no woods sense, was apt to go in circles. He could walk right up on her. That's why he kept the shotgun resting easy across his arms as he walked. The dogs fell into a loose line behind him, moving like shadows under the heat of the sun.

When they got to the edge of the swamp, there was an old wooden dock the sheep farmers had used. Jeb was waiting.

"Beat you," Jeb said, smiling.

"Kennel up," Dave said, pointing to the boat, and again the dogs spilled in with just the click and whisper of nails and pads.

"Good for you," Dave said, stepping in and tipping the boat nearly to the waterline with his awesome size.

Jeb started the motor and wove through the swamp to the grassy finger where they'd found her tracks. Dave got out and squatted down next to them, scanning the earth ahead, shading his eyes from the sun. He followed them a little ways into the woods, reading the disturbance of leaves and sticks the way others would read a yellow road sign.

"You motherfuckers scuffed it up in here pretty good."

"We was looking," Jeb said.

Curly came up, his bald head red as a three-ball, his arms and chest pink beneath the green army vest he wore with army shorts, boots, and knee-high socks. In his hands was that Tech DC-9 that he loved so much.

"She started to run here," Dave said, pointing to a bed of ferns. "She lost a shoe somewhere back there. In the water."

"Damn, I thought I'd get a shot at her," Curly said, his dark eyes sparkling as he wiped his sweaty brow with the back of his bright pink arm.

"You will before it's done," Dave said, turning back toward the boat.

With a whistle, the dogs poured out and danced right up to Dave, ears back, stubby tails aquiver. Dave took the sheet from under his arm and held it out for the dogs to smell. They growled as he pushed the sheet into their muzzles, washing them with the scent.

"We'll comb south behind the dogs," Dave said over the canines' rumbling. "Curly, you take the east. Get close to the water. Jeb, you go down west about two hundred meters. I'll stay right behind the dogs."

From his pocket, he removed a thin silver whistle. He tooted it once and said, "Fetch her up."

The dogs took off like bullets, snarling and snapping at the air, which still carried the girl's scent. Dave straightened up and offered a rare smile to his men.

"We got ourselves a little manhunt, boys," he said, then looked at his watch. "And I'll bet anyone a cold drink we'll be home before supper."

CHAPTER 37

The truck rumbled and coughed. The AC was on as high as it would go, but for some reason, the air being pushed into their faces was tepid at best. Mike sniffed and detected a hint of burned diesel fuel. He looked at his watch. Twelve-thirty.

When a blond in a white dress stepped out of the law offices, a quiet whistle slipped out from between Mike's lips.

He clamped his mouth shut, feeling stupid.

Tom looked blankly at the building, as if he hadn't heard.

It wasn't long before Kestrel came out too. He looked both ways and set off up the sidewalk at a healthy clip. Tom put the big truck in gear, but waited to pull away from the curb until Kestrel had turned the corner. Then he went fast, cutting off a Volvo and getting an earful of its horn.

From up in the cab of the 350, it was easy to spot Kestrel's yellow hair. Plus, even though he was moving fast, he stopped every thirty feet or so to look around.

"Is he looking for us?" Tom asked.

"Someone," Mike said. Their plan was to follow him to wherever it was he was having lunch, wait until he went into the rest room, and put a gun to his head. It was Mike's plan, the best he could come up with until Kestrel dodged into the Marriott on 22nd Street.

When they pulled up in front, Mike saw the blond dish in the white dress get up from a chair in the lobby and head for the elevators.

"Straight to dessert," he said.

"What?"

"That blond I goggled at?" he said. "I just saw her inside there."

"And?"

"Kestrel ain't here for the chicken quesadillas," Mike said. "That blond was somebody's secretary at Duffy & McKeen, and I promise you Kestrel's got a room. Plan B."

"What's Plan B?"

"It's the Mike Tubbs special," Mike said. "Pull into the garage. Over there."

Tom pulled in and parked in the deepest darkest corner.

"Should we check on him?" Tom said, nodding toward the back as he shut off the engine.

"Better to ask for forgiveness than permission," Mike said, hopping out. "Let's go."

They found the elevator and went up into the lobby. In the gift shop, Mike bought a disposable camera.

"This way," he said to Tom, leading him past the front desk and nodding a signal toward a young pimple-faced bellman. The kid followed them around the corner. Mike took the roll of hundreds out of his pocket, peeled off two, and looked around.

"Here," he said to the kid, tearing both bills and handing the kid half of each. "You see that tall blond guy in the suit? Him and the hot blond in the white dress are in here at least once a week, am I right?"

"Yeah, but what's this?" the kid said, holding up the torn bills.

"That's half the job," Mike said. "You get me the room they're in, just the room number, and you get the rest."

"What are you gonna do?" the kid said, his eyes scanning both of them top to bottom.

"Look," Mike said, holding up his camera. "I'm a private detective. I know it looks stupid, but I'm working for his wife and I caught his ass first time out and I don't have my regular stuff. Woman's got cancer, you know? So all you'll be doing is saving her money by telling me where this guy is and saving me the trouble of staking him out for another couple of weeks to get a shot through the window with my regular equipment. Sound good?"

"Well . . . ," the kid said.

Mike wasn't worried. He could see the greed in the kid's eyes as clear as the little red bump on the tip of his nose.

"Okay," Mike said, reaching for the bills, "you don't have to."

"No," the kid said, drawing them out of reach. "Man, for a lady with cancer? What do you think I am? Wait here."

The kid disappeared around the corner. Mike put his hands in his pockets and began to whistle.

"He's not calling the cops, is he?" Tom said, edging toward the lobby, peeking around.

"Nope."

Mike was right. The kid came back and walked right past them to the elevator. He stopped and stared at the door without a word until it arrived. Two people got out. Mike and Tom followed the kid in and up they went, stopping on seven.

"Seven twenty-eight," the kid said, pointing the way. He held the elevator doors open with one hand and extended the other, palm up.

Mike tucked the two remaining halves of the bills in his hand and thanked him.

The kid looked around sharply and said in a hurried whisper, "For two more, I'll give you a passkey."

"Deal," Mike said. He took out another pair of bills and gave them to the kid, taking the passkey in return.

"You're not going to do anything crazy, right?" the kid said. "I could lose my job."

"Just pictures," Mike said.

The door closed, and Tom turned to him.

"That's scary," he said.

"Yeah," Mike said. "And it works wherever you go."

"No wonder they have that sign telling you to chain your door," Tom said.

"Those chains aren't shit."

At room 728, Mike took out his camera and ratcheted home the first picture. He slipped the card into the lock. It beeped. Green light. Kestrel did use the chain. Mike kicked once, snapping it and bursting into the room. They were at it, right on top of the bedspread with the blond riding high and Kestrel, pants to his knees, blinking up at her through his glasses. The lawyer's narcotic smile snapped into a mask of horror at the white explosion of the camera flash.

CHAPTER 38

Jane's throat was dry and burning. Her face wet. She had a cramp in her side. So bad she held it with both hands. Dizzy. The snakebites throbbed quietly now; the bleeding had stopped. The trees were swaying, their leaves hissing quietly in the breeze. Jane turned her face toward it, letting it dry some of the sweat.

She started up again with a quick bolt. Fear. Hair fell into her face in ratty strands. She no longer had the energy to push them back, so she saw the woods now through the bars of her own portable prison. Maybe that was why she stepped into the rabbit hole and twisted her ankle.

Still, something pushed her on. Limping. Pain now a permanent guest. She began to move downhill. Every step was a choice. She took the easy way, regardless of direction, trusting herself to blind luck. Around this tree. Under those branches. Through the thinnest patch of brambles. Sticks snapped beneath her. Thorns snagged her shirt and the bare skin on her legs, tearing them both.

A sharp snarl startled her. She scrambled up into the closest tree. A silver beech. Her hands gripped the smooth bark on the branch and she swung her legs up into the air. The snapping shadows flowed from the brush and threw themselves at her buttocks just as she heaved her hips upward, clenching her knees around the branch. A frightened gasp escaped her.

Somehow, seconds later, she found herself up on the next branch, safe, but looking down into the snarling teeth of four big dogs. They leaped skyward, barking hungrily now and filling the woods with an amazing din. In the distance, she heard the shouts of men.

CHAPTER 39

Mike clicked off shot after shot, spinning the film advance with his thumb so fast it made Tom think of the blackjack dealers at the Turning Stone Casino. Mike bobbed and wove as he clicked off the shots, getting all the different angles. The shrieking blond—a blur of silky hair, painted nails, and tight flesh—didn't seem to faze him. And even though Tom put his fingers in his ears, he supposed that Mike had heard and seen it all before.

"What? Hey! Stop! Get out!" Kestrel yelled, clutching a pillow over his privates. His torso was pale white, in contrast to the golden brown golfer's tan on his arms and neck. His glasses were askew, their gold frames flashing in the light like the wedding ring on his left hand.

"Okay, I'll go," Mike said, turning. "But this'll be on the Internet by five, so you may want to give your wife and your law partners a little heads-up."

Mike started for the door. Tom wasn't going anywhere. He was thinking about a thumb hold that would make the naked lawyer talk. The man had no honor.

"Wait!" Kestrel said. "Just wait. Wait a minute. Don't go. What do you want?"

Mike turned to him and said, "Mark Allen. Who is he? Where is he?"

The blond was sitting on the chair beside the TV now, her hand covering her face, the white dress clutched to her body. She was crying.

"He's a client, for God's sake," Kestrel said. "He's not with the firm. I don't know anything about him."

"You know who he works for," Tom said, leaning in. His hands curled into weapons.

"So, Kale Labs," Kestrel said, backing into the corner of the bed, knocking the telephone off the little night table with a crash. "They're a client. A big pharmaceutical company based up in Watertown, New York. We represent them in health care issues on the Hill. He's a big executive with them up there and he needed an office. I don't have a damn thing to do with him. I set him up with an office, for God's sake."

"What's that got to do with Senator Gleason?" Tom asked.

"We lobbied Gleason months ago for a vaccination contract that Kale Labs is lined up for," Kestrel said. "He wasn't budging on it and we gave up. That's it. I don't know anything else about him."

"And Mark Allen?" Mike said. "Where is he now?"

"Honestly," Kestrel said, "I don't know. I haven't seen him since yesterday. Sometimes he doesn't show up for days."

"Where's he staying? Where's he live?" Tom asked. He was at the bed's edge, ready to launch himself. Wanting to smack this guy silly. Tickle his nerves.

"I have no idea where," Kestrel said.

"Seventeen fifty-seven L Street," the blond said suddenly.

"How the hell do you know?" Kestrel said, glaring at her.

This caused her to look up from behind her hand. Her eyes were puffy and red and scowling.

"Because he asked me to have some equipment shipped there, you son of a bitch," she said.

"I didn't mean anything," Kestrel said.

The blond's face went back into her hand.

"What else do you know about him?" Tom asked.

"Look," Kestrel said, whining now, "I've told you everything I know. I've told you more than I should have. Would you give me that camera? You're not going to use that, are you?"

"What was he doing down here?" Tom asked.

"Honestly," Kestrel said, pleading, shaking his head. "I have no idea. Please."

Mike tossed the camera onto the bed, and he and Tom left the room.

"Excellent strategy," Tom said as they waited for the elevator to take them down. "Much better than putting a gun to his head in the bathroom of a busy restaurant. Not that that wouldn't have worked . . ."

"'Those who win every battle are not really skillful—those who render others' armies helpless without fighting are the best of all,'" Mike said quietly, looking down at his shoes.

"Sun Tzu," Tom said, smiling until he looked at his watch. 11:14:51. Too fast.

They got the truck out of the garage. It took them less than ten minutes to reach Mark Allen's apartment. One of a dozen narrow brick row houses. There was no place to park on the street and they were afraid to double-park with Gleason in the back of the truck. The closest garage was two blocks away.

By the time they reached Mark Allen's door, Tom's knees

were aching and his breathing was difficult in the humidity. The sun was a blinding ball of heat at the top of the sky. Even the trees lining the street had gone limp beneath its glare.

"You okay?" Mike said.

Tom put his hands on his knees and drew deep breaths. His limbs felt heavy, and if he'd thought his daughter was safe, he might have lain down right there on the sidewalk and fallen asleep. Instead, he looked up the steps and studied Mark Allen's front door.

"I'm fine," he said, removing the .38 from his ankle and stuffing it in the waist of his pants as he straightened. "You?"

Mike patted the bulge of the Taurus 454 Raging Bull beneath the hem of his black T-shirt.

They went up to the door, both of them with their hands on their guns, and knocked. No one. They knocked again. Then again. Mike looked around. He dropped his hands to his side and waited for a middle-aged woman with a baby stroller to go past, then dug into his pocket and took out a small metal tool. In half a minute, the door swung open. They scanned the street, then slid inside.

The instant they got in, their guns came out. Tom heard Mike's heavy breathing.

The lights were on, but the apartment was still.

Tom listened. Silence.

It was upstairs that they located the small table by the window loaded with electronic equipment. A leather headset hung over the edge, suspended by its coiled cord.

Mike threw the headset on and began punching buttons.

"Holy shit," Mike said, taking off the headset and handing it to Tom, "listen to this."

Tom hesitated, then put it on. It was Gleason. He was talking on the phone. Describing his problems. Something about a King of Clubs. Then it hit him. Ordering death like it was take-out. A rush order.

"But Thorne said he didn't get her," Tom said, tearing off the headset, "and you believed him. Right? So Mark Allen got there first."

Mike slipped the reflective disk out of the player and held it up so Tom could see a distorted glimpse of his own weary face. "And this is our 'Get Out of Jail Free' card."

Tom didn't care about that. Didn't care that they'd abducted a senator. Scared the shit out of him. Roughed him up. Transported him across state lines. What was just wasn't always legal.

"Keep looking," Tom said.

Mike moved into the bathroom. Tom rifled the clothes drawers. Jockey shorts. T-shirts. Polo shirts. Socks. All neat. Nothing buried.

Mike came out of the bathroom shaking his head. "Nothing."

Mike started going through the clothes closet. Tom lifted the mattress and checked under the bed. Mike started checking the air ducts. There were no picture frames on the wall to move. Tom went to the desk. Empty drawers, until the last.

"I've got something," Tom said, holding up a thin stack of mail and a checkbook.

"Can I see?" Mike said, hurrying across the room.

Tom handed them to him one at a time.

"Power. Cable TV. Water. Phone—"

"The phone bill?" Mike said, reaching, then pulling his hand back. "Sorry."

Tom handed it to him and Mike tore into it.

"I always tell the husband, or the wife," Mike said, "'Get me the phone bill.' That's the first thing. People are stupid. It's like a trail of bread crumbs."

There were five pages on Mark Allen's phone bill. Mike scanned them each, top to bottom, front to back. He looked up at the ceiling for half a second and said, "Two hundred ninety-six calls. Two hundred forty-five to the 315 area code. Eighty-three percent. Two numbers make up ninety-seven percent of those. That's where we start. Just call them and see what we get."

What they got was Mark Allen's office at Kale Labs.

"Is he traveling back from Washington today, do you know?" Tom asked the secretary.

"I believe he's already here," she said. "Just out of the office."

Tom left his name and cell phone number and said he'd call back. The second number was only two digits different from the one for Mark Allen's office.

Another secretary. "Dr. Slovanich's office."

"Is the doctor in?"

"He's in the lab right now. Who's calling?"

"My name is Tom Redmon," he said. "I'm supposed to meet with him and Mark Allen. I'm pretty sure they're expecting me. Bob Kestrel set up the meeting."

"You mean the dinner meeting tonight?"

"Well," Tom said, "I'd like to see them before that, if I could."

"Dr. Slovanich can't be disturbed now, but can I give you Mr. Allen's secretary?"

"No thanks. Do you know when he might be out?"

"When he's in the lab, you never know," she said with a friendly laugh. "Sometimes he's in there all day."

Tom hung up. He looked at his watch. 10:52:33.

"We've got to get there," he said.

"Kale Labs?"

"Yes."

"Drive?"

"No, fly," Tom said, dialing on his cell phone.

Kapp was back from Vegas and told Tom he could have the plane for whatever he needed. He described his pilot, Will Munch, as a kid with a sketchy military background.

"Kid flies my Falcon like a fucking bumblebee, though."

Munch answered his cell phone on the first ring. He was polite, but his voice was more adolescent than adult and Tom felt like he was talking to one of Jane's high school boyfriends.

"I'm at the Falcon right now, sir. Just finished a maintenance," Munch said. "I can mount up and be down to Manassas—that's the closest private airfield to D.C.—in . . . fifty-seven minutes."

"We'll be there," Tom said. "Waiting."

He turned to Mike and said, "On the way to Manassas, there's one person we haven't asked about Mark Allen . . ."

"Gleason?" Mike said.

"Got your pliers ready?"

CHAPTER 40

M ark tilted his head away from the wind and cupped a hand over his ear. He thought he heard the dogs. Baying. Yes, there it was.

They had her.

The radio on Mark's belt spit and hissed. The volume was low and he couldn't make out the garbled words, but there was no mistaking the tone of excitement. Mark put both little fingers in his mouth and whistled hard. The piercing sound split the wind. He let it linger, dip, then pitched it up high before cutting it sharp. He stepped up onto a fallen ash tree and cupped his hand to his ear again. No dogs.

He started moving in the direction of the barking, hunched down and careful about where he placed his feet in order not to snap sticks, his eyes sweeping the forest in front of him. He didn't know what Dave would do if he caught him interfering. He didn't want to find out.

Carson had always stood between them. But the way Carson had looked at him this morning. The tone of his voice. Its mocking. On the outcrop, sitting until he'd heard the gunshot, Mark had come to the conclusion that something had changed.

The dark shapes of the Dobermans came streaking at him

186

through the rich green undergrowth. He saw their liquid blackness even before he heard their guttural grunts. Their mouths hung open, pink tongues lolling, flipping white spit onto one another's sleek flanks. They surrounded him in a snarling whining pack.

"Heel," he said.

They lowered their heads and frantically licked at his hands.

"Good boy," Mark said, scratching the top of the male's head. He called them by name and rewarded them with thumping pats on their ribs. The youngest female trembled and peed.

Mark took a rope out of his backpack and strung it through their collars. He wasn't certain how they would react if Dave called them with his whistle. He knew what they'd want to do, but he'd seen Dave's shock collar roll their eyes into the backs of their heads. He'd seen them trembling for thirty minutes even after the punishment.

He no sooner had them looped together than that sweet low whistle came floating up somewhere from the woods below. The dogs spun around, tangling Mark in their makeshift leash. He grabbed hold of the rope and tugged them back. The little female began to bark. Mark heard the whistle again, and the male howled.

"Heel up," Mark said sharply. He had regained his feet and was tugging at the rope. At first, their paws dug up fresh black dirt in great hunks, but Mark's gentle voice prevailed. He talked to them. They continued to bark, and that was okay. He wanted that.

He tied the rope off around his waist, anchoring his leash in case they tore the rope from his hands. The radio squawked and he lifted it to his ear. He didn't catch it all, but it was something about the dogs. Dave was following them.

Mark marched on hard and fast, letting the dogs bark. Dave would follow the sound as long as the dogs gave him a direction. If he heard barking every couple of minutes he wouldn't slow down to examine the ground. If he did that, Dave might see Mark's boot prints. Then he'd know. Mark avoided soft ground, instead stepping on rocks and leaves where they lay in thick beds.

It was an hour before Mark was halfway up the rocky ridge overlooking the South Swamp. Even from there, the ripe scent of rotting vegetation and thick mud infused with sulfur floated up to greet him. Here, Mark tied off the dogs to a sturdy hemlock as thick as his own waist. He was breathing heavily now, and sweat had drenched his clothes. He backed away from the dogs. They rolled their eyes at him and began to whine. The little female yelped.

"Fetch 'em up," he said.

The dogs shot to the end of their short rope and lurched back with staggered yelps. Then they began to bark. Mark covered his ears and backed away, down the rocky path, through the trees. When he got to the bottom of the hill, he stopped. The sound of the dogs echoed through the swamp. One second, their baying came from the south. The next it came from the east. It bounced around crazily, the way he knew it would.

Mark had entertained himself for hours as a boy sitting beneath that hemlock, calling out swearwords and his own name, only to have them bounce back at him several heartbeats later.

Dave and his cronies would slog through this swamp until dark.

Mark hitched up his pack and set off to the east. There was a game trail that ran up the lakeshore that would take him all the way back to where the dogs had treed the girl.

CHAPTER 41

Tom pulled around in back of the Motel Six and backed the truck right up to the door. Mike tossed a blanket over Gleason, and Tom carried him into the room under his arm, promising to be nice if he was good.

They got Gleason propped up on the bed in his Speedo and cocoon of tape before Mike ripped the gag off his face. His cheeks were pink now and worn partially away from the glue. Instead of cursing, Gleason began to blubber.

"I didn't hurt her," Gleason said. "I know I was wrong, but I didn't hurt her and Thorne didn't hurt her either. Can't you let me go?"

His hair was sticking up, mussed about at crazy angles with the dark roots of his plugs exposed. Tears welled in his red eyes and a flow of bloody snot seeped from his swollen nose.

"Tell us what you know about Mark Allen," Tom said.

"I can tell you about him," Gleason said. "I want to help you. Don't you see? I can help. Will you cut my hand loose? I have to scratch my nose. I've had to scratch my nose for an hour."

"Then tell us."

"I couldn't sleep for three years after that thing with Sook

Min," Gleason said. "You've got to understand. I thought she liked me, and things got out of hand. That almost ruined my life."

"Mark Allen," Tom said.

"He's a bastard," Gleason said, bobbing his head. "A no-good bastard. Is he the one?"

"You tell us," Tom said.

"Carson Kale," Gleason said. "Allen is his adopted son or something. Does the dirty work. They threatened me to get some big contract. I didn't take that shit. . . . I . . . I wanted to do the right thing. . . . Can I use the shower? I smell."

Gleason shook his head and started to cry again. "I don't want to die like this."

"When you've told us about Kale," Tom said, "you can wash up. Is he in Watertown?"

"He's always there," Gleason said. "A place called Galloo something. He has a hunt club there. A huge old mansion. I was there. They flew a bunch of us in there for a big party. It was a conference. Kind of."

"Where is it?"

"Right near Watertown," Gleason said. "I don't know exactly. They just flew us in. We took two planes. There's a little runway. They're a crooked bunch. Kale would do anything for this contract."

"Why would they take my daughter?" Tom asked.

"I don't know," Gleason said, his voice breaking. "You're not going to kill me, are you?"

Tom pumped Gleason for more information until his watch read 10:28:23. The man knew nothing else of value.

"You've got five minutes to wash up," Tom said. "Cut his tape, Mike."

Mike freed Gleason. Tom kept an eye on him while Mike booted up his computer and logged on to the Internet to download some information about Kale Labs.

At 10:24:01, Tom banged on the bathroom door.

"Hurry up," he said.

The toilet flushed and out came Gleason, wrapped in a towel with his hair slicked back. His limbs were trembling and when he saw the Super Ball between Mike's fingers, he began to bawl again.

"Just put this in there," Mike said. "We're not going to hurt you. You just behave yourself and you'll be fine. I've got a disk of you and your hit man on the phone, so you can't press charges against us anyway."

"I won't press charges," Gleason said, eagerly nodding his head. "I won't do that. I'm in the wrong here and I know it."

Mike held out the Super Ball.

"I'm cold," Gleason said. "Can I have some clothes?"

"You put this in your mouth and I'll take care of you," Mike said.

A tear spilled down Gleason's cheek. "You believe me when I tell you I'm sorry, don't you?"

"We do," Tom said. "Now let's go."

"You wrap him," Mike said, after the senator was gagged up. "I'll get him a shirt."

Mike returned in a moment with a black *Star Trek* T-shirt and slipped it over Gleason's head. The shirt came down to his knees and his arms remained inside. As a courtesy, Tom wrapped a belt of tape around the shirt at the waist to keep Gleason's privates private. Gleason nodded his thanks and Tom tipped him onto the bed, reassuring him that he'd be fine before covering him with the blanket and toting him back out to the truck.

CHAPTER 42

Jane thought she heard a distant whistle. When the dogs took off in that direction, she remained standing where she was, the branches swaying, her brackish hair catching in her mouth, and the odor of her clothes making her turn her head into the sharp wind. She shifted to a sitting position, and was clutching the trunk of the tree, thinking about getting down when she heard men's voices coming toward her.

She dropped quickly to the ground. They were close. Her eyes searched the woods. A huge fallen tree lay not twenty feet away, brown and eaten by years of decay. Jane limped over to it, moving without a noise, climbed over, and threw herself down on the ground. She burrowed up under the damp crumbling wood as far as she could, then froze.

She heard their footsteps crackling twigs and leaves. They were just on the other side of her fallen tree.

Jane tried not to breathe.

"Where the fuck are those dogs?"

It sounded like the deep voice of Dave, the man who had appeared at Mark's apartment. As if in answer, the sound of barking came from the direction in which the dogs had fled.

"There," Dave said.

Jane heard the scuffle of feet, then the snapping of branches as the two men crashed through the woods toward the sound. She let out a big breath of air, almost too big; after a series of short gasps she was afraid of hyperventilation. She breathed into her hands. She shut her eyes and tried to calm herself. She was exhausted. She fantasized about just keeping her eyes shut and going to sleep. Maybe she'd wake up in her own room.

Instead, she forced them open and wriggled out from under the dead tree. She staggered to her feet and hobbled away. The sun now cast short shadows through the trees. She followed their line. They were pointing away from where the men had run, and if she followed them it would keep her from going in circles.

Jane reached the water's edge, the slate-colored water chopping offshore and long shadows cast long and pointed across the stony beach. She looked both ways, up and down the shore. No one was in sight. After the two men, she hadn't seen or heard a sign of anyone. It was as if she'd imagined it all.

When she stepped out of the trees, she gasped. Off at an angle on the water was a white boat. A boat with six long poles bent to the whitecapped water and orange planing boards bobbing a good distance behind. Jane could even make out the tiny shapes of the people in its stern.

She began to scream into the wind at the top of her lungs. She jumped up and down, forgetting completely the pain in her ankle and the bite in her leg. She howled until her throat was raw, but the boat kept going. When she finally gave up, she realized that she was waist-deep in the cool water, the waves slapping her midriff. Tears spilled down her cheeks. She turned away from the speck of a boat and saw something that kept her from coming completely undone.

From her new vantage point, just beyond a point of land to the south, she could see something that wasn't trees or rocks, but just the edge of some structure. She pushed through the water toward it, slipping on the algae of the rocky lake bottom, splashing with her hands to keep upright, swallowing a mouthful of water, then another on purpose. Soon she could see that it was a cabin, nestled in a stand of tall old pine trees at the water's edge.

When she reached the point, she could see that the cove separating her from the cabin extended quite a way into the island. Instead of walking the shoreline, she plunged headlong into the water to swim the narrow neck of the inlet. She came out of the water, sputtering and barely able to walk. The sight of a thick black wire strung from a large pine tree to one corner of the cabin's roof gave her new hope. Maybe there was a phone. She stripped down to her bra and shorts, wringing out the jacket she'd tied at her waist and the T-shirt and laying them on the porch railing to dry in the sun.

Inside, it was neat but musty. Her one shoe squished with water and her sock left a dirty puddle on the floor. She flipped them off. There was a small front room with a worn leather couch and a card table. Old hunting pictures covered the wainscoted pine walls. The wood was shiny and golden orange from varnish. Over the cobblestone fireplace, the dusty face of a ten-point buck stared down at her.

A door on the other side of the room led to a small bedroom filled almost entirely by a brass bed with a frilly shaded lamp on its nightstand. Ahead was a short narrow hall that led to the kitchen. Another bedroom was on the right, a broom closet on the left. The door to the closet was ajar, and the black empty space within was somehow sinister. The hair on the back of Jane's neck raised up and she felt a small chill.

"Hello," she said. The squeak of her voice echoed through the empty cabin. After a careful search, she was convinced that the line outside carried electricity, but not a phone line.

In the kitchen, open shelves held rows of canned food. Their labels were faded, but the images of ripe tomatoes and a split pineapple made her mouth water. She hadn't eaten in a day.

She took down a can of pineapple juice and one of tomatoes and set them on the counter next to the sink. She began yanking open drawers in search of a can opener. She found a large butcher knife, tarnished with age. It wasn't what she wanted, but it would do. She poised it above the can of juice and stabbed down, puncturing it with a sweet sucking sound. She dropped the knife and drank, ignoring the tangy hint of rust. She'd had no idea how thirsty she was.

When the can was nearly empty, she set it down. Calmer, but now fully aware of just how hungry she was, she eyed the can of tomatoes. The knife was sharper than she'd realized and this time she tempered her strokes. After several steady thrusts, she had a rough-cut circle in the top of the can. She pried at the jagged hole with the knife until it was large enough for her to slip her fingers inside and extract a tomato.

She'd fished around and nearly had one out when she heard a sound. Footsteps on the porch. Her stomach somersaulted. She scooped up the butcher knife and looked frantically around. There was no place to hide. Through the curtain on the window of the front door, she could make out the shape of a person. The door handle rattled.

Jane slipped into the darkness of the broom closet and the

sour smell of mothballs. The front door creaked. Someone walked into the front room and the footsteps stopped. The closet door sagged open. A two-inch shaft of light ran the full length of her body. Jane wanted to pull it shut, but knew it was too late.

She remembered her shirt and jacket hanging on the porch. Her shoe, sock, and the small puddles on the floorboards. The knife began to tremble in her hand. There was a hook pressing into her back. Her breathing had become so ragged and so loud that she was all but certain that whoever it was knew that she was there. The footsteps, quiet shuffling on the dusty floor, began moving her way.

CHAPTER 43

When they got to the airport, Mike went in to check the schedule. Tom waited in the truck to keep an eye on the new and improved Gleason. While he waited, he looked at his Ironman. He watched as it rolled from 10:00:00 to 09:59:59.

The stink of jet fuel poisoned even the air inside the truck. Limousines swung through the circular drive in front of the airport at regular intervals, unloading men and women in suits. Tom began to crack his knuckles. When he came to his wedding ring, he stopped and spun it around and around. The ring was a part of his hand. He forgot he even wore it.

He brought its perfect smoothness to his lips and caressed it as he watched the steady traffic of private aircraft taking off and landing. Appearing and disappearing into the indigo sky like white slivers, with barely a minute passing between one's screaming in and another's screaming out. Tom counted nine before Mike reappeared.

"Munch just landed," he said, climbing into the truck and turning the key. "I cleared it for us to drive the truck right out on the tarmac."

"There was another jet, a Lear 60. It took off this morning at five A.M. Same flight plan as us. Watertown."

"Was it Mark Allen? Did they see Jane?" Tom said, gripping the wheel.

"There's a whole different shift of people now," Mike said, shaking his head. "No one knew."

A man in a gray mechanic's jumpsuit let them in at the gate and directed them to the other side of a hangar where a Falcon 50 had just arrived from Ithaca. When they pulled up, a young man with a blond crew cut was jogging down the steps of the plane. He was dressed in a white V-neck T-shirt, faded jeans, and a pair of reflective Oakley wraparound sunglasses.

Tom got out of the truck and extended his hand.

"Munch?"

"Yes, sir, I am," Munch said, with a firm grip. The orange wind sock across the runway filled and sagged behind him amid a picket of blue lights on short yellow posts. Heat waffled up off the runway, bending the light. A jet screamed past.

Munch was shorter than Tom imagined him. His freckled cheeks and gap-toothed grin reminded Tom of a schoolmate from his childhood who spent more time in the principal's office than the rest of the kids combined. His hair was nearly white and cut short, military style.

"This is Mike Tubbs," Tom said. "We got a ticket to Watertown."

"Here's the locator number and a flight plan," Mike said. "I'm a pilot. I worked it out inside."

"Fellow flier, huh?" Munch said, making his hand into a kind of airplane, adding the noise, and flying it into Mike's outstretched palm. "Good to know you."

Munch studied the paper and nodded his head.

"Looks good," he said. "I've got enough fuel, so we can be wheels up as soon as I get clearance."

"Will," Tom said to the pilot, "I know if you work for Randy Kapp, you're used to bending the rules a little, looking the other way?"

"Like I tell Mr. Kapp," Munch said, "as long as we come down with the same number that go up, I'm blind as a church mouse."

"You mean bat?" Mike said.

"Anything you want," Munch said, showing them his picket-fence row of teeth.

"I've got a package to load up that would probably be in your best interest not to see," Tom said.

"Not a problem," Munch said. "I can wait in the cockpit and close the door. You gents let me know when you're ready."

Without the slightest hesitation, the young pilot turned and climbed back into the plane.

Tom looked around and then opened the back of the truck. Gleason lay there, wide-eyed. Tom touched his leg and said, "Everything's fine, Senator. You just relax. We're taking a little plane ride. When I get my daughter back, we'll put you right back where we found you. It's not that I don't trust you, but . . . I don't trust you."

He wrapped Gleason up in the hotel blanket and bound it with five more long strips of duct tape.

"Jesus," Mike said, looking around.

"I don't have far to go. I'll just load him up," Tom said, straightening and scanning the fuel-stained tarmac up and down the rows of metal birds. "You take the truck back to the parking lot. If anyone asks, tell them we got a great deal on a rug."

He scooped Gleason out of the truck and threw him over his shoulder. The F–350 rumbled away. By the time Tom tossed his load down onto the Falcon's couch, he was breathing hard and his forearms were damp with perspiration. He wiped his brow on the short sleeve of his shirt and took hold of a seatback to keep from staggering. He saw stars.

"Whoa," he said.

"You okay back there?" Munch asked without looking.

"Fine," Tom said.

He unwound some seat belts on the couch and crisscrossed them over Gleason. He took another blanket from the drawer below and spread it over the entire couch, tucking it in between the couch back and the oval windows to anchor it down.

Gleason started to moan.

"Uh-uh," Tom said in a low tone, "no noise."

He knew that if Munch worked for Kapp, he was trustworthy. Everyone who worked for the contractor knew the story of the limo driver who once talked to a newspaper. They found him dead drunk in an alley two weeks later with bullet holes in each of his feet. And of course, there was Kapp's wife's boyfriend, whom the contractor had nearly beaten to death with a lamp. Still, their abduction of Gleason had been a clean operation so far. There was no reason to sully it by being sloppy.

The jet gave a lurch and the stairs began to rattle and shake. Mike appeared red-faced and sweating beneath his duffel bag.

"Right there," Tom said, pointing Mike to the plush leather seats facing the front.

Mike set his bag down behind the seat. He snapped his gum and sat down, removing his computer from the briefcase.

"Hey, Will," Tom said, buckling in, "we're all set back here now. Thanks. You want to button us up and roll?"

Munch popped out of the cabin, retracted the stairs, and pulled the door shut behind him. He returned to the cockpit, this time leaving the door open.

"Not much pussy up in Watertown, you know," Munch said. "Got some decent whores across the border in Kingston, though. Nothing like Vegas. The boss threw a little of that stuff my way on this last trip. Vegas is the place to be. You guys all set?"

Munch pulled a headset into position over his ears.

"Let's go," Tom said. He looked at his watch. 09:29:09.

Munch nodded and let the headset snap closed on his ears. Soon Tom could hear him talking to the tower, jabbering about coordinates as he began flipping various switches among the riddle of lights and levers on the control panel in front of him. After a minute, Munch took the headset off and angled his head slightly toward the back of the plane and said, "We got a little hitch, guys. Some serious weather moving in across the Great Lakes."

"No," Tom said, stiffening. "We have to go."

"We will, sir," Munch said, turning in his seat. "But we can't get clearance. They're not going to let me take off."

"Time is of the essence here," Tom said, raising his voice. "Tell them it's an emergency."

"Change the flight plan," Mike said.

"What?" Tom said.

Munch looked back and frowned. "You don't want to go to Watertown?"

"We'll go to Watertown," Mike said. "Just tell them something else to get us off the ground."

"Yes," Tom said, slapping his hand on the armrest of his seat. "Do that like he said."

"It's not just the tower," Munch said. "It's real bad what's coming."

"Randy Kapp told me you could fly this bird like a bumble-bee," Tom said. "That's what he said."

"I can, sir, but you don't see any bumblebees in a storm."

"I'll do it if you're afraid," Mike said.

"Are you licensed to fly a jet?" Munch asked.

"I really don't give a damn about that. You want me up there? I'll be glad to take the controls," Mike said.

"Kapp told me I'd get whatever I need, son," Tom said. "I need it."

"It's not about being afraid," Munch said with a small giggle. "That's bullshit there. I just don't want to be responsible. This isn't taking politicians and hookers to Detroit. This is risking lives."

"You going to make me call Randy?" Tom said.

"Hey, don't start threatening me," Munch said, his face turning red. "Fuck that. You want to fly into a storm? You two better buckle up."

Munch jammed the headset back on and started talking. He pulled out a booklet and made some notes. Mike gave Tom the thumbs-up, and the Falcon began to roll across the tarmac. They waited in line, four planes in front of them. Tom tapped his foot and touched his ring to his lip.

Finally, it was their turn. They stopped briefly at the head of the runway and then began an acceleration that pinned Tom into the back of his seat. He felt the plane leave the ground and heard the landing gear grinding until it thumped up into the Falcon's belly. It seemed to Tom that they were ascending too steeply. He looked over at Mike, who smiled.

Tom nodded and did his best to smile back.

Soon the plane settled out and they banked in a gentle circle until the sun came glaring in through the windows on the left. Mike pulled the shades and opened his computer.

"I got the address of Kale Labs and a bunch of information from their Web site. Some stuff on that Dr. Slovanich, too. I downloaded it all."

"Good work," Tom said, his stomach dropping as the plane tilted so sharply he was staring straight down at a big red barn and a duck pond.

"I didn't mean it like it came out," Tom said, projecting his voice up to the cockpit. "Me calling Randy. It's just that my daughter is missing."

"No big deal, pops," Munch said. "It's just that I'm a big Lynyrd Skynyrd fan, you know. I know I seem a little young for it, but my older brother was wacky for them and I got hooked myself."

"What's Lynyrd Skynyrd got to do with it?" Tom asked.

"Oh, they went down in a storm just like the one we're going into," Munch said. "But your friend is right. You can't live your life chickenshit."

"Well," Tom said. "Be as careful as you can."

Munch gave a little cackle.

Mike looked up from his computer and blinked at Tom.

"Kale was an army colonel," he said. "He got out and got his hands on an old Squibb pharmaceutical plant. Started making drugs for the army. They got into the biotech world in the mid-nineties and grew like hell. Bought up a bunch of drug companies all over the world. They do about ten billion a year, but they leveraged the whole thing with a bunch of expensive biotech acquisitions and their stock hit the shitter with the crash. They sold a lot of Cipro—the stuff they give you for anthrax. Best I can tell, if they didn't have a couple big government contracts, they'd be bust by now."

"Wow," Tom said. "Hey, are you up on Lynyrd Skynyrd?"

"Ooo, that smell," Mike sang, off-key. "Sure. I was a biker, remember?"

"Not the music, though," Tom said. "The crash."

Mike waved his hand in the air and turned back to his computer. "Pilot was crazy," he said.

"Oh," Tom said. "That's comforting."

The plane dipped into a long deep slide. Munch giggled.

"You ever been in a sandwich, Mr. Redmon?" the pilot said, raising his voice over the drone of the engines. "With one girl licking the bottom of your feet and the other one on your crank?"

"I never had a hooker, son," Tom said. "I'm kind of old-fashioned that way."

"For real?" Munch said, snapping his head back. The jet banked and he turned his attention back to flying. "I'd hate to have a man pass into the next life without a taste of that."

"Twenty thousand employees worldwide. Two thousand jobs in Watertown," Mike said, looking up from the computer again. "Their share price went from a high of seventy-four down to around a dollar. If Kale Labs went in the tank, they'd probably cancel Christmas for everybody north of the Thruway. You think they got anything to eat on this thing?"

"You're hungry?" Tom asked, fishing in the pocket in front of him for a barf bag.

"A little."

"There's a galley right there," Tom said. He'd flown with Kapp on a trip to Florida once to close on a big glass contemporary home on the Intercoastal. That was when Kapp had bought a cigarette boat for three hundred thousand in cash. Tom could still recall the backpack full of hundreds.

Mike struggled up out of his seat and started digging into the small galley. He found a bag of pretzels, then bent down and opened the little refrigerator, removing a bright gold can of Molson to get to a diet Coke. Tom wet his lips.

"Maybe I'll just have one of those Molsons," Tom said. "Just one."

"Sure," Mike said, opening the can and handing it to Tom as he sat back down with his pretzels and soda. He offered over the bag with a gentle rattle.

"No thanks," Tom said. He tried to sip at the beer, but it was gone in four swallows. He crinkled the can and looked down at his hand. It was shaking.

"You want another beer?" Mike asked.

"Maybe just one," Tom said. "I'm not a great flier."

"Better drink it now, before we hit that front," Mike said. He hopped up and got Tom another.

Tom nodded his thanks and looked at the golden can. He took a sip and sighed.

"I used to put guys like Randy Kapp in jail," he said under his breath. "Now here I am, drinking his beer."

"Ever think about going back to that?" Mike asked.

Tom took a deep breath and let it out. "No. Not really. I try to fight the good fight in my own way."

"I'm wearing your colors," Mike said, smiling big.

"You're family, Mike," Tom said. "I want you to know that."

"I know that," Mike said.

"But I never told you," Tom said. "I just wanted to tell you."

Mike rattled the pretzels again. On his face was a look of hope. He offered over the bag. Tom shook his head and closed his eyes for a moment. He reclined the seat, took a deep breath, and let it out.

"*Sleep is the best meditation.*'"

Tom smiled at her. He couldn't exactly see her, but it was more than just her voice. He could feel her.

"Dalai Lama," he said to her.

"*Yes, my love.*"

"What?" Mike asked.

Tom's eyes shot open.

"The quote," he said. "It's the Dalai Lama."

"What quote?"

"Nothing," Tom said. "A dream. I think I fell asleep."

"You should for a minute," Mike said. "I got some stuff I want to read on that guy Slovanich."

"I think I will."

Tom settled in. The empty beer can clicked quietly under the loving flex of his fingers. After a while, Munch chortled in the distance. The airplane began to rumble gently, rocking him to sleep.

Tom was ripped from blackness by a cry. Someone was shaking him violently. His eyes shot open. The plane. It was bucking and weaving. Out of control. Mike was clutching his computer. His eyes wide. Only the seat belt kept Tom from smashing his face into the bulkhead. His heart pumped wildly and his stomach flew up into his throat. He groped, unthinking, for the vomit bag. The plane plunged.

They were going down.

CHAPTER 44

Jane stepped away from the door and held still. Again, she thought back to her father. The motions seemed slow, weighted, but the sound of his voice rang clear.

"Sometimes the best defense is a good offense," he said.

He never mentioned the reasons why she should learn to protect herself, but Jane knew.

"A baseball bat or anything heavy that you can swing," he said, "delivered to the base of the skull, back here . . . That's where the brain stem is, that's where even a big man will crumple."

"What about a knife?" she asked.

"A knife? Where would you get a knife?"

"Well, if you had one."

"You use it like this," he said, picking up a pen from the little desk where he would fill out his weight-lifting card in his flourishing script. He placed the pen in his palm, as if he were holding a small sword. "You don't stab down like they do in the monster movies. You thrust it like this . . . straight into their chest, between the ribs, like a punch. You nick something vital like that and they'll go down like a bag of rocks."

Jane eased away from the hook that was sticking in her back. She shifted the knife in her hand and held it parallel to the floor. She cocked her arm back, her knuckles pressed up against her ribs. She would let him step past. Then she'd lunge out and stab him, straight in, between the ribs, just to the left of his spine. She'd nick a lung, maybe even the heart.

Now her hand was still, but her knees were trembling. The footsteps were coming closer, slowly. Just outside the broom closet, they stopped. She could *feel* him there, and she wondered if he could feel her, too.

In the crack of the door, the barrel of a gun appeared, steady, waist-high, and pointing toward the kitchen. Then came his hands. Then him, blotting out the light. He was past her. She inhaled sharply, too sharply.

She swung open the door and stepped out, but he was already pivoting back toward her while at the same time feinting away. She knew her thrust would never reach him, but she tried, lunging.

The black pit of the gun barrel flashed. There was no pain, only shock, and the deafening and disorienting explosion of the shot.

CHAPTER 45

I told you. We dropped about five thousand feet," Munch said over his shoulder from the front of the plane. He sounded jubilant. "We hit a hell of a pocket."

With that, the plane shook and dipped, buffeted by a new bank of clouds. Again, Tom felt the grip of panic. For two full minutes his fingers were fused to the seat. Munch took them on a steep ascent. Tom felt his stomach rise up into the back of his throat. They broke through some clouds with a wicked wrench that seemed like it had to be the end of them all, but then the plane steadied out, trembling like a cold wet dog.

Munch let out a whoop and then cackled, "Who's scared now, boys?"

It was quite some time before Tom was breathing normally again. He looked over at Mike. He was eating pretzels and working his computer. He grunted abruptly.

"What's that?" Tom asked.

"Just this guy Nicholas K. Slovanich," Mike said. "Interesting guy. Back in the mid-nineties, seems he ran a biochem lab in the Ukraine. Get this. He's mentioned in this article about a village near the plant. . . ."

Mike looked up, staring hard at Tom.

"Yeah?" Tom said.

"They died."

"Who?"

"The village. Everyone in it. It was near this guy's lab," Mike said. "I also found a paper he published. Some scientific mumbo jumbo about something called Filoviridae."

"So you're like the Encyclopedia Britannica," Tom said. "What's that?"

Mike shrugged. "Numbers are my thing. I never heard of it."

Their landing was rough. When they finally came to a stop next to the hangar, Tom pulled the curtain between the galley and the cabin so Munch could leave the plane without having to see Gleason.

"We made it," Tom said.

"I told you it was going to be rough," Munch said. His cheerful exuberance was gone.

"Can you wait for us inside?" Tom said.

"It's not much of an airport," Munch said as he forced the cabin door open into the stiff wind and put down the stairs. "Couple soda machines and a couch. Not a girl in sight. But I'm working for you today, right?"

"I guess you are," Tom said. The wind felt good after the heat of the capital. The glaring summer sun was cloaked in a thick blanket of clouds and their dark rolling underbellies promised more than just wind. As Tom made his way for the one-story brick building that was the airport, he squinted his eyes against the grit whipped up off the tarmac. The grass bowed and the trees showed the silver underside of their leaves.

Inside, Tom dusted off his shirt and gave his credit card to the kid from Thrifty. The kid gave him back the keys to a silver

Dodge Intrepid, as well as directions. He knew right where Kale Labs was.

"Everybody knows," the kid said.

Mike tossed his bag in the backseat and navigated. Tom drove and used Mike's phone at the same time. Mark Allen still wasn't in and the secretary got even nastier with him. He didn't give a damn. He tried Slovanich. Unavailable. Yes, she had given him the message. Ten minutes later, they were there anyway.

Kale Labs was a monstrous brick facility surrounded by a high fence topped with concertina wire. The faded and broken parking lot held a thousand cars at least—late model Fords and Chevys, lots of pickups pocked with rust and patched together with NRA bumper stickers. Three different stacks stabbed up at the charcoal sky from the tangled fortress of brick. Plumes, endless and white, spilled from the stacks, trailing off at sharp angles in flight from the coming storm. Red lights pulsed steadily on their crowns.

At the guard shack, Tom asked where Mark Allen's office was. The guard pointed out a three-story reflective glass annex on one end of the factory as the corporate offices.

"That entrance is over on Field Street," he said, pointing. "Go to the light and make a left, then it's your first left. There's no guard shack, but you'll have to check in with security inside."

The driveway and the circle around the offices were freshly paved, the sidewalks white. Inside the circle were a flagpole surrounded by junipers and some flower beds. There was a rectangular lot of no more than a hundred cars off to the side of the circle. Tom stayed out on the street.

"Are we going in?" Mike asked.

Tom drummed his fingers on the wheel. His watch said 07:41:10.

"What time do you have?" he asked Mike.

"Quarter to five," Mike said.

"Do you have a picture of Slovanich in any of that stuff on your computer?"

"No."

"What about his car?" Tom asked. "Could you find out what he drives somehow?"

"Sure," Mike said. "I can hack right into DMV. Done it plenty."

"'If you possess the high ground, let your enemy come to you,'" Tom said.

"Sun Tzu?"

"Chen Hao," Tom said.

"Oh . . . so we wait until he comes out?"

"He's got a dinner meeting with Mark Allen," Tom said. "If you can get me his vehicle information, we can ID him and follow him to it."

"I gotta have a phone line is all," Mike said.

Tom drove back down the road until he came to a fading single-story building with an insurance agency, a printer, a real estate office, and a company that called itself Kwik Tech. They pulled into the narrow lot.

The Kwik Tech guy was just locking up.

"My name is Tom Redmon," Tom said. The narrow man's Adam's apple bobbed and his eyes shifted nervously to Mike and back again.

"This is my friend Mike Tubbs," Tom said. "We're investigators and we're in an emergency situation here. We need access to the Internet, and we're willing to pay you to give us your phone line for just . . . what, Mike?"

"Ten minutes," Mike said, pulling the fat roll of money from his pocket. "No more. I've got my own computer. All I need is the line."

The man swallowed at the sight of two hundred-dollar bills.

"How about it?" Tom asked.

"Sure," the man said, fumbling with his keys. "You can hook right up to my cable modem."

Inside were a small table and chairs next to a dusty curtain and a counter with shelves of disassembled computer equipment behind it. The man pulled the cable right out of the computer behind the counter and snaked it to Mike. Tom stood over Mike's shoulder as his friend's fingers flew across the keys.

"Got it," he said after less than five minutes. "Blue Cadillac Seville. License CET-899."

Mike spotted the car through the fence just as people started pouring out of the glass office building. The secretaries came first, holding their hair against the wind, checking with their palms for rain. Men began to blend in with the women. Some with ties. Some with dress shirts open at the collar. Most carried their jackets over their arms. The parking lot emptied out, but the blue Cadillac remained, along with a handful of others.

The stream of workers trickled out. Tom looked at his watch. 07:08:57.

Mike looked up from the big binoculars.

"He'll come," Tom said.

Mike put his eyes back to the lenses. Five minutes later, he said, "Bet this is him."

CHAPTER 46

Through the ringing in Jane's ears she heard a tremendous crashing and kicking of wood. Disoriented, she spun halfway around and saw another man through the doorway to the cabin. Bald. Pink arms and legs flailing. His boots striking the door over and over. There was a crimson bloom in the center of his pale chest, where a green army vest hung open. Blood had already leaked through the vest into an expanding pool on the porch. His eyes stared up and his mouth opened and closed as if he were choking.

Jane looked back at Mark Allen. Even as the gun went off, she knew it was him. Now she knew that his target was not her.

Mark lowered his weapon. His grimace faded and he reached for her.

Jane pulled away. "No."

"Do you see that?" he said. He stabbed his finger toward the man on the porch. His eyes were crazed, burning. "Who the hell do you think I did it for?"

Jane saw the man's gun now, lying haphazardly across the threshold.

"You're them," she said.

"I'm not. Would I do that?" he asked, pointing again. The man had stopped moving.

Jane shook her head no.

Mark moved past her and out onto the porch. He lifted the man up under his arms and dragged him down the steps and out of sight. A bloody swath glowed in the golden light of the afternoon. When Mark returned, he stepped around the mess and shut the door behind him. He took her hand.

"You're exhausted," he said, leading her through the bedroom door. "You can rest here. It's all right. We'll stay here until dark."

"They'll come," she said. Her eyes were losing their focus.

"No," he said. His voice was soft, soothing. "Sit. It's okay."

She sat on the edge of the bed, its softness sweet beneath her aching joints. Weariness was tugging her down into the pit of sleep.

"That was Curly," he said, nodding toward the porch. "He must have seen you or something. Dave is following the dogs. They had you treed, right? When I called them? I took them to the other side of the island. He won't find them for a while. We'll move when it's dark. We'll get a boat and I'll get you out of here."

Jane pressed her fingertips into the bite on her neck. Tears spilled down her face.

"They bit me," she said.

Mark moved her fingers gently aside.

"Black snake?" he asked. "Big?"

Jane nodded, biting her lip.

"Northern Water Snakes," he said. "Very aggressive, but not poisonous. You'll be sore, but fine."

Jane took a deep breath and let it out. She put her legs up on the bumpy cotton bedspread and put her head back on the pil-low. Mark sat down on the bed's edge beside her. He touched her cheek. She pulled the bedspread over from the other side of the bed, covering herself. Clasping it tight around her neck.

"I'm sorry," he said. "I never meant for this to happen."

"What did—"

"Shh," he said, putting a finger to her lips. "Not now. You rest—you'll need it. There'll be plenty of time. Everything will be okay. You're safe now."

His face was close to hers, his voice low and hoarse. Jane was numb. She felt a small shock when he brushed his lips against her. She was too tired to turn away when he let them linger. In-stead, she took a deep breath, shut her eyes, and dropped off to sleep.

CHAPTER 47

L et me see," Tom said.

The man headed for the Cadillac was built like a bear, with wide hips, a thick chest, short bow legs, and a lumbering gait. He wore an ill-fitting blue single-breasted blazer with brass buttons, gray slacks, and a blue tie. He opened the car door, tossed in his briefcase, and tugged at the collar of his pink dress shirt, where black hair sprouted like the edge of a doormat. His eyebrows were dark and thick, like his hair. His face was shadowed by stubble.

Tom fired up the Intrepid. He let the doctor get out in front, then pulled away from the shoulder and followed him down the road. Fifteen minutes later, Slovanich pulled over next to a meter on Fort Street in downtown Watertown. Tom stopped a block farther down and pulled over on the other side of the street. The brick and stone buildings, like the sidewalks, were drab and soiled by years of having gone without cleaning.

Slovanich got out of his car and disappeared beneath a thin red neon sign on the corner. A man on a gondola. Little Venice. Tom and Mike got out, both of them instinctively feeling for their weapons. The traffic was thin; there was plenty of parking on the street. Papers blew by, and a Pepsi can rattled along before it clattered off the edge of the curb. Wind hummed through the buildings and whipped the dirty yellow awning of a Chinese restaurant that had gone out of business.

They crossed the street and went in. A narrow bar area with two big round tables by the window. A black and white tile floor that led to the main dining room in back. A family sat at one table, dishing pasta and calamari with red sauce out of a large blue bowl. Tom smelled stale beer, fried fish, and cigarette smoke. His shoes stuck lightly to the floor. A decrepit set of people who appeared to be regulars slumped on their stools at the bar while a white-shirted man with bushy black hair and a mustache followed Tom with his bloodshot eyes as he wiped out a glass on his apron.

"Drinks, gentlemen, or dinner?" he asked. His accent was more Mexican than Italian.

"Dinner, thanks," Tom said, moving through.

The old patriarch at the table looked up at him through thick plastic glasses. Spots of sauce stained the white napkin that hung from his neck, and his tongue whipped around the inside of his mouth as if he were feeling for his dentures. Tom nodded at the man but got only a scowl in return.

A narrow wood-paneled hall where the bathrooms were opened up into a large dining room lined with red plastic booths along the wall and linen-covered brass tables. Slovanich was sitting in a booth by himself with a basket-bottle of Chianti and a snifter of clear liquid in his hand.

The big burgundy-haired hostess nodded when Tom pointed to the Ukrainian and said, "We're with him."

Tom walked right up and extended his hand. "Dr. Slovanich?

I'm Tom Redmon. Mark Allen told me I was supposed to meet you guys here."

"Mark say nothing to me this," he said in a thick accent, his mouth, like a creature separate from the rest of him, red and strained beneath the heavy mustache, the teeth lopsided and gray. Tom saw now that the burly man's hair was peppered with gray and that the skin around his eyes was creased. A white napkin was tucked into the collar of his shirt. It hung limp down his front without covering the bronze CCCP pin that rested at an angle on the lapel of his blazer.

"This is Mike Tubbs," Tom said, sliding into the booth. "We work together. With Mark."

"Vodka?" Mike said, pointing to the snifter.

"In Soviet Union," Slovanich said, staring flatly at Mike, "Party members drink grappa. Russian czar was Caesar from Rome. Roman Empire is good until 1990. You understand?"

"Three grappas," Tom said to the waitress, who had appeared without a sound.

Slovanich sipped at his grappa; then, closing one eye, he slugged it down and said, "How long you work Mark?"

"Just getting started, really," Tom said.

"So. You hunt on that Galloo?" the doctor said, taking a fresh glass from the waitress's hand. The nails on his fingers had been gnawed to the quick and their tips were white under his firm grip on the glass.

"Galloo?" Tom said.

"Yes. You hunt ducks. American all like guns. They hunt many ducks. They want me work. Take me Galloo. We hunt ducks. Now I work. They no take me. You hunt today Galloo?"

"We talked about it," Tom said. "I didn't know Mark was at Galloo."

"Yes, yes," Slovanich said. "He Galloo. I speak to him. Always there. Hunt many ducks. Big-shot men go there. Like Soviet Party. You no big shot, eh? No Party?"

"So he's there today?" Tom said.

The doctor narrowed an eye and said, "Yes. I no speak good English? I tell you this."

"Is the girl with him?" Tom said, edging closer to the table. "Jane Redmon?"

"Girls?" Slovanich said, grinning wide, his eye sparkling. "Oh, yes. Many many girls from Kingston they bring on boat. Many hookers."

"No, just one girl," Tom said. "Dark hair. About five foot five . . ."

"This hooker have name?"

"No, not a hooker. Just a girl."

The doctor shrugged, looked at his watch and said, "We eat. No wait. Mark Allen knows this."

Tom ordered spaghetti with meatballs, as did the Ukrainian. He listened to the doctor's broken description of the glory of the former Soviet Union as he slurped up pasta and washed it down with wine that he poured into a small water glass.

"When state ask people die in Soviet Union," he said, wiping his mouth on the napkin and pitching down another glass of grappa, "they give life. Millions. Hundreds village. No now. Now is weak like West. People die, every people cry like woman."

Tom looked at the door, then at his watch. Time was burning away and still no Mark Allen. Then the doctor said something about quarters.

"You play this?" the doctor said as he pulled a smudged coin from his pocket and bounced it up and into his grappa glass with one swift movement.

"A little," Mike said.

"Sure," Tom said.

"I good, no?" he said.

"Once," Tom said. Mike shook his head no.

"You get sick?" the doctor said. He started to laugh through his nose, a loud snorting noise that made the waitress look their way.

The doctor's body shook and he dabbed at the corners of his eyes with the brass-buttoned cuff of his jacket as he laughed.

"Every cruise I take," he said, his dark eyes twinkling. "Every people sick. But . . . I learn this game. Is very good."

The doctor ordered a pitcher of beer from the waitress. While they waited for it to come, Tom listened as the Ukrainian explained away the 1980 defeat of the Soviet hockey team to the Americans as part of the Brezhnev conspiracy to destroy the Roman Empire. When the beer came, he poured some into his empty wineglass and bounced the quarter into it. He pointed at Tom with his elbow.

"Only elbow, no?"

"I've got to drive," Tom said, draining the small glass of beer. "I think that's it for me."

"First cheesecake from New York," Slovanich said, signaling the waitress and holding up his empty snifter. His words were slurred. "Is famous this restaurant. And Folgers coffee from Italy."

"I need to find Mark," Tom said, shaking his head. "Mark Allen."

"So you go get him Galloo, no?" Slovanich said. "This why I eat. He do this many time. Mark Allen is very big shot."

"I don't really know how to get there," Tom said. "If you could give me directions, I could drive over and get him and bring him back."

This sent the doctor into a new fit of heavy laughter and tears. The waitress set down a fresh grappa and looked at him sideways.

"You have car with wings?" the doctor said when he could talk. He slugged down more grappa. "Boat or plane. You no Party member. No. You hunt Galloo to be big shot. Galloo is island. Little Galloo, birds and shit. Big Galloo, duck birds and other kind shit. Boat or plane is all you go. Very big shot. They fly plane."

"What about Filoviridae?" Mike said suddenly.

The doctor stopped and closed one eye. He looked around and leaned closer to them.

"You no talk this bug," he said in a low drunken voice. "You drive truck for Mark? You do that only. No talk bug. Very stupid American talk. No talk. No."

The doctor clamped his mustache down tight against his thick lower lip and folded his arms across this chest. Tom tried to pump him some more about Jane and the island and Mark Allen, even Carson Kale. But, either because of Mike's mention of Filoviridae or because of the grappa, the doctor remained virtually silent.

By the time they reached the airport, Tom's watch read 05:05:08. The wind was strong enough now that Tom had to fight for control of the Intrepid's wheel. Munch was inside the airport's small lounge. He'd found a dirty magazine somewhere. He sat on the torn couch with his feet on a chair and a Fanta grape soda on the cushion beside him.

"Do you know where Galloo Island is?" Tom asked.

Munch looked over the top of his magazine and shook his head no.

"Is there anyone around here?" Tom asked.

"Ground handler over in the hangar. Cute girl. Got her name," Munch said with a wink. "Alison. She's it until the morning."

"Come on," Tom said. "Show me."

Munch sighed and got to his feet.

Beyond Kapp's jet was a corrugated metal hangar bearing a faded sign: BROWDIE'S AIR SERVICE. As they approached, the girl named Alison came out of the office door in red coveralls. Her face was round and pleasant and she had dark shoulder-length hair that matched her eyes. "Galloo Island," Tom said to her, raising his voice above the wind. "Do you know where it is? How long will it take to fly there?"

Alison held the windswept hair out of her face and looked at them sadly and said, "It's a seven-mile-long right foot with a long big toe. A five-minute flight due west, if you could do it."

"Strip too small for the Falcon?" Mike said.

"No," she said looking at Mike. "They fly charters in there for duck hunts in the fall all the time. There's a thirty-five-hundred-foot strip. You guys have that Falcon 50, right? You could make it in, but not in this." Her eyes swept the sky.

"But it's possible, right?" Mike said.

"Anything's possible," she said.

"Yeah, too bad our pilot is a little capon," Tom said.

"What the fuck does that mean?" Munch said.

"Rooster without stones," Mike said. "Don't worry, I'll fly us. Just give Mr. Kapp a call and tell him we needed a big man to do the job."

Alison bit her lip and covered her mouth.

"Hey, fuck you both," Munch said, throwing his shoulders back and glaring up into Mike's eyes.

Tom looked up and around, "Yeah, not fair. I don't see a single bumblebee out in this stuff."

"Okay, you two stupid motherfuckers," Munch said, rolling up his magazine and turning toward the plane. "You want to go for a little ride on the Wild Mouse? Let's go."

CHAPTER 48

When Dave saw the howling dogs tied off to the big hemlock, he spit a command for them to heel up.

Jeb came up behind him, out of breath, and said, "What the fuck?"

When the little bitch emitted a yap, Dave whipped out his nickel-plated .45 and shot her in the head. The other three dogs rolled their yellow eyes and whimpered. Their tails were pinned to their backsides. The shot echoed through the swamp and back. The big male had scuffed his neck against the rope down to the meat.

Dave cut that rope away, cursing Mark Allen out loud.

"You think it was him?" Jeb asked.

"Don't be so fucking stupid," Dave said as he cut the last dog free. "Who the fuck else do you think did this? The girl?"

"I guess she don't know them dogs," Jeb said quietly.

"I fucking knew something was wrong," Dave said. "I told you they didn't sound right. God damn, I'll strip the skin off his fucking back."

His face felt hot and his breath choked. The sun was gone. The red wound that stretched across the dark horizon had bled itself nearly dry. The trees above him hissed and swayed in the wind. He'd need a flashlight before long; he felt mocked by the coming darkness.

At the sound of engines, his eyes darted into the sky. A small white jet passed overhead. Dave squinted as it banked out over the water and disappeared toward the north.

He took the radio off his belt.

"Carson, do you read me? Carson?"

There was no answer, only static. Dave tried again, then put the radio back on his belt.

"Come on," he said to Jeb. He began jogging toward the footpath that ran up the west side of the island. It was a rough track, but without his jeep it was the fastest way to both the airfield and the main house.

"Who do you think it is?" Jeb asked as the plane circled over them again, this time slower and with its landing gear down.

"No fucking idea," Dave said.

The dogs were skittering along at his heels. Massive as he was, he still leaped through the woods with the grace of a young Iroquois brave. When they reached the rocky footpath, Dave took out his flashlight and turned to the north. The water crashed against the shore, throwing up the rich smell of fish and seaweed into the wind. Ten minutes later, he cut the light and pulled up short at the edge of the airfield. Jeb was still huffing along the trail.

The sky above was black, but there was still a weak yellow glow from the west that allowed Dave to differentiate the long grassy strip from the dark woods that bordered it. At the other end of the airfield, the white jet rested in front of the small hangar with its running lights on.

Dave saw no sign of anyone. He held his finger to his lips and motioned with his head for the exhausted Jeb to follow. As he skirted up the tree line, he could see that the stairs to the jet were down. Warm light spilled out onto the grass in a perfect rectangle.

"Stay," he said to the dogs. "Quiet."

To Jeb he said, "Stay right here and cover the stairs to that jet."

Jeb nodded and took the shotgun off his back. Dave took out his pistol and circled the hangar. He entered through the back door and listened. Only the wind. He flicked on the light and swept over the big shapes of a tractor and an old Cessna 187. Satisfied no one was there, he slipped back out into the night and rounded the corner of the hangar to where the jet was parked. Sitting up in the cockpit was a man reading a magazine.

Dave shook his head. It wasn't unusual for the important executives Carson hosted to fly in on their own planes. A jet, he hadn't seen. The Falcon 50 was the only one even remotely capable of landing on their short strip.

He stuck the gun back into his pants, circled the plane, and quietly mounted the steps. His hand crept close to the pearl-handled pistol. He peeked into the open cabin. On the leather couch in back, someone lay under a blanket with just the top of his blond head showing. Dave narrowed his eyes and sniffed. Something fetid lingered in the air. The smell of fear. Nervous sweat.

He looked toward the cockpit, gripping the pistol firmly now.

"Hello," he said.

The pilot—he looked like a kid—jumped and spilled his magazine to the floor as his hand flashed away from his body. Dave detected shiny pages and the pale images of flesh. He smiled at the red-faced boy.

"Hey," the pilot said, bumping his head. "I'm Will Munch. You kind of caught me with my hand in my pants."

Munch came out of the cockpit and extended his hand.

"Who's that?" Dave said, disregarding Munch's hand and heading for the back.

"Hey," Munch said. "That's not— Can I help you? Hey, you can't go back there."

Dave ignored him. He tugged the blanket off the figure lying on the couch and sucked in a sharp breath of air. He knew that face, had seen it before. A guest of the lodge . . .

But the black *Star Trek* T-shirt and the duct tape and the swollen nose? Dave had an impression of arrogance, but these eyes were wide with fear and eager obsequiousness. The head bobbed as though anchored by a cheap spring. He studied the dark plugs of hair sprouting from the scalp. Dave snorted at the bad hair transplant.

Then he knew.

"Gleason? What the fuck?"

The words came out of Dave's mouth low and soft. The senator's head bobbed wildly. His eyes straining and moist. An urgent wheezing escaped his throat. It sounded like "Help me."

"Hey," Munch said. "No one's supposed to go back there."

Dave turned and smiled. Munch was standing there in the galley, averting his eyes, a well-trained soldier. Or just scared shitless at what he'd seen.

"That's okay," Dave said. He removed his gun from its holster and pointed it at the kid. "Who else is with you?"

Dave moved closer, putting the gun up to the kid's ear. Munch's eyes widened, then he winced.

"Hey," he said, straightening and backing away. "My clients are none of your business."

"You just sit the fuck back down and read your girlie magazine," Dave said.

Munch sat down, and Dave leaned his head out the hatch and hollered. Seconds later, Jeb stamped up the stairs with his shotgun ready.

"Watch him," Dave said. "I'll be back."

Even if he could get Carson on the radio, he wouldn't relate what he'd found over the airwaves. He put his gun away and descended the stairs. He had a lot to think about. Mark Allen. The girl. Whoever Munch's "clients" were, not that it mattered much. After what he'd seen, Dave knew they were outlaws. Most likely they were headed down the road toward the main house. On the footpath, even with their head start, Dave would beat them by half an hour.

He whistled to the dogs and started off down the runway at a steady jog.

CHAPTER 49

The massive stone dining room was long and cool. Carson's fork shimmered in the light of the chandelier. He said nothing, just stabbed at a piece of red meat and put it in his mouth. A fire crackled behind him in the fireplace. Dave stood waiting. His stomach rumbled quietly, and he felt the saliva begin to pool up under the back of his tongue. Carson swallowed the meat and reached for his wine. He let it linger in his mouth, savoring it, before he swallowed. Dave had to admire the coolness with which he'd received the news.

Dave cleared his throat. The fire snapped.

Carson wiped his mouth on a lace napkin, then finally looked up and told him what to do.

Dave tried to keep from smiling, but couldn't because of the beauty of it.

"Your moonlighting can finally come to some good," Carson said. He sniffed.

"I could have killed Gleason from the start if you wanted," Dave said.

"You don't just kill a U.S. senator," Carson said. "But whoever brought him here did our work for us."

"Can I use your Land Cruiser?" Dave asked. "My jeep is at North Pond."

"Of course," Carson said, then turned his attention back to his plate, as if Dave had simply inquired about which side of the island he wanted to drive on a deer hunt.

Dave left through the kitchen. Danny, the cook, and his young wife Katrina were sitting on stools at the butcher block, having dinner before they left for their home on the mainland. They looked up from their plates without speaking. Dave smiled at them as he grabbed the remainder of the roast up out of the pan and began tearing away at it with his teeth as if it were a loaf of bread.

"Not bad," he said, his mouth full and nodding their way. He tore a paper towel away from the roll by the sink and headed out the back door, wiping grease from his hands and letting the screen door slam behind him.

In the Land Cruiser, he returned to the kennel and put up the dogs, then went to the bunkhouse and beeped his horn.

Vern stumbled out in an apron, drying off a frying pan.

"Get a gun," Dave said.

Vern looked at Dave in surprise. He was sixty-two, an infantryman in the Korean War. Like the rest of Dave's crew, he'd done some time in the brig. But he was the one who did the cooking and cleaning, not one of the young Turks who helped guide the hunters and run the weapons.

"I don't know where the hell Curly is," Dave said. "Jeb's got a post. Quentin's half-dead."

Vern nodded. He came out of the bunkhouse moments later with a heavy goose gun, an Ithaca .10-gauge. They got into Carson's vehicle and set off toward North Pond.

"There's four people on this island that we can't let get off," Dave said as they bounced along. "Mark is one of them."

"Mark?"

"You heard me," he said, glancing over.

"Carson knows?"

"You worry about me," Dave said, glowering. "There's the girl I'm huntin', and a couple of other strangers that I don't know nothing about—just that you can shoot them if you see them."

"I can shoot any of 'em?" Vern said. "But you don't want me shooting Mark?"

"You shoot him in the leg, Verny," Dave said. "I'll do the rest."

"I don't know about shooting Mark," Vern said, mumbling to himself.

Dave whipped out his pistol and put it under Vern's eye. "You do as I say, Vern. That's a direct fucking order."

Vern's eyes grew wide and teary.

"I didn't mean nothing," he said.

"Good," Dave said. He stuffed the pistol back in his belt.

They rode in silence the rest of the way to the Coast Guard Station. Dave backed the Land Cruiser up to the building he used as his warehouse. He went inside and came out with a long wooden box. Vern helped him load the box into the back of the Land Cruiser, then took up his position in a rocking chair on the porch of the main house.

"What if this storm hits?" Vern asked.

Even with the glow from the headlights of the truck, Dave could barely see him in the dark shadows of the porch.

"You just sit tight until I get you. I don't give a damn if it starts raining buckets of shit," Dave said. "You got your radio on channel two?"

"Yup."

"Okay, don't use it unless you see someone," Dave said, climbing into the Land Cruiser. "And don't you forget what I said, Vern. There's still a warrant for you on the mainland and if someone gets by you, I promise you'll be spreading your saggy cheeks for half the cell block in Attica. Even crooks don't like a child molester."

Dave continued to scan the roadside in the headlights of the truck as he bounced along toward the airstrip. He picked up his radio.

"Carson," he said, "this is Dave. Everything okay?"

"This is Carson. Just fine."

"No sign of our guests?"

"Not yet. I'll be sure to let you know."

Dave pulled the Land Cruiser right out onto the airstrip next to the jet, nose in toward the hangar. Jeb leaned out of the hatch as he got out.

"Everything okay?" Dave asked.

"Miss July ain't too bad," Jeb said. He raised a can of beer in the air.

"I'm glad you made friends," Dave said, climbing the stairs.

He looked at the unconscious senator lying on the couch before he said to Munch, "Okay, time for you to leave now."

"What?" Munch said, blinking at him and smiling. Two empty beer cans lay on the floor of the cockpit.

"Time to go," Dave said. "You heard me."

"Where?"

"I don't really give a fuck," Dave said, "but you're trespassing, so you'll have to leave."

Munch's smile faded. "But . . . I can't."

Dave put his .45 up to Munch's ear. The cabin resounded with the metallic click of a hammer being pulled back.

"O-kay," Munch said, slowly reaching for the control panel and flipping on some switches, "as long as you promise to take care of my clients. They'll need to get back somehow."

"Don't you worry," Dave said. "We'll take care of them for you."

"Okay," Munch said. "Well, I can't stay if I'm trespassing."

"No," Dave said. "That would be unhealthy."

"It's pretty rough weather."

"Yeah. Bad night to fly. Be careful."

Dave and Jeb went down the stairs and then, as Munch retracted them up into the plane, Jeb gave him a friendly wave.

"Pretty good kid," Jeb said at the door.

"What are you, the fucking welcome wagon?" Dave said. "Help me with this box."

The jet's engines were whining loudly now, blocking out the sound of the heavy wind in the trees. Munch turned the plane around, facing it into the west and the wind.

"And they were never seen or heard from again," Dave said.

"What do you mean?"

Dave flicked up the metal latches on the wooden box.

"Jeez," Jeb said. "That's one of them Stingers for the Indonesians."

"Yes it is," Dave said in a pleasant singsong voice as he lifted the long metal tube from its packing foam and rested it on his shoulder.

The jet was screaming now. Jeb covered his ears and yelled something to Dave, who smiled back at him. The whites of Jeb's eyes had grown large and his mouth was a circle of wonder. The jet started off down the runway and lifted up into the inky sky. Its lights twinkled on and off. Dave put one eye up to the sight, closing the other, lining it up perfectly. Not that it mattered. This was one of the good ones. Fire and forget. A heat seeker.

The jet was well out over the water now. A good mile away.

"Jesus," Jeb said, his shout ringing loud and clear now.

"Feel free to call me Dave," Dave said.

With a chuckle, he released the rocket. Sparks and a pungent chemical aroma filled the air. The rocket streaked through the night with a deadly hiss. It was nothing more than the distant ember of a cigarette when it touched the blinking lights of the jet.

A beautiful orange ball of fire burst from the darkness. Seven seconds later, the roar of the explosion washed over them.

Dave couldn't help the giddy hoot that escaped his lips. He slapped Jeb on the back. He laughed so hard, the corners of his eyes were damp.

Between gasps, he said, "I told that kid . . . it was a bad night to fly."

CHAPTER 50

Jane pulled herself free of the arm around her waist and the tangle of sheets. She padded to the bathroom of the cabin in the darkness, closed the door, and found the light switch. The room was all light pine and slate, trying to make you feel like you blended into the woods.

She did. She didn't know where she was or what time it was. Her source was sleeping in her bed, and she smelled like swamp funk.

She searched through the drawers of the bathroom cabinet and found it stocked with new toothbrushes, toothpaste, soap, aspirin, and deodorant. She sighed and turned on the shower, let the room steam up, and removed her soiled clothes, peeling out of her bra and panties as she made sure the door was locked.

Naked, she stood before the steaming mirror and washed the caked black mud from her freckles and tied her hair into a knot with a rubber band she found. She washed off her taut stomach and her breasts.

After she showered, she rinsed her underclothes and returned to the room where Mark slept. She kept the door cracked, and the shower steam escaped into the room.

With her towel around her, she slid back into her damp underwear. In a closet, she found a small man's pair of khaki pants and a flannel shirt. She dropped the towel.

When she turned, Mark was awake. Propped up on one elbow, shirtless.

"You're beautiful," he said. "More than just your neck. My mother was beautiful like you."

"Is that supposed to be charm?"

"It's a compliment. She was beautiful inside and outside. You have the same long neck. The dark hair and eyes . . ."

Jane hustled into the clothes, cuffing the pants, rolling up the sleeves, buttoning up her shirt.

"Sit with me . . ."

She walked to the front door and heard the rain hammering the top of the cabin. Dark-as-hell skies turning the forest floor into a river. The thunder shook the house. A jolt of lightning illuminated his angular face as he stood and grabbed her hand. "Sit," he said. "Let's talk."

"What's it have to do with Senator Gleason?" she asked. "Let's really talk or I'm gone."

Mark drew in a breath and blew it out slowly. She sat.

He stroked her hair and removed a loose strand that had plastered itself against her wet face. She grabbed his hand, stared into his eyes, and said: "Tell me."

"I don't want to talk anymore," he said. "I'm sick of all of it."

"Well, you brought me into the middle of it."

"Not now."

Jane stood and turned back to the door. She was reaching for the handle when he spoke.

"The government is about to award a massive contract," he said. "Billions of dollars. To inoculate the entire country."

"So?"

"It's a ten-year deal against bioterrorism. My company, Kale Labs, was going to get it. We're the only ones who've done this kind of thing. For the military. Carson was a colonel in the army. That's how he started. But Gleason is being paid off; we know he is. You know him—you've seen the things he does."

She sat back down on the bed with him. He grabbed both of her hands and stroked her fingers.

"And he's the chairman of the Senate Committee on Health and Human Services," Jane said. She allowed him to touch her. He was talking. That's all that mattered. "So he controls the contract."

"Yes," Mark said, holding her hand and slipping his arm beneath her back. "It won't be awarded until the first of the year. If Gleason loses the election, Kale Labs will get it. Easy."

She could hear his breath. Labored and slow.

"Gleason is a pig," she said. Her voice raspy. His fingers lacing into hers. She peered down at her hands and noticed that her top two buttons were undone. Her bra wet and clinging to the curves of her breasts.

"We also have a two-billion-dollar loan that comes due in September. If we don't get the contract, everything Carson and I have worked for will be ruined . . ."

The thunder broke again. The rain sounded like tiny pebbles spilling onto the roof. She needed him to keep talking.

His arm caught her back as he leaned her into the bed. "It's still light outside," he said. "We can't move until dark."

"You were going to use me to save it all."

"It's more than just us," Mark said, his face within inches. She could smell his sweat. See her own hand reaching across his wide shoulders. "We've got twenty thousand people working for us. Thousands of them are right here. If something happened to Kale Labs, this whole area would be ruined."

He kissed her. And she let him.

"You used me," she said.

"Maybe I wanted to be around you."

"No you didn't."

"You are so beautiful."

No one had ever said that before. Not like that. He kissed her again and in the darkness unbuttoned her shirt. Her breath a steady rhythm as their chests touched and he slipped his fingers under her bra.

"You know," Mark said. They were under the sheet, kissing, their naked bodies twisting together. "Everything I gave you about Gleason was true. And I could have gotten anyone to break that story. I chose you because I knew you felt the same way about him . . ."

She grabbed his face and pushed him onto his back. "Quit talking."

CHAPTER 51

Mark grabbed a shotgun, punched in two cartridges, and said, "There's a path to the airport road and then it's only about half a kilometer to the nearest boat. Come on."

He looped his arm around Jane's back, taking the weight off her ankle. In his free hand was a small flashlight. By the time they reached the road, the darkness lay thick beyond the yellow beam of light. At the top of the driveway leading down to Dave's cabin and the bunkhouse, Jane watched the sky behind them suddenly glow. Mark spun around just in time to see the dying orange flash. Several moments later, the air rumbled from the blast.

Jane gripped his shoulder tight.

"Jesus," Mark said. "He's lost it. Dave has absolutely lost it."

They hurried down the gravel drive to the bunkhouse, dark except for a single light in the kitchen. Down past Dave's cabin to the narrow dock, where up on a lift waited a thirty-two foot Formula cigarette boat, glowing yellow even in the darkness.

"Unsnap that cover while I lower it down," Mark said. He tugged at one of the snaps until it popped loose to show Jane how it was done, then started the winch motor.

Jane was up on the swim platform in the back when head-lights swung over their heads. Even with the wind, the clatter of gravel could be heard as a vehicle came tearing down the drive.

"Get down," Mark said. Jane disappeared in the back of the boat and he dropped down flat on the dock. He scooped up the shotgun and tried to hide his profile as best he could behind the housing of the heavy winch motor.

The vehicle soon appeared, jouncing through the air past Dave's cabin and sliding to a halt at the end of the dock. Dust spun up, filling the beam of the headlights with smoky white clouds that were quickly whipped away by the wind.

When the doors opened, Mark fired three shots at the driver's side and the final two at the passenger's. The roar of the short-barreled shotgun left his ears ringing. Behind him, Jane was silent. As the dust settled, nothing stirred. He lay still for nearly a minute, marveling at his apparent luck.

Mark fished into his pockets and reloaded the gun. Taking careful aim, he shot out both headlights, then jumped to his feet. He sprinted the length of the dock with his finger on the shotgun's trigger. By the time he reached the vehicle—it was Carson's Land Cruiser—he could see the dark shapes of two men crumpled on the ground beneath the open doors.

Mark kicked the passenger-side door closed, and there lay Jeb. Even in the dim light that crept from the cabin, Mark could see the inky hole in the middle of his forehead. Blood poured everywhere. Cautiously, he rounded the back of the vehicle, and there was Dave, sprawled awkwardly on the ground, facedown and still.

Mark eased up and flicked his toe at Dave's massive hand.

It came to life.

A jolt of panic. A vice on his ankle. Bone being compressed.

Mark pulled the trigger. Too late. The shot ripped into the truck frame.

Falling. Swinging the gun. Pulling off another shot.

Stars and a sharp pain in the back of his head. The gun torn from his hands. A blow to the side of his head. The weight of Dave's knee on his chest. The smell of garlic and meat. Dave's hot breath. His face eased forward. Bulbous pale eyes. Reptilian. Empty. Grinning yellow teeth, fading.

"Been looking for you," Dave said. "Boy."

Then blackness.

CHAPTER 52

Tom had seen the big house when they circled before landing. It blazed with light, and he knew instinctively that the answers were there. He hoped Jane was too, but for some reason he was less confident about that. There was no other way to get there than walk. Exhaustion was lurking on the perimeters of his conscious, but strangely, the walk was invigorating. Maybe it was the sharp wind, or the way the thin beam of the small flashlight from the plane so boldly cut through the darkness, or the sound of crashing surf that could be heard from the road. Whatever it was, Tom felt a spring in his step.

When the headlights of a vehicle suddenly shot around a bend, Tom didn't have time to think. He snapped off his light, grabbed Mike, and plunged into the trees. The vehicle—it looked like a Land Cruiser—shot by in a blur of taillights and dust.

"Why did we hide?" Mike asked. "My feet are killing me."

"'In making tactical dispositions, the highest pitch you can attain is to conceal them.'"

"Sun Tzu?"

"Yes," Tom said. "The big house is our objective. I feel it."

Mike had wrapped a piece of cloth around his big head like a sheik and carried a fallen branch as a walking stick. Moses leading the way.

They stepped back out onto the stony dirt road and continued their march. After a time, Mike's labored breathing could be heard even above the howl of the wind. Tom passed the small yellow beam of light over Mike's face. It was beaded with sweat.

"Do you want to stop for a minute?" Tom asked.

"No," Mike said, "we're almost there."

Tom pushed the light button on his watch. 02:57:03. The notion of having less than three hours gave him a jolt and he pressed ahead, dipping his head into the wind.

There was a sudden flash over the treetops to the west.

Tom stabbed the beam of his small flashlight toward the dying fireball.

"That wasn't lightning," Mike said, gripping Tom's shoulder.

"A bomb," Tom said.

"Munch?"

"No," Tom said.

"It was something," Mike said.

"Stay focused."

Tom kept walking, watching and listening now for more fireworks. After a few minutes, he said, "Munch wouldn't have left without us."

Mike nodded; he was apparently breathing too hard to comment. They rounded a bend and saw a dock out in the water. A single light on a pole illuminated a shiny blue powerboat resting on a hoist.

Down the road, they found a place where they could see the large stone building. The road wound up ahead, but there was a long wide swatch of grass that ran right up the side of the hill.

The Hunt Club on its top, shining gray in the beams of its accent lights. Its rough-cut limestone blocks were staggered and stacked sideways, unlike Tom's blue beer cans, which rose vertically end to end. But this was the real thing. Intricate crenels topped the battlement, narrow openings through which medieval archers launched their arrows.

Tom felt heat spread through him. Beside the battlement ascended a round tower. Atop the tower's pointed hexagonal roof a red pennant fluttered. On the other side of the triangular parapet and the column-studded veranda below stood a stout curved bay, topped by a half-round balustrade. The perfect place for the lord of the castle to sit and observe the battle below.

Tom licked at his lips and raised his .38 over his head as though it were the hilt to a sword.

"We'll storm it," he said, leaving the road and starting up the hillside.

"Tom," Mike said, hustling up from behind, the tail from his ragged headpiece spiraling in the wind. "Let's look around."

But Tom was already bent into the wind, trudging steadily up.

"Tom?"

"'When time for action has arrived, stop thinking and go in,'" Tom said.

"That's Napoleon, but you told me the first part of that quote is 'Take time to deliberate,'" Mike said. "And we haven't deliberated."

Tom didn't even bother to turn around. He kept going and held his wrist up in the air.

02:49:48

"Two hours forty-nine minutes and forty-eight seconds," he said. "That's all the deliberation I need."

Mike started to lag behind, and even Tom was breathing hard by the time he was three quarters of the way up. The wind howled. Tom stopped only briefly as they ascended a set of stone stairs and crested the hilltop. There was a stone path that curved its way from the stairs to the front porch. Halfway along it, the stones had been pulled up. A small mixer, a pile of sand, and some masonry tools lay in the grass.

Tom marched past the project, along the path and up the front steps onto the veranda. He heaved the thick cast-iron lever that opened the thick-beamed doors. It was locked. Tom stepped back and kicked with all his might. A shudder of pain rocketed through him. The door held fast.

Tom looked around the veranda. Wicker furniture and clay pots filled with geraniums. Mike stood at the top of the steps, his hands on his knees, trying to catch his breath. Tom skipped past him, down the steps, and jogged back to the mixer. Among the tools in the grass was a rusty six-foot crowbar. Tom returned to the veranda and jammed the pointed end of the bar into the crack of the doors.

He wiggled it deeper and deeper until it would go no more. With his hands out on the far end of the bar, Tom heaved his weight against it. The bar bent. The door groaned. Still, nothing happened.

"Help me, Mike," he said.

Mike rose up and put his hands on the bar next to Tom's.

"Ready," Tom said, "set, go."

Together, they strained against the bar. It bent and the door groaned. There was a sharp crack as it moved an inch, then stopped.

"Your weight," Tom said. "Put your weight into it."

They leaned and pushed. Their faces grew shiny with sweat;

the air was filled with their groans. Just as Tom thought his arms would give out, the door burst open and they tumbled to the veranda floor.

Tom hopped up and dusted himself off. Mike got up slowly.

"This is it," Tom said. He marched straight through the broken doors with his weapon raised. The ceiling in the diamond-shaped reception room stretched twenty feet high and was lined with dark oil paintings. To the left was a library, to the right a drawing room with tasseled furniture. Tom kept going, in through a great hall bursting with stuffed animals whose shadows trembled in the light of a blazing fire.

Tom felt almost as if he'd been there before, and proceeded without stopping until they were standing just inside the entryway of a long stone dining room. A smaller fireplace crackled at the other end. A grand mahogany table ran the full length of the room, surrounded by leather high-backed chairs. At the far end, behind a glittering silver coffee service, sat a silver-haired man with dark eyes and a strong angled chin.

"You're just in time for dessert," the man said.

CHAPTER 53

Jane gasped and ducked down, ready to dive into the water if he came for her. But Dave was busy with Mark. She watched from around the corner of the boat's broad stern, her hand gripping the thick chrome exhaust pipe. She watched Dave tie Mark's hands. Watched him drag Mark to the wooden beam stretched between two trees just off the corner of the cabin's porch. A beam used for hanging deer carcasses.

Jane had seen pictures growing up. Animals split open. Tree branches wedged between the silvery ribs, cooling the meat. Tongues lolling purple from the corners of mouths. Men in coats and hats. Standing proud with guns.

Up went Mark. His hands bound together. Hanging from his wrists. Fingers splayed. His body swaying in the wind. Dave heaped firewood into a nearby circle of stones, doused it with fluid from a can, and set it ablaze. Orange sparks sailed up high and far, giving a face to the windy darkness.

Dave went into the cabin and returned with something long and black, writhing like the water snakes. A knife gleamed in the firelight. Jane nearly cried out, but Dave only used it to cut away Mark's shirt. The hose made a sickening hiss as it whipped through the air. The slippery sound of rubber tearing into flesh. Mark's eyes jolted open. His agonized cry pierced the howling wind.

She jumped as Dave reared back and thrashed him again.

Just what Dave was saying, she couldn't make out in the wind. But she could detect the growl of his voice and the curses. She knew that Dave was going to kill him.

Jane looked behind her at the dark swells of water as they crested and licked at the underside of the boat. She took a deep breath and plunged in. Shocked by the water, she burst to the surface and sputtered, treading hard to keep her head above the swells. She got her bearings by the light of the fire, swam through the piers of the dock, and angled in toward the shore.

When she was nearly upon the crashing surf, she tested the bottom with her feet. She was in no more than four feet of water, so she stood and swept the water past her, keeping her eyes on the cabin. In the flicker of the fire, the black whip licked away, but Mark was no longer crying out. Jane dug her hands into the water. A wave sent her forward and down, spinning her. Another smacked her directly, filling her mouth. She sputtered but turned and continued to drive for the shore, scrabbling now with her hands as well as her feet, buffeted by the roaring waves.

When she got to the thin rock beach, she climbed immediately up and over the bank. In the dark shadows of the trees, she stumbled uphill and toward the back of Dave's cabin. The wet clothes hung dripping from her. When she could no longer see the fire, she came out of the woods and ran along the grass toward the bunkhouse. There was no time for caution and she burst right in, her heart thumping hard.

In the kitchen, she found a knife. By the stove was a box of matches. She grabbed those and a newspaper off the counter, then flipped on each of the four burners atop the stove. The windows were open and Jane closed them tight, along with the back door. She shut the doors along the hallway that led from the kitchen to the main room, where there was a fireplace. Jane pushed some wooden chairs into a jumble up against the wall. She crumpled the papers and lay them in a heap under the chairs. Then she took some split kindling from a bucket beside the fireplace and laid it atop the papers.

She moved halfway back down the hall and sniffed. No gas yet. When she returned to the great room, she struck a match and lit the papers, then bolted out the door. She shut it tight and didn't stop to look back until she'd reached the gravel of the main drive. Through a small window, she could clearly see the flicker of orange light. She blew out a quick breath and turned away. Skirting along the edge of the drive, she came to the opening where Dave's cabin looked out over the water. She pressed herself against the rough-hewn siding on the back of the cabin, clinging to its coarse surface, making herself small. Smelling tar and wood, she rounded the rectangular cabin slowly. The kitchen knife from the bunkhouse was gripped tightly in her fist.

CHAPTER 54

Tom aimed his .38 with both hands to steady the trembling. He stalked the length of the table with the man's head in his sights.

The man clucked his tongue.

"A gun?" he said, raising just one silver eyebrow. "I've had guests hunt deer with pistols but the season's closed."

"I'm Jane Redmon's father," Tom said. "I want her back."

Both eyebrows went up this time.

"Her father?" he said. "It seems my ward has been impertinent again."

"Your ward?"

"I'm Carson Kale. This isn't the first time Mark has brought a young lady to our island for a romantic . . . getaway," the man said. "But it is the first time a father has shown up with a firearm."

Tom felt his stomach turn.

"She's . . . missing," Tom said. He felt the vigor draining away from him. His arms drooped to his sides, the gun now limp in his grip.

Carson's eyebrows stayed up. He pulled down the corners of his mouth and shook his head gently from side to side.

"Not . . . really, I don't think, Mr. Redmon. I think she's fine. She's with Mark, so they could be anywhere on the island, but she's fine. There are several waterfront cabins. Dave will know. He's the caretaker, and he should be back soon. Why don't you sit down."

"We found a shirt of hers in Mark Allen's apartment," Mike said, stepping forward, fists clenched. "It had blood on it."

Tom nodded and raised his gun.

Carson's frown deepened.

"Maybe it was Mark's," he said with a shrug. "He's always been prone to nosebleeds, but I can assure you that she's fine. Dave will help you. Really. Please, that gun is absurd."

"Absurd." Tom had heard that word before. Whispered behind his back as he walked through the courthouse halls. "Fool." He'd heard that as well, and now he felt it all coming down on top of him. He had been something once. Had fought for good. Now . . . How had Jane put it? Fighting noisy battles against giants who swatted him down like a gnat?

Maybe it was the exhaustion, finally taking hold. Maybe it was making an ass out of himself at Friendly's. Maybe it was the epiphany of what his life had really become. Tom let the gun drop to his side. He sat down and put his face in his free hand. His shoulders started to shake.

"Please," Carson said. "Would you like some coffee? My help have just gone home for the night or I could offer you something more . . ."

Without taking his face from his hand, Tom nodded that he would.

"Yes," Carson said, pouring a cup of steaming coffee and placing it on a saucer before pushing it across the corner of the table, "and a napoleon?"

The creamy layered pastries, perfect rectangles of yellow and brown, sat in an orderly row on a gleaming salver. Carson already had one in front of him. Its corner was gone and flaky crumbs littered the plate.

"No," Tom said shaking his head, trying to hold it upright like a man. He heaved a sigh.

"And your friend?"

"All right," Mike said.

Mike sat down, and Tom felt his friend's hand pat his shoulder.

"It's okay, Tom," Mike said quietly, gripping him. "She was in real danger. We didn't know. We did the right thing."

Carson slid the napoleon and a silver fork across the corner of the table on a small plate. Mike overloaded his fork and took a quiet bite.

Carson sipped his coffee and sighed.

"Well," he said, "if there's nothing else I can get you, I'll go and see if I can raise either Dave or Mark himself, although part of the reason he comes here is to get away from everything . . ."

Carson rose from the table and dabbed at the corners of his smiling lips.

"Jesus," Tom said when Carson had disappeared through a small open doorway adjacent to the fireplace. He felt like he was coming unraveled. "Just that she's all right . . . my God, Mike . . ."

"Yes," Mike said absently. He shoveled the last bite of pastry into his mouth and got up from the table.

"I'm an ass," Tom said. "Jesus, and Gleason . . ."

Tom stared at the flames. Ellen.

"Don't, Tom. You're strong. Be strong."

Tom took one of his lips gently between his teeth. He felt for his wedding ring. Its smoothness.

"I will," he said to her silently.

Mike peeked around the corner of the doorway where Carson had disappeared.

"Mike?" Tom said from his seat at the table. He got up and followed his friend around the corner. A narrow stairway rose halfway up the wall before doubling back.

Mike was standing at the foot of the stairs, his finger pressed to his lips. Tom heard voices from above. They flared to an angry pitch. Tom pointed up the stairway. He moved past Mike and motioned for him to follow.

CHAPTER 55

Know what he called you?" Dave asked. Sweat shining on his brow. Breathing heavily.

Mark tried to talk. He would do anything to stop the whipping. A croak came out.

"What?"

"A failed experiment," Dave said. "Like a bad feint in a war game. A failed maneuver. A disaster. That's you, and now *I'm* going to strip your back to the bone."

The black hose whistled through the air and thrashed him again. Mark grimaced and ground down on his teeth.

"Everything is over, you weak little fuck," Dave said. "That's all you ever were. Poor orphan boy. I wasn't fooled. An officer's commission—"

Dave spat.

"Fuck that. You were a spoiled little pretender. Weak like a woman . . ."

Thrash.

"Now cry like a bitch. Cry like that girl's gonna cry when I give it to her . . ."

Thrash.

Just as Mark opened his eyes, a blue ball of flame flashed brilliantly behind and above the trees. The concussion of the explosion jarred him.

"What?" Dave said, staggering two steps forward and dropping the whip. He scooped up the shotgun leaning against the tree and started jogging toward the bunkhouse. Orange flames now showed through the trees and danced in the night sky. A cascade of sparks spilled up into the wind.

Mark jumped when he felt someone touch him from behind.

"It's me," Jane said, her voice urgent. Frightened.

"Quick," he said. "There's a rope tied off to that cleat . . . Yes, that's it. Untie it."

Jane bent over the trunk of the tree, her elbows moving spasmodically in the firelight. Mark suddenly dropped to the ground. His legs buckled. He fell sideways and struggled to right himself.

"Here," she said. She was beside him, cutting away at the bonds on his wrists. The rope snapped free and Mark pushed himself upright, fighting to regain his feet.

"Did you do that?"

"I turned on the gas stove and I lit a fire in the other room," she said, cutting the bonds around his ankles.

"I knew I liked you for a reason," he said, smiling.

He was stumbling now toward the Land Cruiser. There was his shotgun lying in the grass. He scooped it up and fumbled with the box of shells in his pocket. Blood trickled down his back. His eyes worked between the weapon and the driveway, which was backlit by the burning bunkhouse. Flames now swept upward in massive sheets, fueled by the dry wood and the strong wind.

The fifth shell slipped into the gun with a final click.

"Stay here," he said.

"No, I'm going with you."

"He has a gun. You stay, goddamn it. Right here."

"I don't need protection," she said. "You do."

"I have a gun too."

Jane nodded. "Point taken."

"I'll be right back," he said.

He limped up the drive toward the fire, keeping under the dark shadows of the trees. He saw a big shadow moving up ahead and dropped to the ground. It was Dave, slogging slowly down the drive, glancing back at the fire at every other step. Mark steadied his elbows in the gravel, wiggling them in. His back burned with pain. He looked through the aim-point sight and put the tiny red dot in the center of Dave's massive chest. He took a deep breath, settled himself, then fired.

Dave sprang into the trees on the other side of the road.

The sound of twigs snapping and branches breaking could be heard even over the roar of fire and wind. There was a scuffle of leaves, and then nothing. Mark held his breath, straining for a sound. He knew Dave's skill. It would take the big man less than a minute to silently outflank Mark and open fire from a superior position.

Mark rolled off the road and into the shallow ditch. He crawled up the slope, his bare belly scuffing the damp ground, stopping only when he believed he'd reached the spot where Dave was when he'd fired. He peeked over the lip of the ditch and listened, scanning up and down the dark woods that lined the drive. He tried to see not with his direct vision but with his peripheral vision, which he knew was twice as effective at seeing in the dark.

The treetops swayed in the wind, but down below, nothing moved.

CHAPTER 56

Slowly, Mark army-crawled up onto the drive. In the firelight, he saw a dark splash of something. He put his tongue to a stone in the patch. Blood.

He crawled farther. There was another splotch. Farther. More. He was up on his knees now. The patches were growing in size. He leveled his gun in front of him and backed slowly down the driveway.

Jane ran up to him. She grasped his naked shoulders.

"What happened?"

"I shot him."

"Did you get him?"

"Yes," Mark said. "I don't know how bad. Run back to the Land Cruiser. There'll be a flashlight in the console between the front seats."

Jane disappeared, then returned, scuffing up fountains of gravel as she did. Mark kept his eyes on the drive.

"Thanks," he said, flicking on the flashlight. "When we get back to D.C., dinner is on me."

She smiled. "I'll give it some consideration."

He swept the woods as he moved up the hill, shotgun ready.

When he reached the blood, he heard Jane suck in a breath. The splotches were deep red. Rich and shiny. He followed the trail into the woods. The patches of blood were growing, creamy red pools caught in the bellies of dead leaves.

Mark swung the beam through the trees, scanning the forest floor. Up ahead lay the dark mound of a body.

"Hold this," Mark said, handing the light to Jane. "Point it there. No, over there. That's right."

"What are you—"

Her words were cut short by the blast of the shotgun. Jane shrieked and the light stabbed up into the treetops.

"What are you doing?" she asked.

"Fool me once, shame on you," he said. "Fool me twice . . ."

He took the flashlight from Jane and started to walk. As it turned out, the second shot to the head was unnecessary. The one on the road had struck Dave in the center of his chest. Jane looked away. Mark knelt down beside the body and, using his handkerchief, yanked the pearl-handled pistol from Dave's belt.

"Come on," he said, sticking the gun, handkerchief and all, into the waist of his pants. He took Jane by the hand and led her back toward the driveway.

The bunkhouse flames were already diminishing; the fire in front of Dave's was waning as well. Mark led her up onto the porch and in through the front door. Warm amber light from a small table lamp filled the front room, along with the apple-tinted scent of pipe tobacco. Mark sat her down in a mission oak chair with thick leather cushions and a velour pillow.

"Do you need something?" he asked. "I'll get you some water."

He started for the kitchen.

"Oh my God," she said. "Your back."

Jane got up out of the chair and started toward him.

"No," he said, raising his hand. "Don't. It's all right. Sit. Please."

He turned and went quickly into the kitchen, removing a bottle of water and grabbing a box of wheat crackers from the countertop.

"What are we doing?" Jane asked as he handed them to her.

"*You're* staying right here," he said. He ducked into a bedroom and pulled a thick flannel shirt off a hanger. The metal rang against the bar as Mark slipped it gingerly over his shoulders. As he buttoned it, he returned to the great room.

"You can't come with me now," he said. "I have to do something. Two things. I . . . I think Dave already killed Carson . . .

"I've got to go back to the main house, and I don't want you to see that. Then I have something else I have to do . . . ," he said, kneeling down in front of her. "It will make everything all right. I'll be back soon. You have to trust me."

He picked up his shotgun off the coffee table and slipped two more shells into it. He handed it to her.

"I don't know where Vern is," he said. "Probably not around. Just an old guy anyway. The cook. But in case."

He kissed her on the lips, his fingers slipping beneath her hair, touching her neck. Then he backed away from her and opened the door.

"I'm locking it. See?" he said. "I'll be back."

"You better call out before you come through that door," she said, bringing the gun up to her shoulder and sighting it in.

"I'll remember," Mark said. "You'll be okay."

"It's you I'm worried about," she said, lowering the gun.

Mark smiled at her, then slipped out into the night.

261

CHAPTER 57

Tom pressed his finger against his lips. Mike nodded. It was silent except for the complaining of the stairs under their weight. When he reached the top, Tom drew aim with his .38, one by one, at the suits of armor, almost expecting them to move. The long hallway was lined with carved wooden doors, each with a snarling gargoyle for its handle. Behind the landing was a double set of glass-inlaid doors that apparently gave access to the battlement. The first door on the left was where Tom stopped.

He could hear talking from within. It turned to shouts. Mike pressed his ear right up to the cold metal of the keyhole.

"What the hell are you doing?" Tom said.

"Trying to hear," Mike said. He put his finger to his lips and angled his head. Tom pressed his own ear to the door, but without crouching down.

"Dave came for me," a voice said.

"The man does his job." It was Carson.

"He tried to fillet me like a deer."

"You're insane," Carson said.

"I want no part of you anymore."

"Breeding," Carson said.

"What?"

"When one breeds a mongrel to a mongrel they get trash," he said. "Even with my training, you're a mutt. Just like that slut you called your—"

Tom jumped back away from the door at the sound of the gunshot, his ear ringing. Mike had staggered back as well. They aimed their guns.

Mike tried the door, quietly at first, and then rattling the gargoyle's head noisily.

"Back," Tom said.

Mike stepped aside. Tom took two steps and kicked the door.

"Ow! Shit!" Tom yelled, holding his knee. The door hadn't budged.

"Here," Mike said, taking a battle-ax off the wall.

"Let me," Tom said. He took the ax from Mike and swung it at the doorknob. He hacked away for several minutes, then kicked it again. The door sagged inward. Tom kicked it once more, and it burst open.

He was breathing hard, but he pushed Mike back and drew his gun, going in first. Mike crouched down next to the doorframe, ready to cover him.

There wasn't a sign of anyone amid the heavy antique furniture, the musty smell of books, and the tang of gunpowder. In the far corner of the room, cut into the shelves of books that stretched to the ceiling, a doorway was ajar. Aiming at the door, Tom crabbed his way into the room. Mike followed.

"He's here," Tom said, leaning over behind the desk.

He felt Mike peering over his shoulder. Carson lay facedown on the floor in a pool of blood. The back of his skull had been broken open. The exit wound. A striking scarlet divot. Tiny droplets clung to the silver stalks of hair.

Halfway between the desk and the side door, a pearl-handled .45 lay on the wooden floor. Mike walked over to it.

"Leave it," Tom said. "Just leave everything."

Tom tilted his chin toward the ceiling and cupped his hands. He stumbled into the hallway and bellowed until his face turned red.

"Jane!"

CHAPTER 58

Tom heard stones clattering off metal. Rubber spinning grit and the roar of a vehicle's engine. He dashed out into the hall-way and out onto the battlement. The bloodred taillights of a truck whipped around the corner and down the drive.

Tom ran back into the house.

"What?" Mike said as Tom sprinted past him and down the stairs.

Through the dining room. The great hall. The entryway. The front door and out onto the veranda. He heard Mike shouting his name, but he was halfway down the hill. The truck appeared and screeched to a stop beneath the blue light beside the dock.

The dark shape of a man flickered out of the truck and into the boat.

"Jane!" Tom yelled. The howling wind battered him. His eyes strained for a second shape. There was only one in the boat.

Tom tumbled and rolled right up onto his feet, still striding long, eating up ground. The boat hoist creaked, and the waves began to pitch the hull as it was lowered into the water.

"Stop!" Tom yelled.

The figure in the boat never looked up. He was at the wheel

now. The engine revved and a plume of smoke burst from the back and quickly disappeared. Tom hit the road, sprinting. The boat shot backward, out of its crib, the figure's arms spinning the wheel. Tom was at the dock, beneath the light. The boat rocketed away, out into the dark heaving water. A young man stood anchored to the wheel, mounting the crests of water in an explosion of spray.

The night swallowed him.

Tom checked the truck. Empty. He went back to the house. Mike was halfway down the hill.

"What happened?" Mike asked.

"He's gone," Tom said. "I think it was Mark Allen. I don't know."

"Jane?"

Tom bit into his lip. He shook his head and said, "I don't know."

He marched back up the hill. They searched the house for her. It was enormous. Closets and hidden doorways. Tom newly afraid at each new nook that they would find a body. They checked the dusty attic, with its thick rough-hewn beams. They scoured the cellar, its stone walls damp and discolored.

The phone line had been cut, but Carson's body was the only one.

One of the bedrooms on the third floor belonged to Mark Allen. His West Point diploma hung on the wall next to a picture of him in his uniform with his arm around a beautiful woman with long dark hair and a long white neck that made Tom think of Jane. The woman looked older than Mark Allen; otherwise the warmth of their smiles would have made Tom think they were a couple.

There was a leather briefcase beside a desk. Mike looked inside and pulled out some papers.

"Lab reports," he said, sifting. "Signed by Slovanich."

Tom couldn't bring himself to care. He had to find Jane.

"What do we do?" Mike said, stuffing the papers back into the briefcase and slinging it over his shoulder.

"Carson said there were cabins all over the island," he said. "We'll search them. Every one."

They descended the side stairs into the dining room. The fire had died down to a bed of coals cloaked in gray ash. Mike looked at the dessert and coffee resting on the table.

"I should have done something," Mike said.

"No," Tom said. "I should have. I began to doubt."

"Look," Tom said, pointing.

On the wall was an old map in a wooden frame. The paper was faded and its edges were worn. On the map, the Hunt Club was represented by a large rectangle that matched its footprint. Across the island were other footprints. Cabins and buildings. Tom held it out in front of him and studied it.

"She's on this island," he said. "We'll go through every single one of them until we find her. Come on."

Tom lifted the frame from its hook and smashed the glass against the stone wall. Part of the glass remained, so he smashed it again. Glass tinkled to the floor. He jiggled the map free, then folded it and stuffed it into his pocket.

Without looking back, he strode through the cavernous hall and out onto the veranda. The wind was gusting even stronger. Looking out from the veranda, they could see the narrow dock below at the water's edge. In the single cone of blue light was the boat hoist. Empty.

They started back down the grassy lawn. When they got to the road, Mike pointed at the truck. The maroon Land Cruiser.

"At least we won't have to walk," Mike said.

Tom opened the driver's door and fished around.

"No keys," he said, striking the wheel. He looked at his watch. 01:17:08. "Can you hot-wire it?"

"I can't," Mike said.

"Well, damn," Tom said. He struck the wheel again, slammed the truck door, and started off back up the road at a steady march. His legs were already tired, but that didn't matter. He'd push them until they seized up.

He took out the map and shone the flashlight on it without stopping. Mike hurried up behind him, puffing.

"What are we doing?"

"Besides the main house," Tom said, pointing to the map, "most of the other structures are on the north end of the island. It's about four miles to the first group."

He looked at his watch again. 01:13:53. He showed Mike.

"My legs," Mike said.

"If you can't make it," Tom said, "don't worry. But I can't slow down."

"I'll be right behind you," Mike said.

Tom clapped him on the shoulder, then doubled his pace, fighting the urge to jog or run. He knew that if he did that, his legs would seize up.

Tom put his head down. At 00:57:42 he could no longer hear Mike's shuffling feet and his labored breathing. The wind was his only company until Ellen joined him. They talked. It helped.

CHAPTER 59

Jane stirred. There was an ancient oak clock on the mantel. Bold Roman numerals and a yellowing face. Its ticktock could be heard above the wind moaning in the chimney. The apple-scented tobacco had lost its charm; it smelled dirty to her now.

She was tired still, but determined to remain alert, though she didn't really know how long she could. Maybe until the morning. Maybe until the storm passed. If it died out, she would take that formula and find the mainland. She was no expert with a boat, but she'd seen her father do it often enough to try. She wasn't going to remain here any longer than she had to, no matter what Mark Allen wanted.

The light from the one lamp let the shadows linger malevolently in the corners, and she had finally worked up the courage to leave her chair and try the switch by the door when a shape passed by the far window.

Jane gasped and gripped the gun. Her hands grew slippery with sweat, but she knew enough to fumble with the safety, clicking it off. She slipped out of the chair and knelt down behind the arm of the couch, resting the barrel of the gun. Pointing it at the door. Footsteps moved slowly along the porch. A shadow passed the window. The door handle slowly began to turn.

Random drops of rain were starting to fall from the sky. Tom checked his watch. 00:29:37. He looked back, shining the light. Its beam was fading, and there was no sign of Mike. Tom had no idea how much farther he had to go. His chest was aching now; his legs were numb. Only the sharp biting blisters rubbed raw by his leather boots let him know he was moving at all.

Soon the wind brought the rain down in sheets. The road grew wet and sloppy. He glanced at his watch. 00:13:56. His heart gave a jump and he slogged on, his feet sloshing now in his boots. His shirt clung tight to his skin. He started to shiver.

When he reached the driveway, he directed the dying beam of his flashlight at his watch again. It was too weak to read by. He fumbled for the light on the Ironman itself. 00:01:47.

He drew the gun from his waist and started down the drive. The air grew rancid with the sharp smell of damp smoke.

He stopped at a small clearing. The weak beam of light, flecked with rain, illuminated the fallen shape of a burned building. Heavy smoke was still floating upward into the downpour.

He looked at his watch. 00:00:31. He started to run, stumbling down the muddy drive.

That's when he heard the shot.

Tom started, and inhaled a ragged breath of air and rain. He saw a warm yellow square of light through the trees. Mud and stones splattered up from his heavy feet. He stumbled and fell, plowing up a puddle. A cabin came into view. More smoke met his nose. Somewhere his mind recognized it as the clean dry scent of burning firewood.

In the faint yellow light that spilled from the window, Tom saw a figure slip off the porch. It had a shotgun. It stood in front of the window and raised the gun. Tom set his feet, aimed, and fired.

The shotgun went off too. The window blasted to pieces. The figure fell. Tom shot again. The dark shape thrashed in the puddle, droplets of water spattering up into the face of the rain, glinting in the yellow glow of the window. Tom fired again and again. The dark shape lay still.

"Janey!" Tom screamed.

He staggered to reach the fallen form, and then he peered through the broken window. The quiet *beep-beep-beep* of his Ironman protested feebly under the press of the storm.

CHAPTER 60

Jane's scream rose above the sound of the watch and cut through the heart of the rain and wind.

"Dad!"

She leaped from the porch. Her gun clattered off a stone as it fell to the ground. Tom dropped his .38 and staggered toward her. She hit him like a linebacker, buckling his knees. They grabbed each other and squeezed. Tom rolled to his side and over on his back in the mud, hugging her and crying with joy.

"Janey."

He shifted his hands across her back, wanting to squeeze every inch of her. He stroked her hair, then let her go and stood, drenched from head to toe, laughing from deep in his chest. Even the sight of the dead old-timer with the big goose gun didn't dampen his spirits.

The watch continued to beep. That beautiful Ironman. He led her by the hand and they walked up onto the porch.

"What is that?"

He showed her. 00:00:00.

"The first forty-eight."

"What?"

He shook his head and laughed some more, hugging her again. Then he held her at arm's length. Her eyes gleamed in the porch light as she looked up and out into the rain. Tom shifted his feet and looked down at the floor, then jumped. His wet shoes were slipping and mixing with the dark patch of dried blood. Little rivulets of water swirled red.

"What happened?" Tom asked.

Jane looked down at the blood.

"I got away," she said. "They tried to kill me. Then Mark . . . he shot that man. There's another in the woods . . ."

"Tom?"

They both turned toward the driveway. Chugging down the lane was Mike. Dripping wet. His red goatee plastered on his chin. His ragged sheik headdress tangled down his thick neck. The briefcase still slung across his back.

"Tom?"

"I'm here," Tom said. "I've got her."

Mike stepped up onto the porch. Dark wet strands of hair were plastered to his head. Water dripped from his small beard. His eyes were aglow.

"Jane," he said, hugging her.

Tom hugged them both. He savored the warmth of his daughter and the heaving form of his big friend. Their heads rested together, skulls bumping like wooden blocks. Mike breathing loud and hard. Tom huffing too. Laughter bubbled up between them.

Tom's eyes were closed. His face warm.

After a minute, an insane chortling swelled up in the midst of their laughing like a bad joke. Tom's laughter ebbed. So did Mike's. Jane's stopped. It wasn't coming from them. Tom's eyes shot open and he spun around.

The laughter became a howl. The monstrous form of a man, scarlet with blood, pink foam seeping from his nose. He staggered toward them, his hair and thick beard matted, his clothes torn. The long silver blade of a knife glinted above his red eyes, then slashed down through the yellow porch light.

Jane crossed her wrists and stepped in, stopping Dave's forearm in midair. Tom dropped to one knee and threw a full body punch at the solar plexus. A bloody spray erupted from Dave's mouth as he fell back. He doubled over, and Mike pumped a quick shot into the top of his head. The enormous man shuddered and rocked, then dropped to the porch floor and went still.

CHAPTER 61

Even the burning welts across Mark's back seemed to have their place, keeping him awake through the night. He yawned and pulled off the exit to get gas, coffee, and a cheap rain poncho. The man behind the counter had a mouth full of brown holes and bent yellow teeth. He smiled sharply at Mark and then winced and splayed out the inside of his lower lip in a strange tic. He rubbed the dark stubble on his chin and wiped his hand on the red vest that bore his name: CARTER.

"You want a Danish to go with that there coffee?" Carter asked. "You get two for one before six. They's yesterday's, but they ain't bad."

"Yeah, sure," Mark said.

"There you go," Carter said with a nod. "Some people, they turn they nose up at day-olds, but man, way I growed up, you'd be at the gates of heaven to get yourself one of these Danishes."

"I hear that," Mark said. He turned and saw a thick stack of newspapers with Senator Gleason's face taking up the top half of the page. SENATOR MISSING.

Carter opened the plastic case. He put a thin sheet of wax paper over a Danish and scooped it up, handing it to Mark. The

275

frosting had grown crusty and whole chunks of its swirls lay broken in the creases of the paper. The smell of the blueberry filling floated up into Mark's nose. He took a bite.

"Here's your other one," Carter said, reaching in and holding it forth.

"You have it," Mark said.

"You don't like it?"

"No, I like it fine," Mark said. He took a gulp of the hot black coffee.

Carter angled his head away and partially closed his far eye. He splayed out his lower lip and winced, then rubbed his stubble and wiped his vest.

"Look," Mark said, taking another bite. A thin line of the syrupy filling dribbled down his chin. Mark swiped it up with his finger and stuck the finger into his mouth.

Carter smiled.

"Awful nice of you," he said. He took a bite.

Mark nodded and dug into his pocket for the money.

"You want to top that coffee off, you can," Carter said, handing back his change. On the corner of the dollar bill was a flaky crumb.

"That's okay," Mark said, shaking the crumb free.

"No, you ought to. I don't let everybody."

"Thanks," Mark said. He removed the plastic cover. Coffee gurgled in up to the brim of the foam lip.

"You have a good one," Mark said, raising his cup. The bells on the door tinkled as he left.

Mark stood for a moment and breathed in deep. Even the scent of gasoline somehow seemed full of promise. The sky was just beginning to brighten in the east. Dark blue instead of black. The breeze brought with it a small mist. Cool but exhilarating. In the rear of the white Bronco the black sixty-gallon drum gleamed under the halogen lights at the pump.

Mark got in, sitting with care, not leaning back, and drove out onto the highway. He shook his head, thinking of Carson. Everything the man had wanted was within reach. Not just the contract. That would revitalize Kale Labs; Mark's plan went beyond that. It made him personally rich. Filthy rich. And it would make Kale Labs a company to rival Microsoft.

Mark snorted and gulped some coffee. Carson had actually doubted his resolve. His craftiness. His fortitude. Mark had planned to surprise him with his plan. The millions he had used to buy Kale Labs stock on margin would become billions. When people started puking their guts out all over New York City? When old people started to die? Bioterrorism . . . It didn't matter who got the blame. And when Kale Labs stepped in with a hastily conceived antidote? How much would the stock be worth then?

Soon Mark rounded a bend in the gap between two massive hills, and there before him stretched the Tappan Zee Bridge. A massive web of steel, it snaked for nearly four miles across the flat dark Hudson River. The pointed peaks of its ridged back glowed with blinking red lights. A stream of taillights pulsed to the east while an opposing flow of headlights came west.

On the far side of the bridge, the queue at the tollbooths had grown thick. Mark craned his neck to see what was taking a tractor-trailer so long to pay. By the time he was through, all remnants of night had been washed away by the thin gruel of dawn. The exit for the Central Westchester Parkway was 7. Lucky seven.

He finished his coffee and stroked his lips with the tips of his fingers, thinking that it was destiny for him to have killed Carson. Carson had no right to talk about his mother like that. And now that Carson was gone, Mark understood an ancient adage. The king was dead. Long live the king.

CHAPTER 62

The kitchen in Dave's cabin was neat and orderly. Tom found the coffee and made a pot. They sat at the kitchen table, as far away from the bloody mess on the front porch as possible. Jane found some pancake mix and made stack after golden stack. They drowned the cakes in some real maple syrup from a shiny metal can Mike found in the refrigerator. Even Jane wolfed down her food, drinking hot black coffee in big gulps.

Jane and Tom exchanged stories about what had happened, how, and why, until most of the pieces had been put together. Mike wiped his plate with the last shred of pancake and pushed back his plate. He removed the papers from Mark Allen's briefcase and silently spread them out on the table.

After a few minutes, he said, "Holy shit."

Tom and Jane stared.

"All these lab reports signed by Dr. Slovanich? It's all about this Filoviridae. How it thrives in water. And check this out. This is the freaky thing . . ."

Mike held up a map of the New York City area. Small round stickers—bright yellow ones—marked the different reservoirs surrounding the city. One site was circled in red ink. The Kensico Reservoir. A straight purple and white line ran from it into the city. The Croton Aqueduct.

"Is this what this is all about?" Mike said. "The main water supply to New York? The truck Slovanich talked about?"

Tom stood up and nodded his head.

"It all makes sense," Tom said. "If Kale Labs can start the virus, they can stop it too."

"People get sick," Mike said. "Not cruise ships—the whole city. They step in and save the world."

"They get the government contract," Tom said.

"More," Mike said.

"Mark Allen," Tom said. "We've got to stop him."

He looked at Mike, who nodded solemnly back at him. "Mark Allen."

"Kensico Reservoir?" Mike asked.

"He's already two hours in front of us," Tom said. "You feel like taking another plane ride?"

"What are you talking about?" Jane said, wiping her face on the sleeve of her baggy shirt.

"Come on," Tom said. "I'll tell you while we go."

Tom finished his story. Rain dripped down off them and puddles bloomed on the concrete floor beneath their feet. The thin and fading beam of Tom's flashlight passed over the gleaming white plane with burnt orange stripes backed into the corner of the hangar. The wind howled and the rain clattered against the metal roof. Sweat shone on Mike's face beneath his headpiece.

"Dad," Jane said, "you're making a mistake about him."

Tom shook his head, shined the flashlight up at his face, and said, "Have you been listening to me? He's planning to do something."

"What about Friendly's, Dad?" Jane said.

Tom furrowed his brow and waved the light toward Jane. "You said yourself you didn't trust him."

"When?"

"On the deck cooking steaks," Tom said, "when I told you about Gleason. 'A man I met but don't trust.' Your words, Jane."

"He saved my life, Dad," she said. "If he's so horrible, why would he do that?"

Mike was watching them, his head moving from one to the other.

"He's insane," Tom said, clenching his fists. "He killed his own father."

"Why do *you* have to stop him?" she asked.

"Because . . . ," he said, straightening himself and raising his chin.

"That must have been Randy Kapp's plane we saw get blasted out of the sky," Mike said.

"With Gleason in it," Tom said. He turned to Jane. "Maybe you should stay. This weather is bad."

"I'm going," she said, pushing a wet strand of hair from her face, her back as straight as his.

"Come on, Tom," Mike said, tugging him by the sleeve. "Don't. We don't know for sure what he's doing. We should stick together. I've flown in weather like this."

Mike walked over to the Cessna and opened the door. He reached in and flipped on the control panel.

"Looks good," he said. He reached into the pouch behind the pilot's seat. "Sectionals are all here. I'll get the coordinates."

Mike pulled one out and unfolded it.

"Do you want me to pull these chocks out from under the tires?" Tom asked, bending down and grabbing the rope threaded through the thick rubber triangles.

"Yeah," Mike said over his shoulder.

Tom went over to the hangar doors and pushed them open. The water cascaded in, drenching him.

After less than a minute of scrutinizing the map under the dome light of the little plane, Mike told them to hop in.

When they were sitting together in the backseat, Mike put his foot on the step and sucked in his breath. He plunged forward and got stuck.

"I'm okay," he said, holding up his hand at Tom.

He wiggled and squirmed. His face grew red. He stopped and took a couple of deep breaths. He began to wiggle again. A low growl rumbled in his chest. He twisted violently, popped through, and bumped his head on the roof.

"Ow."

"Are you okay, Mike?" Jane asked.

"Fine," Mike said, turning his face away from them and squirming into the pilot's seat. As he reached for the controls a groan escaped him.

"You okay?" Tom said.

"Yeah. Fine."

Mike fired up the engines and ran his fingers and eyes over the instrument panels. He put on the headset and taxied the plane out into the storm. As soon as they cleared the hangar doors, a gust of wind and rain lifted one wing, almost flipping them over.

Tom cried out.

Mike fought for control. The plane crashed down on its landing gear and shot forward. Mike turned and kept going down the runway. He pushed the throttles to the floor. The end of the airstrip was coming fast. The wind groaned and the rain clattered against the windshield.

"Hang on," Mike said.

He pulled back on the controls. The plane lurched up and then got slammed down by a wicked squall. They bounced off the runway with a horrible grinding crash, then rose back up into the air. Tom grabbed a hold.

Mike peeled Tom's fingers off his shoulder. They were up and climbing steadily. The wind buffeted them back and forth as Mike wrestled with the controls. The sides of his face were slick with sweat.

"I'll have to fly at about fifteen hundred feet, just below the cloud ceiling," he said, shouting back at them through the noise. "It'll be rough, but safer, believe it or not."

After only a few minutes, he announced that they were over Watertown and he was switching to hone in on the signal from Syracuse. He called it a VOR.

Tom's forearms ached from grasping the edge of the seat. His head hurt from scowling. Mike suddenly gasped and clutched his chest. He pawed at his collar and began to shake.

The weather rocked the plane.

Tom grabbed Mike's shoulders with both hands and yelled for him to hang on.

CHAPTER 63

Mark went north, through a little strip of gas stations, dough-nut shops, and hair salons that called itself the Town of North White Plains. He looked at his map to make sure before veer-ing off onto Route 22. The road began to rise. The landscape grew precipitous, and jagged rocks began to expose themselves beneath the dripping leaves of the trees.

West Lake Drive came upon him fast. He took a left and crossed over the narrow bridge. The guardrail was a series of rectangular limestone slabs seamlessly set end to end. Straight ahead, the road ran through the center of a classic stone ro-tunda.

It was all so perfect, coming to him like it had in the dream.

He was Carson and Carson was him.

He'd dreamed of this in a flood of images, like paintings he'd once seen in Greece. Why was everything so familiar?

When he saw the cop car, it was already too late to turn around. The cop, leaning against the car door, dressed in a dark blue jumpsuit and cap, looked directly at him. Mark waved and accelerated on by.

He passed through the rotunda and its thick Doric columns,

catching a glimpse of the thick woods through its open arches before the sky and water opened up before him. To the left, rich green hills sprawled on into the distance. On the right was the reservoir, a dark tranquil body of water bordered entirely by trees.

Mark checked his rearview mirror for signs of the cop. Halfway across, he switched his focus to the rotunda ahead. A set of headlights spilled out of it and crept toward him. Mark strained to see if there was a rack of lights on its roof. There was something. His stomach tightened.

A ski rack.

Through the second rotunda, there was another cop car, this time a white Jeep, nose out to the road behind a set of orange cones. Two cops leaned against it, staring at him as he went past. Just before he lost them from sight in his rearview mirror, they were still there. He took a deep breath and exhaled.

He had seen a newspaper account in the White Plains paper about how patrols by Department of Environmental Protection police around the reservoir had returned to normal after a funding cutback from Albany. Normal meant almost no police presence. The local fishermen were happy. They left their boats along the shore on state property, using the reservoir as their own private fishing spot. Mark shook his head and snorted. No police to protect the water supply, but two officers stationed on an old stone dam. That was the government.

As he rounded the bend the mist turned into a light rain, and he flipped on his wipers. Ahead at the traffic light stood a brick church with a thin white steeple that melted into the flat gray sky. To the right, up on a hill looking out over the reservoir, was the great stone filtration plant. Its flat hip roof covered a gallery of enormous arched windows. An iron fence surrounded the property and a guard gate blocked its driveway.

At the light, Mark glanced down at his map. The plant was no longer used to filter the water. He smiled. Now it only served as offices for the Water Authority, but the intake pipe for the Delaware Aqueduct ran right through it. That aqueduct was the main source of drinking water for New York City. They'd start filtering it again after this gig. Six hundred meters into the water was the intake valve. He would row out and dump his barrel directly over it. The Ukrainian's virus would spread like a red tide in the ocean, only this would be colorless and odorless.

No one would know what it was or where it came from until the outbreak was well under way. Thousands of people would flood New York City's hospitals. Hysteria would flood the entire country. Kale Labs stock would go from a dollar back up to the seventies. Maybe higher. Everyone would want a piece. And, since Dave went insane and killed everyone on the island, the leadership of the company would fall to the executive vice president. Him.

The light turned green and he continued on past the filtration plant. The water disappeared from sight. To stay on West Lake Drive, Mark had to make a right-hand turn, and he did. The trees leaned in over the road. Large homes appeared on either side among the tall pines. Mark passed several cars, men in shirts and ties with cups of coffee. The vehicles were big, their grilles shiny, Escalades and Mercedes sedans.

The road wound down toward the water. A yellow NO ENTRANCE sign on an iron gate warned him away from a small pump house built in the same fortress style as the filtration plant. Mark kept going, circumventing a cove and climbing up again. Black chain-link fence stretched along the guardrail just to the other side of the road.

Mark kept going until he passed an area where two other residential drives came in on the left. A blue Cape Cod rested on a bright green lawn. Another yellow sign. DEAD END. At the end of the road was a dirt turnaround. No one else was in sight, and he stopped and got out.

Three different paths led off into the pinewoods. Three weeks ago, Mark had had a pleasant conversation with a woman named Pat who worked in the Valhalla Town Hall. He asked about boat rentals, and she told him that there were none. Apparently, the local fishermen simply left their aluminum skiffs at the water's edge. No motorboats were allowed on the reservoir.

Mark stood for a moment, smelling the rich pine needles. Water fell in fat silver drops from the trees. Emerald ferns grew up among the undergrowth, giving the woods a soft inviting feel. He took a final deep breath through his nose and exhaled through his mouth. The place was heavy with solitude.

He opened the back of the Bronco and rolled the barrel out onto the ground. Its sides were slick and the fresh paint gleamed, even in the gray rain. He slung the shotgun over his head, covering it with the poncho. Then he shut the back of the truck, chose a path at random, and set off down it, rolling the barrel before him.

CHAPTER 64

I'm okay," Mike said, gasping. He shrugged Tom's hands from his shoulders.

"What happened?" Tom asked.

Mike took a deep breath and exhaled.

"I don't know," he said. "I'm fine. My head hurts a little."

Mike shook his head the way a dog shakes a sock. He did it again, and Tom saw him squeeze his eyes shut hard, then open them. He did this several times, and Tom began to wonder if they would make it.

"Mike, are you all right?"

It was Jane.

"Yes," Mike said. He straightened his back and lifted his shoulders. A firm frown was fixed beneath his scowl as he did battle with the wind.

Thirty minutes southeast of Syracuse, the clouds began to tatter above them. Soon stars winked down and in the light of the crescent moon, Tom could see the dark shapes of mountains. In the flats of the valleys, tiny farms and houses lay asleep beneath the halos of their light poles.

At this moment it was hard to believe they had nearly

crashed—but the pleasant weather was short-lived. Soon there was nothing to see out the window but a thick gray soup, illuminated by the plane's flashing lights. Nearly two hours later, Mike told them they were close and began to talk to someone at the tower. Tom thought he detected a quaver in Mike's voice as he received his instructions. When they finally came down onto the runway, Tom felt light-headed. Mike exhaled and turned his head to show them his smile under the hearty claps that Tom smacked down onto his back.

Jane gave a little cheer, and Mike's cheeks went red again.

Tom was already dialing his phone.

"Who are you calling?" Jane asked.

"The police," Tom said.

He got through the dispatcher to a sergeant. Tom told him who he was and demanded a full-scale operation.

"I'm talking about a terrorist plot," Tom said.

The sergeant asked for his driver's license number and put him on hold for a minute. When he came back, he said, "Okay, Mr. Redmon, I know all about you, sir. Why don't you just come down to the station and we can talk this over."

"This is an emergency, Sergeant," Tom said. "Every second counts."

"I know it does, Mr. Redmon," he said. "I know all about it. You have a very impressive past and I'd love to talk with you, but you'll have to come down here. How about eleven-thirty?"

"You dumb-ass," Tom said. He snapped his phone closed and shook his head.

Tom was still shaking his head in disbelief as they taxied to a stop. He climbed out of the plane and onto the wet tarmac. A small jet raced down the runway beyond, deafening him.

"What now?" Mike said, squeezing out after Jane.

"We go it alone," Tom said.

The woman at the car rental desk eyed Mike suspiciously. Tom put his credit card down and looked at his damp, mud-stained pants and boots. He tried to tug the worst of the wrinkles out of his shirt. The few other people who were in the small airport wore business suits.

Mike was a disaster. Hair flat on his head. Eyes red and sagging. Pants smudged with dirt and his black T-shirt looking and smelling like it was ready to walk away on its own. Jane also seemed suddenly conscious of how she looked. She hitched up her tan trousers and held her hair back with one hand.

The credit card was good, though, and the woman behind the desk said it was easy to get to Kensico Reservoir.

"120 North takes you right to 22," she said. "Go left and you can't miss the dam. You go over that and you'll see the water plant on the right."

Tom asked for a map. Outside, he got behind the wheel. Jane scooted in back, so Mike took the other seat in front.

"Locked and loaded?" Tom asked Mike.

"Okay," Mike said, patting the bulge of the Taurus on his waist.

"I've only got two shots left," Tom said, feeling for his snub nose.

"Will you two stop it?" Jane said. "You're going to feel stupid after I talk to him."

Tom looked from Mike to his daughter, then back to Mike.

Mike shrugged and cast a guilty sidelong look at Jane.

In about fifteen minutes, they came to the old dam at the head of the reservoir.

"What about them?" Jane said, pointing at the white cop car.

Tom set his jaw and kept driving.

"Dad?"

"They'll think we're loony," he said. "Did you see the way people looked at us in the airport? You should have heard the cop on the phone. Like I was a nutcase. By the time we get someone to believe us it could be too late."

"It could be the right thing to do either way," she said.

"That's not what my gut tells me," Tom said. Out of the corner of his eye, he saw Mike looking straight ahead, but nodding his head in agreement.

They passed the cop and crossed the long narrow dam. The wind was picking up again. Rain spattered the windshield.

"There's another," Mike said as they passed through the rotunda.

"Just don't look," Tom said.

The two stone-faced cops were just climbing into their white Jeep and out of the rain.

Soon they saw a church, then the old filtration plant.

"As far as I can tell," Mike said, tugging the map from Mark Allen's briefcase out of the big pocket on his leg, "the pipe will go straight out into the reservoir from here."

"Look for a truck," Tom said, casting his eyes along the roadside. "The Russian said something about a truck."

He pulled into the filtration plant and drove up the road. They saw the gate and another guard. Tom took a deep breath and kept going on past. There was another building up on the left, an empty education center. Tom stopped in the parking lot and they looked out over the expanse of the reservoir.

"He wouldn't be here," Tom said, "but maybe we can see something on the shore."

He rolled down his window and looked out at the reservoir. The dreary scene of water and pines was partially obfuscated by a thin mist. Raindrops pricked the water's black surface, bringing it to life with an endless population of tiny ripples. He scanned the shoreline.

As he did, an enormous cat's paw crept across the water toward them from the north. The mist above it was roiling and turbulent.

Tom narrowed his eyes and started to roll up the window. The gust rocked the truck. A bucket of rainwater hit the windshield and it just kept coming. The wind was moaning outside now. It was as if they were suddenly back on the island.

"Now what?" Jane asked from the backseat.

Tom sat and thought.

"If he's not right here," he said, "I've got to believe he's parked somewhere close. He'll want to get a boat. Does that map show the exact location of the intake valve?"

"Out there somewhere," Mike said, nodding. He looked down at his soggy map, then up, pointing. "Right in the middle, where you get the least amount of turbidity."

"He's got to be close," Tom said.

Mike kept studying the map.

"If we go back to the road," Mike said, "there's a right up there that goes right down by the water."

Tom nodded. He put the truck in reverse and backed around. They turned right on the main road, then made another right. Soon they could see the water again. They passed the gates of a small pump house with a warning sign. They slowed down in front of every driveway they came to and craned their necks, looking for a suspicious truck.

A woman in a Volvo pulled out of one brick driveway and eyed them suspiciously before heading for the main road.

"This is crazy," Jane said. "He could be anywhere."

"He's got to be close," Tom said for the second time. "He's got to be."

Rain clattered on the roof. They rounded the bend and continued on, straining their eyes, willing the truck to appear. They came to a crossroads. Straight ahead was a dead end.

"Now what?" Jane asked.

"Go down there," Mike said.

Tom crested a small rise, and there it was.

"Look," Mike said, pointing ahead.

The road ended in a turnaround that was surrounded by towering pines swaying in the wind. Tucked under their eaves was a white truck. Behind it was a sandy-colored Buick sedan. Tom whipped the Excursion around and pulled up alongside the truck. He rolled down his window. Rain danced on his cheeks and nose and spattered half his body.

A green and blue Kale Labs symbol was painted on the door.

"The Holy Grail," he said.

CHAPTER 65

The drum fit nicely in the bottom of the boat. Mark tucked the edge of the cheap poncho he'd purchased between the black barrel and the gunwale of the aluminum skiff, hiding it from sight. The wind was rising now, gusting up and down. Rain spattered off the side of the boat and tore up the water's surface. Mark placed the 12-gauge on the seat in the bow and lifted the front of the boat, sliding its stern into the reservoir.

"Hey."

Mark's heart jumped, and he spun around.

"Who the hell are you?"

It was an older man in a bright yellow hooded slicker. He scowled behind thick glasses and a long-brimmed Orvis fishing cap that was littered with fly lures. In one hand was a pole case, in the other a small tackle box.

"I . . . I . . . my uncle told me I could use his boat," Mark said.

"That's my boat, boy," the old man said. He took two steps closer and stopped. "Who's your uncle?"

Mark stepped toward the man, slow and easy, but steady. He opened his arms and held his palms up to the dreary sky.

"Carson Kale," he said, forcing a smile. Small stones shifted underneath his feet. There was twenty feet between the waterline and the bank. Mark was halfway there.

"I don't know any Carson Kale, and I don't know you," the old man said. He raised his pole case, pointing like a schoolmaster.

"I just wanted to do a little fishing," Mark said. "This is the weather for it, right?"

"You stay right where you are, boy," the old man said, his voice rising. "Don't come any closer or I'll wrap this pole case around your head."

Still smiling, still gliding, Mark said, "Easy, old-timer, I'm not going to hurt you."

He coiled his body and surreptitiously drew back a fist. He was almost—

Without warning, a nasty rainsquall hit him hard, spattering his face. He lost his balance. His foot slid on the slick mud bank. He staggered. The old man whipped the hard plastic case down on his head. His feet went out from under him and he landed heavy. The sound of a seashell sang momentarily in his ears. His mouth opened and closed.

In a whisk of color, the old man took off into the woods. Mark sprang up and went after him. He slipped on the bank, went down, and sprang up again, cursing. The old-timer was moving fast.

Mark leaped over the tackle box and sprinted hard. The soft path of pine needles wound upward through the high trees. A big boulder, pale with lichen, marked a bend up ahead. The yellow form darted around it. When Mark rounded the corner, he tripped over the prostrate figure of the old man and went sprawling into the scrub brush, gashing his face and hands. His palm split open on the sharp edge of a mossy rock.

The old man had fallen in a heap in the middle of the path, but he was scrambling to his feet now and staggering toward the road. Mark whipped a leg out, hooked him at the knee, and lashed back with all his might. The old man went up and down. Mark rolled onto him, sunk his hands deep into the flaccid skin of the thin old neck, and sucked in a breath. The smell of Old Spice made him want to heave. The old man was wriggling his hand beneath the slicker. Mark tightened his grip. The old man's eyes began to bulge. His throat gurgled.

Mark felt a sudden electric shock in his arm, then another. A distant part of his brain realized the old-timer had a fishing knife. Mark let go of the old man's neck and rolled away just as the knife plunged for his chest. He shot his hands out, gripping the old man's arm and twisting it hard and fast. A bone snapped.

The old-timer shrieked, and the knife fell to the ground. The old man turned and scrabbled away. Mark lifted the long thin knife from the ground. He dove for the old man, and got him by the legs. He worked his way up the old man's back, grabbing his arm, then his shoulder, and finally his neck. Mark grasped the man's forehead, yanking it up and back. With his other hand, he licked the blade across the old man's neck.

The old man lashed his legs out twice. The third effort was a feeble lurch. Then he went limp.

"Stupid son of a bitch," Mark said, blowing the rain from his lips. "Stupid."

He took hold of the old-timer's green rubber boots and dragged him off the path into a bed of ferns. Then without looking, he turned and headed back for the shore.

As he walked, he examined the crimson blade of the bone-handled knife. His blood. The old man's. He wiped the blade on his pants and slipped the knife into the back of his belt.

When he got to the shore, the aluminum skiff that held his drum was gone.

CHAPTER 66

Y ou stay here," Jane's father said, turning back to her as he looked up from checking his pistol.

"Keep your phone on," he said to Mike. "I'll take the path on the right. You take the one in the middle. When you get to the shoreline, check in. We can start working our way to the north. That's left."

"I know north," Mike said. He snapped a shell into the chamber of his gun.

"Lock the doors and just keep down," her father said. He got out and turned to her. "If you see anything, just lean on the horn and we'll be back here in twenty seconds. Why don't you sit up front?"

Jane bit down on her lower lip and nodded. She got out and stood there in the rain, watching them.

"Ready?" her father said to Mike.

Mike looked at her father, the younger man's small dark eyes aglow despite the pallor of his drooping skin. His thin ginger hair was plastered to his skull. In his meaty hand the gun he carried looked tiny and almost comical.

"Yeah," Mike said. He turned and trudged off down the middle path, disappearing amid the undulating tangle of pine branches.

Tom started down the path to his right. He turned back.

"In the truck, Jane," he said. "I mean it."

"All right," she said. She got in and sat down, closing the door behind her. When her father was out of sight, Jane got out. As she walked down the path to the left, she started to shiver. She was soaked and the rain was teeming down. The slashing wind bit right through the baggy clothes that Mark had given her.

She took short gulps of air and tried to fight back the sick feeling in her stomach. She stumbled down the path, scanning the woods in front of her. Her foot with just the sock could feel the stiff slender texture of the pine needles. Even in the rain-squall, the swaying trees had a serenity to them that made Jane wish she could just lie down and go to sleep. Maybe she would wake up and be in the small warm hunting cabin, safe, with Mark Allen by her side.

The foot with the sneaker suddenly slipped from beneath her, and she caught herself just before she hit the ground. She straightened up and flexed her fingers. Pine needles were stuck to her palm, but it was slippery with some substance, too. She raised her hand out in front of her and gasped. It was red and slick with blood. Pink rivulets dripped from her wrist as the rain quickly diluted the clotted gore. Jane gasped and swiped her hand against her dripping flannel shirt, smearing it with a dark stain.

Instead of running back, she hurried down the path. The trees began to thin, and she could see the gray surface of the reservoir. As she neared the bank, she thought she saw a dark shape on the water's broken surface. It was the head and arms of a man, flailing in the whitecaps. He was swimming toward her. Jane steadied herself on the trunk of an ash tree. She stepped down off the bank and crossed the stony beach to the water's edge, wary for more signs of blood.

The swimmer stopped. He dipped beneath the surface, then stood up in the waist-deep water. It was Mark. He waded toward her, pushing the water aside with his hands and gasping for breath. His clothes clung to his body, and she could see the strong shape of his muscular frame. Rain ran down his face. His mouth was open wide, his chest heaving. He came closer, to where the water was only ankle-deep, and put his hands on his knees.

"Mark?" she said, her stomach falling and falling.

He looked up at her with those glass green eyes and smiled.

"It's still okay," he said, gasping. "I'm glad . . . you're here . . . You can . . . help me."

"What do you mean?" she said. "What happened?"

"Great men aren't made, Jane," he said with a misshapen smile, "they make themselves."

"Mark, I don't understand what's happening," she said. "There was blood back there . . . please—"

"All right, asshole!" a voice yelled.

Jane turned. Mike Tubbs, enormous, water dripping off his beard, stood with his feet set wide apart on the stones where the beach met the woods. His mouth was a flat line, his little dark eyes nearly buried beneath his brow. The small pistol was pointed at Mark's chest.

"Mike," she yelled, "wait."

Mike looked at her. His eyes softened. Jane's did too. It was Mike. Everything would be all right. Mike always made things all right. Her throat grew tight, and she felt tears well up in her eyes.

"Mike," she said.

In her peripheral vision, Jane saw Mark shift, then spring forward, his arm like a whip. Something hit Mike with a resounding thud. His eyes, staring into hers, suddenly lost their focus. His gun clattered to the stones, and he fell to his knees.

He felt for the bone handle of a knife whose blade was buried in his chest, just below his neck. Mike's mouth opened and closed. A trickle of blood drooled down the edge of his beard. He choked, tugged at the handle, then fell forward on his face.

Jane heard herself shriek.

She stepped forward. Mark swept his arm around her waist, lifting her off her feet and dragging her up the beach.

"Mike!" she screamed, her feet moving beneath her, instinctively keeping her from falling to the earth. Mark had her by the arm now. He bent down and scooped up Mike's pistol, barely breaking stride.

He dragged her up the path. Jane threw herself from side to side. She dug in her heels.

"Don't," he said. His grip was excruciating. One of his fingers tickled her bone, then pressed firmly down on a nerve. She shrieked and darted forward, wanting the pain to go away. He eased the pressure on the nerve.

"Hurry," he said, dragging her.

"You killed him," Jane said. She was sobbing now, but moving with him, quickly, through the rain and the swaying trees.

CHAPTER 67

"Answer the damn phone, Mike."

Tom held the phone out in front of him and squinted at the number he had dialed to make sure it was the right one. It was. He started moving down the beach toward the rocky point that he knew separated him from his friend.

"Mike," he said to no one, urgently now, starting to jog.

"Mike," he said, raising his voice, desperate, sprinting.

"Mike!" he shouted into the wet trees. A spike of pain pierced his throat. His heart began to hammer against his ribs.

"Mike!" he shouted up the beach. He leaped over a pale blue fishing boat that had been dragged up on the shore. Pebbles ricocheted off the aluminum sides. He rounded the brown sandy point. The torrent of wind and water hit him full in the face, the brunt of the northeaster squall. Caps of white exploded on the water's surface.

"God damn." His chest began to ache. His throat was burning. He leaped over two more boats, pistol in hand, and saw something up on the beach by the dark dirt bank.

Tom got closer and saw two sprawled legs. He raced up and fell to his knees, dropping his gun.

He could already see the blood pooling beneath him in the stones and grit. Tom got his hands under one shoulder and rolled Mike onto his back.

Blood coursed from beneath the knife's handle. Mike's eyes fluttered open. He saw Tom and smiled. Tom grasped his hand.

"Hold on, Mike," he said. Tom's face crumpled with pain. His stomach rolled.

He launched himself up over the bank and into the woods.

Tom ran so hard and so fast that everything went from fire to numbness. He dialed 911 for an ambulance. He began to stumble, but the clearing of the road was coming into view. The foliage thinned. He could make out the shape of vehicles through the trunks of the trees. There was a flash of white, and a set of red taillights sailed off down the road. Gravel bounced off metal. The wet phone slipped from his hand. He kept going.

Tom reached the turnaround and looked left. The white truck's taillights, gleaming through the misty rain, suddenly winked out, disappearing around the bend.

He nearly ripped the door off the Excursion yelling for Jane. She was gone.

He threw himself into the truck. The engine raced. He mashed the pedal to the floor and jammed the truck in gear. In a grind of metal and a shower of flying gravel, the truck rocketed forward.

"It's like you're supposed to be here," Mark said. He smiled and glanced her way, his green eyes incandescent beneath their long dark lashes.

Using his right hand to hold the wheel, he wiped the water from his brow with the other. It left a bloody smear across his forehead. Jane inhaled sharply.

"You're bleeding," she said.

He looked at his left arm, shrugged, and smiled.

"It doesn't matter," he said. "It's all happening. Don't you see? Great corporations. Great people. Great soldiers. They're forged in the hottest furnaces."

His voice was rising on a crest of excitement.

"Think about it," he said, glancing her way at brief intervals. "The old fisherman comes. He almost ruins everything, because my boat gets blown away by that squall. But then, there you are, and that guy. And he has a *gun*. If you weren't there, I don't know what would have happened . . .

"It's destiny," he said. "I'm him, and it's like you could be her."

Jane shook her head, and in a broken whisper she said, "You killed him, Mark. You killed him . . . You crazy fuck."

"Oh, no . . . ," Mark said glancing at her with apparent concern, "no, baby, no. Don't think like that. Don't let that ruin it for you . . ."

He reached out and touched her arm. Jane recoiled.

"Carson always said it," Mark said, "and he's right. It's like war. You have casualties. You have to. But if you look at the greater good . . ."

The windshield wipers slapped wildly against the rain. Mark put both hands back on the wheel. Jane's mind spun.

"I'm actually saving lives," he said, glancing at her. "Don't you see? We're not prepared, as a country. This bioterror stuff is everywhere. The Chinese are messing with it. What do you think SARS is? The Russians have it. The Koreans. Israel. We are so unprepared . . .

"But this will get everyone's attention," he said. "Get them focused. And, in the end, lives will be saved, and the company will do it."

"You are stone-cold nuts. Oh my God," she said. She shut her eyes. "You killed him. You crazy fuck."

"There it is," he said. "Look."

He was pointing out the window, nodding his head. The road was climbing now, heading for the west entrance to the dam.

Jane narrowed her eyes and peered through the drizzle of the driver's-side window. Out on the dark water, a small boat bobbed up and down on the whitecapped waves. It was being blown right down the middle of the reservoir, straight for the dam. They rolled right past the two police who were now inside the white Jeep. Mark waved to them.

Jane saw the cop behind the wheel look up and bobble his cup of coffee. She tried to make eye contact with him, turning around in her seat, but they entered the rotunda and it was too late. The half-dome gave way to the low stone wall that lined the top of the dam. There was the boat, tossing on the whitecapped water. On the other side was the deadly drop to the valley below.

They were halfway across when Mark flipped on his hazard lights and slowed to a stop.

"Come on," he said. He grabbed her wrist and dragged her across the console, tugging her out of the truck.

A car behind them stopped and honked. Mark signaled for the man to roll down his window.

"My engine quit!" he yelled above the weather. "Can you go around?"

The man nodded and waved. Mark waved back, smiling. He yanked Jane up onto the narrow walkway that ran along the northern lip. Wind and rain whipped through her hair. She opened her mouth to yell, but the car was already past.

She turned to look out at the water. The boat was directly in front of them now, maybe three hundred feet out and being swept quickly their way. A car sped past going the other way, its horn blaring.

Mark tugged her to the wall, two courses of massive stone. Jane's stomach hit up against it. She lost her breath and leaned over. The drop made her queasy, and she grabbed the cool wet stone, digging her fingers into the crumbling joints.

"It's a handy devil," he said, raising the sleek black weapon. "A Taurus 454 Raging Bull. It'll punch right through both sides of that drum. When the boat hits the dam, these waves will tip it right over, and then . . . you won't believe what's going to happen."

He led her by the arm to a jog in the wall that afforded them some more room.

Mark let go of her and leaned up over the wall. Steadying the gun with both hands, he took careful aim at the boat and fired.

CHAPTER 68

From the road, Tom saw the white Bronco stop halfway across the dam. He saw Mark Allen dragging his daughter from the truck. Her long hair whipped out behind her in the wind. White water crashed up against the dam, sending geysers of spray into the air. The trees suddenly cut them from his view. The split rotunda lay up ahead. Soaring pine trees swayed, shedding the rain down on the road in fat drops. Tom punched the accelerator just as a white Jeep put on its flashing lights and pulled out across the slick road, blocking the entrance to the dam.

He clenched the wheel and slammed on his brakes. The truck slid sideways and slammed into the car. The horn went off. Tom grabbed his pistol and hopped out of the truck.

A cop was rounding the back of the truck, a shotgun in his hands.

"Hold it!" he screamed. "Put the gun down!"

Tom looked at the cop. His dark blue jumpsuit was being quickly obliterated with spots of rainwater. Blood ran down his cheek. One eye was closed. The other was looking down the sight of a short-barreled shotgun.

"The gun down! Now!"

Tom raised his hands and looked through the truck's window. The cop driving the Jeep was slumped up against the broken window. Beyond, he saw the dark shapes of two figures out on the edge of the dam. Jane and Mark Allen.

"My daughter," he said, his voice cracking.

"Now!"

The cop was moving closer, the gun still aimed, trembling, ready to fire.

Tom looked at the .38 held up over his head. He let it fall. It rattled off the wet pavement and under the truck.

"Now put your hands on the car and spread 'em," the cop said, turning Tom and kicking at his ankles.

Tom put his hands on the Excursion and spread his feet. He could hear the cop fumbling with his cuffs. The cop grabbed one wrist and twisted it down behind Tom's back. The angry pop of a pistol echoed off the water.

Tom took a deep breath. His mind spun like a gyroscope. He twisted his hand, gripped the cop's wrist, ducked, and did a neat pirouette.

Rubber screamed. Metal smashed into stone. Jane opened her eyes. The patrol car from the far side of the dam had skidded to a stop, slamming against the stone wall ten feet in front of her. Smoke curled from the seams of the hood. An officer leaped from the car.

Her ears exploded. She screamed and dropped to the stone walk. Her head rang. She looked up, dazed. The cop was down. Resting up against the wheel of his car. A hole in his chest. Blood bubbling in a steady stream. A dark stain. His head sagged.

Jane looked over her shoulder. Mark was already leaning over the wall again. Instinctively, Jane covered her ears. He aimed and fired once more.

Tom finished his pirouette and lifted the cop's arm up against the joint. He cried out in pain. Tom flicked his foot. The shotgun sailed away. A kick to the nose. The crunch of bone. The cop groping in the empty space. His eyes nearly shut. Tom let go of the arm. He brought the force of his next blow up from his legs, pivoting his hips. Two hundred and sixty pounds behind the chop. A perfect strike. The soft spot between the second and third vertebrae. The first thing to hit the road was his face.

Tom scooped the cuffs off the pavement. A silver Lexus Coupe pulled up, its wipers slapping. A young man with a crew cut and bulging arms got out. He shouted at Tom. Tom picked up the shotgun and fired over the man's head. The man's face lost color and he disappeared behind the car door. Tom dropped the gun and clapped one of the cop's own handcuff bracelets on his wrist, then he dragged him to the front of the truck. The other bracelet went through the hitch ring under the nose of the truck's frame.

Tom scooped the shotgun back up on the run and rounded the truck in time to see Mark Allen kill the cop from the other side of the dam. He saw Jane fall, and a growl burst from his chest. He was sprinting again, closing the gap to get into accurate range. If he pulled up too soon and missed, he might not get off another shot.

Mark Allen fired over the dam. Tom stretched his stride as far as he could. He pumped his arms. His face was screwed up tight. Rain spattered against him. The wind howled.

He saw Jane rise up. She tackled Allen. The Taurus went off. Mark Allen slammed Jane to the ground and leaned back over the wall. He was aiming straight down now.

Tom dropped to a knee and fired.

CHAPTER 69

The bullet spun Mark Allen completely around. Tom saw the splash of blood on his shoulder. Allen fell to his knees. He lurched sideways, then grabbed Jane around the neck. When he stood, she was his shield.

"Drop the gun!" he shouted at Tom.

Tom rose. He walked slowly toward Allen. Jane's face was rumpled and red. Her eyes were swollen. Shut tight. Spilling tears as she shuddered. The rain was teeming down.

"I said drop it!" Allen shouted.

"Think," Tom said as he stepped up onto the walkway, holding the shotgun out over the edge of the dam. "That Taurus is a five-shot. You only have one bullet left . . ."

Allen looked confused.

Tom was close now. Ten feet away.

"You just stop," Mark said, putting the gun to Jane's temple.

She moaned.

"You have what I want . . . but I have what you need," Tom said, hefting the shotgun. "You give her to me and I give you this. Here."

Tom reached across slowly with his other hand and gripped the barrel of his shotgun. He turned the stock toward Allen.

"Go ahead," Tom said. "Sun Tzu said, 'If the enemy leaves a door open, you must rush in.'"

Mark Allen smiled as he let Jane go, shifted the Taurus from his right hand to his left, and reached for the stock. Tom watched Allen's good hand curl around it and lock down on its grip. His finger slipped into the trigger guard.

Tom sidestepped the barrel and yanked it toward him. The gun went off, the shot missing him by inches. Allen was falling toward him. Tom struck him under the chin with the palm of his hand, breaking teeth and bone.

Mark Allen let go of the shotgun and dropped the Taurus. He stepped in and hooked Tom under his arm, lowered his hips, and tossed Tom onto his back up on the stone wall. Allen was on top of him. His hand was under Tom's chin, pushing it back. Tom saw the water above the trees. The sky below. He heard Jane's shriek, and his chin came free.

Jane had Mark Allen by the back of his collar. She pulled and screamed. Allen's face turned red. He gagged and raised up. His hand loosened on Tom's neck. Tom swept it away. He arched his back, cried out, and threw himself up into a sitting position, twisting and pulling with his stomach muscles, struggling to right himself. He saw Allen down now on the stone walk, bending for the shotgun. Tom gripped the edge of the wall and launched himself forward, over the top of Jane.

He struck Allen from behind and knocked him forward. Allen splashed into the puddles on the road, then spun. He had the gun by the barrel. He stepped forward, swinging it like a club.

Tom ducked the blow and hopped backward, up onto the

curb. Allen swung again, closing. Tom ducked again and grabbed the gun.

The roar of the shot echoed out across the valley.

Mark Allen stopped and blinked. He pressed his hands over his stomach. Blood gushed from the cracks between his fingers. He staggered, then lunged for Tom with outstretched red hands. Tom sidestepped him, stuck out his foot, lifted, and kicked as he struck Allen's back with the palms of both hands.

Mark Allen went up and over the wall, flailing for purchase, crying out. Jane lunged for him. Their hands somehow clasped. Jane was slammed down on the top of the wall. Tom grabbed her waist. He felt the force of Mark Allen's weight, tugging them both over the edge. With a sudden lurch, Jane slipped farther, her hips now over the wall. Tom held on, the rough stone surface plowing up the flesh on his arms.

Mark Allen was dangling by one hand. Jane had ahold of his wrist. Tom pressed his knees into the stone wall, fighting to pull them up. His arms burned. He felt a sudden sharp pain in his back.

Then Mark Allen looked up at Jane, his bottle green eyes slitted.

"You have the most beautiful eyes," he said.

His hand slipped free. Tom and Jane tumbled backward. They scrambled to their feet instantly and darted back to the edge. Fifty feet below, where the water crashed against the stone at the base of the dam, there was a white patch of foamy pink bubbles in the turbulent chop, but nothing else. A skiff with a black barrel in its belly suddenly slammed up against the dam's side with a grating noise. The boat capsized and slowly went down. The barrel bobbed like a cork.

Jane threw herself against her father, sobbing. Tom wrapped her in his arms and held her tight.

EPILOGUE

Tom wore a dark suit with a sharp red tie. He ran his fingers over the bristles of his fresh-cut hair. The jury had already given its guilty verdict and now all that remained was the sentencing. The federal judge was a gaunt man with a bald, olive-colored head and wide-set, intelligent hazel eyes. A pair of gold-rimmed spectacles hung from his neck, glinting against the dark folds of his robe. He put them on and picked up a piece of paper off his bench.

Tom inhaled deeply and looked over at the jury. Guilty. The smell of wood polish and dust cooked by the summer sunshine glaring in from the windows filled his nostrils, along with just the hint of his own nervous sweat.

The judge cleared his throat.

"Will the defendant please rise?"

Tom stood along with the lawyers on both sides.

"Because of the magnitude of the crime," the judge said, "and the loss of life involved, I hereby sentence the defendant to life in prison—the maximum sentence that is allowed to me under the law."

Tom felt numb. He tried to force a smile onto his face, but couldn't. He hung his head and let the noise of other people's feet wash around him. When he felt the strong grip of a hand on his shoulder, he sighed deeply and turned.

It was Mike Tubbs, thinner than he'd been two years ago after nearly dying from a loss of blood, but still big enough. His old friend offered a smile and his hand. Tom took it.

"Congratulations," Mike said. "On another one."

He wore a black suit jacket over a *Lord of the Rings* T-shirt.

Tom shook his head as the two of them walked out together. He stopped and turned to see the man he'd just put away for life being led out a side door by two deputies. The man scowled at him with weird blue eyes under big, thick eyebrows. Tom felt the smile he'd been looking for begin to take shape. Just a little. He never wanted to appear smug. Even when he was right.

On the courthouse steps, he addressed the media. Yes, the area was a safer place. Anytime you could thwart organized crime and a dangerous designer drug operation, you had to consider it an accomplishment for everyone working on the right side of the law. He thanked the ladies and gentlemen and rejoined his friend. They walked down the steps and around the building to the parking lot, where Tom's F-150 waited in a reserved spot.

"I found a new spot for my office," Mike said. "Top floor of the old electric company building. I like it. Great digs. All brick. Like a castle."

"Those law firms I sent your way pay that good?" Tom said.

"No more redheaded wives getting busy in the Motel Six."

"No more Home Depot trips either," Tom said.

"God, that poor bastard," Mike said. "They ever find his body?"

"Only his pecker."

"You're kidding."

"Only a false knight lives without jest," Tom said.

Mike looked puzzled. "Malory?"

"Redmon."

Tom started up the truck, still missing the big 350 with its dually tires. The whine of the diesel engine. Its ticks and its shakes. But the 150 was something he could afford on a federal prosecutor's salary and still keep his boat. The old 350 had disappeared two years ago. Tom had reported it stolen. No one had ever seen it. Motorcycle Gang 101, as Mike liked to say.

Less than ten minutes later, they stopped at the marina. The aqua green water stretched out in front of them as far as they could see. The emerald hillsides, rich with trees, seemed as permanent as formations of rock. Just the hint of a breeze worked to cool their faces and stir the thin layer of white dust blanketing the parking lot.

Rockin' Auntie was still in the same spot between the big sailers, still her ugly old self. Worn, but reliable as hell. Tom shed his jacket and tie, leaving them on the front seat of the truck. He unbuttoned his shirt and changed it for a Cornell Law School T-shirt. He waited until they were out on the water before he ditched his shoes and socks, wrapped a big towel around his waist, and swapped his suit pants for a loose pair of shorts. They were anchored in Tom's favorite spot. Mike was putting sunblock on his arms, whistling to himself.

"Talked to Jane today," Tom said suddenly.

"You did?"

"I'm going down there next week on a case," Tom said. "I told her I'd buy her dinner. Want to go down?"

"Heard she got a promotion," Mike said.

"Two."

"She got robbed on the Pulitzer," Mike said. "Next time I need to talk to the committee. Fuckin' morons."

Tom sat down on the seat behind the captain's chair and pulled out a small cooler from under the seat in the back. From inside, he removed a paper bag and took out a bottle of Knob Creek.

"What's that?" Mike asked. There was a hint of alarm in his voice.

Tom held the bottle up to the light and chuckled, letting the sun bounce through the brown liquid, filtering it so he could look up at the sapphire sky without blinking. He took a knife out of the side compartment and used it to cut into the wax around the bottle's neck. He raised it up toward Mike, who stood there stupidly with his mouth hanging open.

"I found it in my old file cabinet," Tom said. "Cheers."

He rested his arm on the side of the boat and tipped the bottle, its contents gurgling out into the pristine lake.

"I thought . . . ," Mike said.

"No," Tom said, taking up his fishing pole from beside the seat. "I just thought we might start marinating them even before we catch them today."

Mike smiled at him and began rigging his pole.

As they cast their lines and brought in their fish, the sun began to move lower in the sky. For a while, they talked while they sipped their iced tea. But then they settled into the kind of comfortable silence that can only be enjoyed by old friends.

Tom thought about that and said, "'Be slow to fall into friendship; but when thou art in, continue firm and constant.'"

"That would be Socrates."

"Smart man," Tom said.

The sun soon melted into an orange pool of light and disappeared behind the western hill. The pop of their lures and the ratcheting spin of their reels filled the quiet. Only the laughter and cheers that came from catching the big ones spilled across the water and bounced back at them.

After a long interval without any action, Mike cleared his throat and said, "Tom, I was meaning to ask you. . . . I mean, it's none of my business, but you giving up drinking and all, I only ask because I care, but I was just wondering . . . about Ellen. Actually, Jane asked me . . ."

Tom smiled to himself and tossed his line out. But instead of reeling it in, he let it float and gazed off into the shadows where the trees met the water and the light swayed in the day's final dance.

"Oh yes," Tom said, his heart full and his throat tight. "We still talk . . .

"It's different now, though," he said, taking a sip from his can of tea. "It used to be she came when I needed her, to build me up, or keep me from falling apart.

"But now," he said, narrowing his eyes and staring hard at the changing shapes of light and water and limbs, looking. "I guess I don't need that, and the things she says are just clips of the things she used to say to me all the time. I don't see her quite as clear as I used to . . . but she's there for me. And I'm there for her. And I know . . . she's just waiting."